# SMOKESCREEN

## MIRANDA FIX

PublishAmerica
Baltimore

ISBN: 1-4241-1938-3
PUBLISHED BY PUBLISHAMERICA, LLLP
www.publishamerica.com
Baltimore

Printed in the United States of America

I would like to dedicate this novel to my husband, Bernie, who always makes me laugh and gives me perspective, to my father, Carmen, with his precious, unconditional love, to my son, Nate, whose motivation and drive is an inspiration, to his fiancé Kayte, welcome to the family you know we love you and to my daughter, Kiralina, who has always shared in all my dreams and never stops believing in me...

I love you all.

A special thanks to Steve Petro RAC SSA/OIG, for his patience and willingness to help me, his expertise and vast knowledge, and his gracious hospitality. If there are any deviations to accuracy, it is purely for the sake of fiction.

In memory of Paul Evans, Detective New York State Sheriff's Department.

# Prologue

Jonathan Thorne paused at the end of the massive iron gate and slowly turned around. The early sun cast lingering shadows across the trees and tangled bramble that wrapped around the rusted post. The atmosphere was crisp and cold; he could see the moisture in the air as he blew out a long cleansing breath.

*A long free breath.*

His features were bitter and calculating as his eyes moved upward, staring at the institution that held him captive for nearly eight years, and then he deliberately spat on the ground by the guard's feet. Sammy Jackson glared a steady, even gawk into the young punk's eyes.

Thorne stared back, a cocky half smile on his lips, intentionally challenging the older man before speaking to him.

"I'll be expecting your phone call, so don't make me wait."

Sammy didn't answer, his eyes narrowed to small slits and as his eyebrows rose in an angry glare as if to say, *who the hell do you think you are?*

Thorne laughed aloud, a mocking self righteous cackle while raising his right hand in a salute and strolling away.

The guard watched the arrogant young man until he disappeared from his sight. His lips turned upward into a slow, calculating grin. But Sammy Jackson was no fool. He knew a lot more information than what Thorne thought he did. Oh yes, and he'd overheard a lot more than what Thorne thought too. Oh yes, he had a few surprises in store for him, and Jonathan Thorne deserved every bit of it. Jackson never believed the crap that Jonathan Thorne fed to a lot of other people. He knew that Thorne was an evil man, with many wicked intentions.

All he needed to do was find this man that many inmates spoke about. He wasn't sure if Dominick Stone was alive anymore, he even wondered if he existed at all. He seemed more a myth, than a man, a legend of sorts and legends have a way of spinning off into a journey all their own. Whatever the case, Jonathan Thorne wasn't going to get away with anything, not with Sammy Jackson around to stick it to him.

The guard spun around and with a confident stride, headed toward the first checkout point. The morning sun was just peaking over the smog filled horizon, changing the natural colors of orange into a deep pink hue. He whistled in an off tune note laughing quietly to himself.

\*\*\*

Thorne couldn't get her out of his mind. He waited a long time to finally have his revenge. He could feel every nerve ending in his body shaking with anticipation. He wanted vengeance so bad, he could almost taste it. It was eight long years that he was planning this, plotting every little minute detail to perfection. This time, he was going to succeed and he didn't have to get his hands dirty at all. This time he was going to kill her.

*The money belongs to me anyway; the bitch tortured me enough.*

Thorne chuckled silently to himself as he thought about how well he had crafted such a believable smoke screen around everyone. Well, maybe they didn't believe it at first, but slowly, as his perfect behavior continued, they started acknowledging his desire to be the 'model citizen'. He attended church regularly and ratted on a few people to make a good deal. Push came to shove in a system that was already over crowded. Oh yea, he knew how to play the game. After all, his biological father was no dummy, he was a doctor.

He boarded the bus marked for Cincinnati and shot his most charming smile at the young woman sitting in the second seat. She quickly smiled back and Jonathan smirked inwardly as he kept eye contact with the woman until he passed her and headed to the back of the bus. He could tell she was disappointed that he didn't sit beside her. He nearly laughed aloud as he thought; *I've got everyone just eating right out of my hand.*

*Bang, Bang, Kerensa Fiori, time is running out.*

# 1

He silently crouched in the shadows watching her dance. Following every movement of her effortless, single lined curves as they perfectly defined her agile body. His eyes slowly glided downward, soaking in every detail of her small waist, and the gentle rounding of her hips. Somehow he had forgotten how absolute she was, but he hadn't forgotten how much he desired her. There wasn't a day that went by without his recollection of their love making. He could feel the trickle of perspiration slip down his forehead and across his temples, but it wasn't the music he was feeling through his veins, it was the fire of her body as he reminisced…

He took a small step forward, and then another. Although he didn't want to make his presence known, he also knew that the sooner he did, the better it would be for both of them. He was certain that she would react with several unpredictable emotions, but none of them would be favorable. He deserved every negative reaction she might have.

*And then some.*

Suddenly a slight sound to his left caught his attention. Stone turned his head sharply in that direction, and realizing he wasn't alone in Kerensa's dance studio, he slowly reached for his revolver. Someone else was there, silently watching her just like he was. He hesitated, aware of the possible danger she was facing. He had come there to warn her, and now he realized it wasn't a moment too soon.

*\*\*\**

Kerensa was lost within the tranquility of her ballet. Her hips gently leaning from left to right, and her arms above her head in perfect unison. She eloquently moved to the music, unaware of anything else around her, just the transfer of her body through the evening air. Dancing alone was the only time she could ponder upon the issues that made her happy or sad. Tonight, she was sad. Perhaps, she was more nostalgic than anything else, but tonight, her thoughts were on Dominick. She was thinking about him a lot lately, and that was frightening to her mostly because she always had a sixth sense, an ethereal feeling, and premonition. Whatever it was, she didn't like it and she hated to admit that she was a little worried about his welfare too. But she was also proud to admit that she could do so without breaking down and sobbing like a fool. Dominick Stone was a long time ago. Slowly she had mended the wound he created in her then, very naive heart. It was hard to believe that her encounter with him and her near death experience was almost eight years ago, but perhaps because she resurrected it frequently the incident still felt like yesterday. Falling in love with Dominick just came with the package deal that year, along with all the other unwanted changes in her life.

It was the year her father died without warning, and she was summoned to Buffalo, NY. She had been living in Florida with her Nana, attending the University of Miami as a dance major. Believing that her father had a fatal heart attack, Kerensa was forced to go to Buffalo to be under the guardianship of her father's colleague until she turned twenty one. Although this seemed tragic enough, having to stay there for a couple months became even more complicated. Living there was far from simple; convoluted and shocking, it created an ordeal for Kerensa that changed her life forever. The incident also brought her to Dominick. Kerensa smiled wryly to herself, recalling what it was like the first time she met Dominick Stone. He was arrogant and crude, capable of doing just about everything; and he knew it. He also did it perfectly. Oh yes, Kerensa hated his over confident demeanor, and him. At least for a little while, *before she fell in love with him.*

And he was gorgeous.

Eleven years older, he eventually told her that he felt the same way about her. Then, one day he simply vanished. This experience left her emotionally murdered, and it was a bitter lesson about the cruelty of love. She wanted to hate him again, oh but she did, at least for a while. A man like him was, well, there were no words to fully describe what he was, but he had saved her life. Maybe that was the invisible attachment she felt from the very beginning. Perhaps, it wasn't love at all. Whatever it was her relationship could never be forgotten. Unfortunately, Dominick was, and always would be, unforgettable. So for three years Kerensa avoided all relationships, afraid to love for a second time. Trust and abandonment became a huge issue with her, until she met Connor.

Fourteen years older than Kerensa, he was unlike the other men she met after Dominick. Connor was mature, settled in his career and confident of what he wanted in life, and he wanted her. At first, Kerensa was leery of a relationship with him. Looking back now, she realized that she was still trying to replace Dominick. At first, their marriage was wonderful. Kerensa continued to teach dance and save as much money as she could to open her own dance studio. They were married almost a year when she found out she was pregnant. At first, the news was a bit overwhelming, but Kerensa was still happy. When she broke the news to Connor, his reaction wasn't at all what she expected. He thought she knew he never wanted to have children, and that his career as a lawyer would more than take care of both of them. So he asked her to have an abortion. Shocked over his request, Kerensa refused. Heartbroken, she began to see Connor and their marriage for what it really was. She was an arm ornament for a man who was heading to the top. A pretty piece of fluff attached to an older, powerful man, what better way to avoid having to face mortality? But Kerensa wasn't a *piece of fluff.* Shortly after his request, their marriage deteriorated. Janelle was two months old when Kerensa packed up her baby and left Connor behind. Life was a struggle, but fortunately Nana was always there to help her and she still had her trust fund from her father's inheritance. Some women would think that the money was enough to live comfortably for the rest of their lives, but Kerensa didn't want to touch that money. It felt good to know it was there, but it was 'blood money', money that people lost their lives over, money that her father lost his life over. The only sibling she ever had, was sent to prison for the murder of her father, and her kidnapping. Unfortunately, her father's trust fund was filled with malevolence.

Kerensa moved back in with Nana, and together they raised Janelle. She returned to dance shortly after the baby was born, and Connor never showed an interest in his daughter. He sent his child support checks without a blink of an eye, the money always arriving on the third of every month. Kerensa figured that he believed he was giving enough, and it left a bitter taste in her mouth. Periodically, she would receive a phone call from his sister asking if she could pick Janelle up and take her to Connor's parents for the day. She always trusted his sister, and whenever she needed anyone to watch Janelle, it was either her Nana or his sister that she counted on. She wasn't given the choice in that matter; the courts had mandated paternity and grandparent rights.

Kerensa cringed when she recalled an incident that happened a few months ago. She contacted Kerensa and arranged to pick Janelle up at 10:00 AM. When his sister was almost an hour late, Kerensa phoned Janelle's grandparents. Apologizing profusely, they asked if she could drop Janelle off at Connor's office, but Kerensa refused. They explained that Connor was out of town on business so he wouldn't be there. When Kerensa still refused, they were extremely disappointed. Feeling accountable, Kerensa reluctantly told them she would do it. When she arrived to his office, she was greeted by his secretary with a warm hug. Confused, that his secretary would act so friendly, Kerensa quietly responded. After a few moments of conversation Kerensa realized that Connor had never told her that they were divorced. Once inside Connor's office, she immediately saw the photographs of her, of Janelle when she was a baby, and of both of them together. Kerensa was furious that he would use their marriage as though it were a marketing tool. Pretending to become violently ill, she ran out of the office with Janelle in her arms. Later on that night, Kerensa spoke with Connor's sister and wanted to tell her the truth. Instead, she continued with the story that she suddenly became ill and had to leave. She could tell that Kerensa was lying, and it put a noticeable rift between them. They still speak to one another often, but not like it used to be. Kerensa missed her; they always got along so well and they considered each other friends as well as sister-in-laws.

It was a little more than a year after her divorce when Kerensa began dating Vance.

He was her sweetheart in high school, and he wasn't about to give up on her despite the difficult time she gave him. He didn't care if she had a child, and Janelle really loved him. Slowly she began to love him too, and when he asked her to marry him a month ago, she accepted. Finally her life was on the right tract again, and she was back in Florida where she belonged. Away from the memories that brought her such heartache. The dance studio was hers, and she had several classes of students to teach. Life was looking up for her now.

*So why the melancholy?*

Kerensa bowed to her imaginary audience, and stopped dancing. She walked across the studio and turned the music off. Then she stood in quiet contemplation, just listening to the silence. A noise behind her alerted her that she wasn't alone any longer. Suddenly she saw the figure of a man, and narrowing her eyes in the semi darkness she recognized him immediately.

# 2

"How long have you been watching me?" she asked, giggling softly.

He stepped out from the shadows, chuckling mischievously in return. "Oh, long enough to get excited. How about we christen the new studio floor?"

"Not now, Vance," she retorted, pretending to be all business but reaching up to give him a kiss. "I have way too much to do."

"Oh yea, right, you know you'll like it."

"Oh really?" she whispered, reaching her arms around his neck and pulling him to the floor. "And maybe you're right."

"So, you can't resist me, can you?" he chided again.

Kerensa giggled, positioning herself on top of him, and slowly kissing him. Vance responded hungrily in return, slipping her sleeveless leotard past her shoulders. Kerensa pulled off the tie that bound her hair, allowing her dark curls to tumble freely down her back. Vance reached out and stroked her hair, loving every last strand of it. He ran his hands over her breasts, pulling her leotard even lower to expose them. Slowly she fluttered her eyes open and began to unbutton his shirt, briefly glancing upward. As she did so she saw the image of another man watching them and gradually advancing toward her. Although he was partially veiled in the darkness of the hallway, she would know that physique, recall that walk, oh yes, she would remember it anywhere, anytime, in her dreams, in her nightmares, in her past...

*No, but it can't be!*

A small scream escaped her lips while she quickly attempted to cover her partially exposed body. Vance instantly stiffened, causing Kerensa to topple over. Vance didn't care about that as he quickly scrambled to his feet and turned around to face this stranger. Reacting to the horror that was written all over Kerensa's face, Vance clenched his fists and swung at the man's face, but the man quickly ducked his head, his arm snaking out at the same time that his right leg kicked forward, tripping Vance as he tumbled to the floor. The man held Vance down with his upper body. He was pinned beneath him, his body so immobile that all he could do was blink.

Kerensa was just as emotionally immobilized, her mouth dropping open, and her eyes glued to his face with shock.

"Who are you, and what do you want?" Vance suddenly demanded, his timbre sounding more like a peep than a man with power.

The man's narrow gaze glared into Vance's face, but quickly changed, shifting the purpose of his visit toward her.

"It's good to see you again, Kerensa," he acknowledged sarcastically, his eyes raking every inch of her body. "Now tell you're a-friend here, who I am and I'll let him go."

*A friend? like hell, he thought, the bastard was ready to screw her blind.*

She didn't answer him, couldn't. Her senses were much too intimately paralyzing for her to respond. She squeezed her eyes closed; wondering if thinking about him made her delusional enough to imagine him standing before her. When she opened her eyes, he was still there, and bigger than she remembered, his broad, thick muscular frame nearly making the man beneath him disappear. And that was no easy feat. She stared into his smooth, strong boned features, and the perfectly angled slope of his chin, but her look still avoided his eyes. She knew that if he captured her gaze it would be deadly for her. Attempting to recuperate, she quickly cleared her throat.

"Let him go, Dominick, right now!"

Stone didn't budge yet; he glanced down at Vance and murmured something Kerensa couldn't hear. Then, he moved and with amazing swiftness, released Vance and allowed him to stand to his feet again.

Vance was furious, actually Kerensa had never seen her even tempered fiancé' so irate.

Kerensa attempted to take control of the situation before Vance could speak.

"What are you doing here, Sergeant Dominick Stone?"

Her choice to formally address him with a title he had shed a long time ago, temporarily caught him off guard, but he recovered quickly.

"I need to speak with you." He glanced toward Vance again, giving her the impression that he considered him the intruder. Stone's behavior immediately pushed the wrong buttons again in Vance. He now stepped forward, forcing Kerensa to take a step behind him.

"Who the hell are you, and what do you want?" he growled.

"Calm down, my business isn't with you," Stone snarled back. "I need to discuss this issue with Kerensa… in private."

Kerensa stood there in shock, recalling how *'Neanderthal'* Stone could be, and she wasn't going to allow him to continue.

"Stop it both of you," she quickly demanded, wishing her voice wouldn't tremble so much.

"Vance, this is—*I'm not really sure who or what he really is.* Sergeant Dominick Stone he's a law enforcement officer and private investigator from Buffalo, New York." She took another breath to continue, but she was interrupted again.

"I demand to know why you're here," Vance crisply retorted, ignoring Kerensa as though she didn't exist.

Stone deliberately didn't respond. Geezus, *this guy just doesn't get it.*

Kerensa parted her lips to speak, but nothing came out.

*Oh God.*

Vance wasn't willing to wait any longer for her to explain. He took another step forward, and spoke again.

"I'm Detective Vance Robertson; now state your business."

Kerensa moaned softly, this was becoming more and more disastrous by the second.

Stone unexpectedly chuckled, his blue eyes piercing into Kerensa's soft brown ones. *A detective now isn't that interesting.* Slowly he nodded his head in response, a glint in his eye as he stretched his arm out to shake Vance's hand. This gesture appeared to be only a professional courtesy.

"I apologize for the -a—interruption, Detective Robertson. There is a very good reason why I'm here, however it does not concern you. If Kerensa wishes to tell you about the situation after she is informed, that is entirely up to her."

*Oh yea, this is definitely a nuclear meltdown.*

She quickly turned to address Vance.

"It's alright, I will meet with him. Please don't make a big deal about this."

Vance could barely control his anger. "Don't make a big deal about this? The guy nearly broke my neck for Christ sake. I am not leaving you alone with this maniac; it's completely out of the question."

Kerensa was feeling besieged. *Maniac, yea, that was a good adjective for Stone. How about narcissistic, egotistical, arrogant maniac, that was even better.* Emotions powerful and long forgotten were suffocating her like a pillow over her face. Stone's smoldering gaze didn't help one bit either.

"I'm capable of taking care of myself; now please leave us alone, Vance."

Vance appeared offended by Kerensa's insistence. She could see the look of embarrassment mixed with hurt reflected in his eyes.

*Great, Stone knocks him on his ass, and now I tell him to get lost.*

To her relief, he finally nodded his head.

"I'll give you five minutes of privacy, Kerensa, but then I'll be back."

Kerensa breathed a long sigh; and watched him turn on his heels, walking out the door. Vance was a well built man, yet he appeared significantly smaller as he brushed past Stone. Then reluctantly, Kerensa turned her gaze toward the man before her. Her heart began to thump in her chest as she stared into his much too handsome, rebel face and wondered if he ever aged. Her gaze automatically shifted to the mouth she kissed so many times before and she immediately pushed those thoughts away. His hair was still a little longer than most men wore and he had it pulled back, fastened neatly to the nape of his neck with a rubber band. This rather *Renegade* appearance always suited him well.

Very well.

*A twenty first century warrior.*

She found herself staring at his thick chest and powerful biceps just bulging from around the black, short sleeved tee-shirt he wore. His sexy well over six foot frame suddenly appeared consuming to Kerensa, perhaps because his body was still so perfectly tuned, sculpted in marble like an equestrian statue.

Then she thought about the sex. *The sex!* Her five month relationship with him literally boiled down to that one thing, *although she didn't think so at the time*. He was her first, and maybe that's why she remembered it with such vivid detail, or perhaps not... Stone certainly knew how to make a woman feel exquisite, sex with him was like morphing into another dimension. He was nearly perfect at it, just as perfect as he was at everything else. Well, actually not everything else. He really sucked at commitment, and he was even worse at relationships. *Not to mention his total lack of refinement...Get a grip!*

She gazed into those dark, midnight blue eyes that glowed like the northern sky. *Oh damn, how long have I been staring at him?*

Kerensa quickly cast her gaze aside, embarrassed. In an attempt to camouflage her discomfort she walked away from him and began to clean up. This purposeful endeavor to ignore him was not going to work, and she knew that. She also knew that Stone was a man who knew no boundaries; he was simply unpredictable as if consequences were of no bearing to him. Her recollection of his nature was correct, and she instantly felt his heavy hands on her shoulders as he firmly turned her around to face him. This action brought Kerensa swirling into a renewed whirlwind of compelling, yet forgotten emotions. She glared directly into his deep blue gaze, her eyes resembling stormy black thunderclouds.

"Don't turn your back on me, Kerensa. Ignoring the fact that I'm here isn't going to scare me away."

Kerensa shook her shoulders free from his grasp.

"You did a good job being scared away eight years ago."

He slowly began to nod his head.

"Kerensa, I'm asking you to give me a chance."

*You can shove your chance up your a....*

She managed to fake a smile, crinkling her nose in the process.

"Oh, like the same chance you gave me, Sergeant Stone?"

"Touché," he quickly responded, his features fixed with an expression she couldn't identify. "But I won't discuss that today; eventually we'll talk about it. Right now I want you to send the, a—boyfriend away and I'll take you home."

Kerensa stared incredulously into his face.

*You are such a presumptuous ass. How dare you act as though what happened between us doesn't warrant a marathon discussion! Oh God, what did I ever see in you?*

"You will not be in my life long enough to discuss what happened eight years ago," Kerensa retorted with renewed conviction. "Vance is my fiancé and he's not going to leave without me."

Stone felt an invisible laser penetrate his heart. He never let on as he crisply retorted. "Well congratulations, now tell him to get the hell out of here, or I will."

Stone's piercing gaze brought back smoking hot memories and Kerensa nearly gasped aloud, but she kept her eyes steady upon his.

"I'm not talking to you, Sergeant Stone."

"Oh, yes you are," he smoothly whispered, with a tone like velvet but would cut like a knife. "Because I'm not leaving without you, Kerensa, and I think you know me well enough by now to know that I mean what I say. Now send him home before I do something you really won't like."

"I can see that time has certainly softened your disposition," she retorted, glaring at him with renewed hatred.

He stared back, his eyes calculating and cold.

"Loose the boyfriend, Kerensa." He flatly retorted, then as an afterthought he added, "please."

Stone was right; his threats were merely a courtesy warning for something bigger and meaner just waiting on the horizon and Kerensa wasn't about to find out what that was.

# 3

Kerensa took several deep breaths in her nose and out her mouth in an attempt to calm down. She refused to allow Dominick to affect her like this, especially since it was so many years later. She was also a little freaked out that she was thinking about him so intently and all of a sudden he appeared. She wondered if he had a crystal ball. She also wondered if he did anything easy. It seemed to her that he had only been back in her life less than one hour and everything was already inside out. Vance was furious with her, she would have to cancel her evening plans with a group of friends, and she didn't know how Nana would react when Stone walked through the door. Hell, she couldn't wait to see what a full twenty four hours could do to her carefully crafted life.

*Be careful what you wish for.*

They drove in silence to Kerensa's house, and she was about to ask him how he knew exactly where she lived. But than again, she didn't want to know the answer to that question either.

Dominick pulled the truck into the driveway. Kerensa quickly exited the vehicle and walked alone to her front door. He didn't seem to care that she was still purposely ignoring him. When she reached the door, she hesitated for a moment. Turning around to face him she replied, "I expect you to state your business here and then leave."

Dominick didn't answer her right away. He stared intently downward into her eyes just the way he used to. It was unnerving, and she found herself shifting slightly onto the ball of her right foot in order to create more space between them, this was no easy task given the size of the man beside her.

"I'm afraid it's more complicated than that, Kerensa," he quietly responded.

Her eyes flashed furiously back. "Then un-complicate it." *Jerk.*

She pushed open the door to the house that she shared with the woman who raised her since she was four years old. The woman she always knew as her mother. Kerensa slowly walked into the hallway, calling out Nana's name.

"I'm in the kitchen, Kerensa," Nana called back.

Kerensa took another deep breath before entering. Nana was standing by the stove, a spatula in her right hand as she flipped over some fried potatoes. Kerensa gave her a kiss on the cheek. She kissed her back, but it was obvious Nana's eyes were on someone else. Kerensa stepped aside to introduce Stone, but before she could do so, Nana spoke.

"You must be Sergeant Dominick Stone," she replied, pointing the spatula at Stone as though it were a weapon before setting it down and wiping her hands on the kitchen towel.

Kerensa's mouth dropped open. *How in the world would Nana know that?*

Stone smirked; glad to see that she didn't plan on plunging the utensil down his throat or across his forehead, and cordially extended his hand.

"Hello, Mrs. Drago, it sure smells good in here."

Nana smiled for a brief moment in return.

""I know it does," she finally replied, studying him thoughtfully, with full, round lips pursed together and eyes practically squinted closed. "I've heard a lot about you Sergeant Stone."

"I imagine you have, ma'am."

"Some of it wasn't very good."

Stone grinned again, he liked this lady.

"Then it's probably all true, ma'am."

"All of it?"

He quickly glanced at Kerensa.

"Oh yes, Ma'am," he slowly responded, catching the angry glint in Kerensa's eyes. "Every bit of it."

Nana laughed aloud, shaking his extended hand. Kerensa was annoyed. Although Nana had a very forgiving heart, Kerensa wished she would have been a little less accepting. Then to make matters worse, Nana said the one thing Kerensa didn't want to reflect upon.

"Thank you for saving my daughters life when she was in Buffalo. I don't think I ever had the chance to say that to you."

*I almost didn't save her life.*

18

Dominick cleared his throat and nodded his head.

"Actually, ma'am, that's why I'm here."

Suddenly there was a noise behind Nana. Kerensa knelt down, holding her arms out in front of her.

"Mommy!" her little girl shouted in glee.

She folded her precious daughter into her arms and gave her a big hug.

"Hi sweetheart, were you a good girl for Nana today?"

Janelle innocently nodded her head in response, her long, dark brown curls bouncing about her shoulders like a toy slinky.

Kerensa took Janelle's hand, and turned around to face Stone. Slowly clearing her throat, she proudly spoke.

"Dominick, I would like you to meet my daughter, Janelle."

If Stone was surprised, as usual he didn't show it. He bent down to his knees and carefully touched Janelle's hand. "Hello Janelle," he answered, in a gentle voice that surprised Kerensa. "How old are you?"

Janelle smiled shyly, quickly looking up at her mommy.

"It's alright, you can talk to him," she reluctantly murmured.

Janelle smiled wider and replied, "Three!"

"Wow!" Stone exclaimed. "What a big girl you are!"

Janelle nodded her head. Kerensa observed how comfortable her little girl was around Stone. She watched Janelle leave the safety of her arms and nudge closer to Stone. He immediately realized this, and asked her if she would like to be picked up. She quickly nodded her head in response. Stone easily hoisted the child into his arms and held her there. Content, Janelle looked down at her mother.

Kerensa's mouth was open in shock. Her daughter had never allowed a stranger to touch her like that; especially a stranger that would be big like a dinosaur but not purple like Barney. Embarrassed that Stone might think she hadn't taught her daughter a thing about 'stranger-danger,' she opened her mouth in defense, except Nana spoke first.

"I've never seen Janelle this friendly!"

"She's as pretty as her mama," Stone reflected softly, his gaze holding hers captive.

Kerensa took a deep breath, but was at a loss for words. *Great, I'm staring at him like a lovesick teenager who just received a compliment from the most popular guy in her eighth grade class. Knock it off!*

Nana glanced at Kerensa as she spoke. "Would you like a cup of coffee, Sergeant Stone?"

"Yes, thank you."

Nana shot Kerensa another quick glance, and Kerensa sighed, reaching for the coffee pot. *I might as well accept the fact that being around this man makes me feel like an insecure child again.*

She quickly poured him a cup and sat down at the table. Nana turned around, preparing to leave them alone.

"No, Mrs. Drago, don't leave. This also concerns you."

Kerensa stared sharply at him, loosing what little patience she had. Reaching over, she took Janelle away from him.

"Look, Sergeant Stone," she interrupted, deliberately addressing him as formally as possible. "I'm very busy this evening, just tell us what's going on and then leave, OK?"

She heard a slight gasp from Nana, and knew that she did not approve of Kerensa's rude behavior. *I'm sorry, Nana, but he's a jerk.*

Stone's gaze rested on Kerensa's soft features and he studied her smoldering, chocolate brown eyes, except they were more like angry hot chocolate eyes right about now. Still, they brought him back to another place, another moment in time. *Sergeant Stone? You weren't saying Sergeant Stone when you were moaning in pleasure, when I was inside your hot, wet body and you were...*

He cleared his throat, pushing the other thoughts aside.

"Jonathan Thorne was released from prison yesterday," he unequivocally replied, his bluntness deliberate.

Kerensa reacted violently to his words. She spontaneously gasped, desperately fighting the urge to vomit. *Breathe, breathe, and breathe.*

"How-how can that be?" she stammered.

Dominick observed Kerensa's reaction. It was all the validation that he needed to remain in Florida.

"He was only given ten years for kidnapping you, and his sentence was reduced to second degree murder for the death of your father. A sentence is rarely served to the end, Kerensa. He had a perfect record, when he went up in front of the judge for parole, it was granted."

"Oh yea, right, what do you mean, a perfect record? He killed my father with his 'perfect record'. Then he decided to kidnap me with his 'perfect record.' But he goes to prison and suddenly he's at the top of Santa's Christmas list? Does the judicial system use a dictionary from another solar system...?

And why wasn't I notified!" she suddenly shrieked.

"You were, but unfortunately the letter went to your old address. It's been over a year since you moved so it wasn't forwarded by the post office."

"Why didn't they notify Dr. O'Brian?"

Stone frowned.

"Dr. O'Brian wasn't the victim, Kerensa, you were."

Kerensa rubbed her forehead with her fingertips. She couldn't believe this was happening and she was scared to death. Nana remained silent, but she watched Stone very carefully. This man impressed her, she could tell that he was worried about this new situation, and he wasn't about to let anything happen to Kerensa. She could also tell something else. Although Kerensa would never agree with Nana regarding this, she knew that Stone still had feelings for her. That simple observation unfortunately was far from elementary in the long run, it was actually quite complicated. While Kerensa remained in silent shock, Nana decided to speak.

"What now, Sergeant Stone?"

Stone smiled grimly at Nana.

"There are secondary options; however I would like to take Kerensa home with me."

*Take me home with you? I would rather be stuck in a cage with a gorilla on Viagra.*

"That is entirely out of the question. Maybe a trick like that would have worked when I was twenty and I didn't have a choice, but I have a life and a choice now. First, and most importantly, I am not uprooting my child or leaving her behind. Second, my students will be performing in competitions in less than three months. They have several days of practice ahead of them, and we plan on traveling to New Jersey." She paused only long enough to take a deep breath. "Besides, if it's protection you're worried about, Vance is here for us."

Stone felt that familiar hot laser through his heart again.

"It sounds like you believe Kerensa is in danger," Nana continued, obviously ignoring her daughter's academy performance.

"Yes, she's definitely in danger. Jonathan wanted her inheritance the first time and he felt he had the right to it as her half brother. I'm sure he still expects this money, and just for the record, Kerensa, I would expect all of you to come to Buffalo with me."

*Oh like that would really work out.*

"Jonathan would be the prime suspect if he did anything to me, shouldn't that keep him away?"

"It didn't keep him away the last time, Kerensa, nothing has changed since then. He may try to harass you, or do things that won't necessarily harm you, but that could easily escalate to a level where you would be in danger again."

*Janelle, oh dear God, Janelle!*

"What about Janelle?" Would he-"she hesitated, the very thought of something happening to her child forcing her voice to slip away.

"I don't know," he softly answered.

*Jonathan Thorne... Sick, demented Jonathan Thorne near my little girl.*

Kerensa didn't say a word; she couldn't speak, hot bile rising to her throat and threatening to force her to loose her lunch. There was complete silence for several moments. The only sound in the room was the little toy weasel that Janelle was playing with. *Ironically enough.*

She took a deep breath, forcing herself not to think about the worst possible scenario. Maybe Jonathan was sorry for what he did.

"Well, what are the chances that Jonathan Thorne has, you know, changed? I mean, don't they rehab people in prison?"

*Oh God, please tell me he could be a better person now.*

Stone looked at Kerensa with the same expression he would use if he were speaking to her three year old daughter. He slowly shook his head from side to side, forgetting how naive Kerensa was. *Did she think Thorne took sensitivity classes to get in touch with his feminine side, too?*

"People don't change, Kerensa, if anything, Thorne only learned how to manipulate the system better than before."

"I definitely realize that people don't change", she replied bitterly, staring calculatingly back. *Just look at you.*

Stone didn't flinch at her caustic words purposely aimed at him. He didn't say a word either.

"So what other options do I have?"

"There are no other options that I'm in agreement with."

She sat upright. Squaring her shoulders and forcing her tone of voice to sound unwavering and determined, as though she were a woman with a purpose.

"Frankly my going away with you isn't going to happen and I won't let you bully me into it."

He momentarily showed his annoyance, so she purposely met his eyes with conviction.

"Maybe you don't care about what I want Kerensa, but Dr. O'Brian is also concerned. All he's asking is that you allow me to be with you until we know what's going on."

"But that's precisely the problem. I refuse to run from this man for the rest of my life. When does a problem like this end and I get my life back?"

"I can't answer that."

"Well that's not good enough for me."

Stone opened his mouth to speak when suddenly the doorbell rang. Kerensa knew it could only be one person. She quickly looked at Stone.

"Does the a-friend know about any of this?" he asked.

"Fiancé, and no, I never talked about it."

'And you plan on spending the rest of your life with this man?" Stone mockingly asked.

Kerensa's mouth dropped open, but she was too angry to form any words. *Yea, because you know everything there is to know about communication, oh wait, that's right you forgot to tell me our relationship was over.*

Nana's mouth dropped open too.

Kerensa glared into his face, and then walked out of the room to get the door. When she was gone, Nana spoke to him.

"Sergeant Stone, I suggest you watch what you say to my daughter and you watch how you say it. She's an independent, intelligent young woman, who doesn't need to be told what to do."

"Yea, so I remember," Stone gruffly replied. "But unfortunately diplomacy has never been my strong point."

Then grinning at Nana he said, "Please call me, Dominick."

Nana barely smiled. "She's not going to change her mind, Dominick."

"I know that too Mrs. Drago, but I'm prepared."

"Prepared for what?"

"I won't leave until I know she's safe. Actually, until I know everyone is safe."

Now she clucked her tongue and shook her head from side to side.

"She's still very angry with you, and she took your absconding rather well. I probably would have shot you."

Stone chuckled, despite Nana's seriousness. *Absconded? That was about the best adjective he had heard thus far.*

"Yes ma'am, I know I was wrong," Stone agreed, attempting to keep his amusement at bay. "But at the risk of sounding heartless, I don't even care about that right now."

Nana liked his style, but she knew better than to ever let Kerensa know that. Dominick Stone was a very sore subject with Kerensa. Nana sat in quiet contemplation and was about to speak again. Suddenly Kerensa came back into the room, with Vance by her side. He looked considerably disgruntled and Kerensa appeared anxious. There were several moments of awkward silence when finally Vance spoke first.

"Kerensa gave me an overview; I would like to be filled in on the details." Of course Vance was looking at Stone when he said this. Kerensa prayed that Stone would be professional enough to accept Vance's request. However, he didn't answer him, his cold blue eyes staring into Kerensa's face instead.

"What have you told him?" he quietly asked.

Kerensa took a deep breath, bound and determined not to let him get under her skin.

"I told him that something happened to me eight years ago and now the person is already out on parole. I didn't explain anything else."

*And he accepted that as an immediate explanation? This guy's a real winner.*

"Well then, it looks like you have a lot of catching up to do." Stone rose to his feet as he said this, stepping away from the table.

"I will be back at seven o'clock, Kerensa."

He extended his hand out to shake Vance's. Vance deliberately hesitated before taking his.

"After Kerensa tells you the details, I will be glad to discuss a plan with you. I apologize about that situation back there at the studio." *The part where I kicked your ass.*

Stone didn't wait for Vance to respond; he took Nana's hand next and held it for a moment.

"Nice to meet you, Mrs. Drago, thanks for the hospitality." Janelle had wandered into the dining room, her little head cocked to one side as she stood between her mama and Nana. Stone saw her hiding there, and he winked at her too. Then, he turned on his heels and walked away.

Kerensa stared in shock at him, and continued to do so until he disappeared and she heard the kitchen door close behind him.

"So let's hear it," Vance replied, forcing her attention back to him. She tried hard to ignore the edgy tone of anger in his voice.

Kerensa sighed, she preferred to forget what happened to her, but in a few short hours it was all brought to the forefront again.

"Eight years ago my father died suddenly by what they first diagnosed as a heart attack. He was a physician at Children's Hospital and living in Buffalo, NY. I was summoned to Buffalo immediately following his death because he changed his will and named his colleague, Dr. O'Brian as my guardian. I was only twenty years old at the time." Kerensa took a deep breath; she was surprised at how difficult it still was for her to talk about the incident.

"Well, Dr. O'Brian hired Sergeant Stone to investigate my father's death because he didn't believe it was by natural causes. It turned out, he was right." Kerensa paused again, fighting back the tears that suddenly had a mind of their own.

"My dad was married before he met my mom and had a son, but I didn't know that. Maybe my mom did, but she died when I was very young, so I guess that will always be between them. My father's son is Jonathan Thorne. He killed my father and he kidnapped me. His plan was to kill my father and inherit his money as the only living heir. He never knew I existed until my father's death and he read the obituaries. Of course I was living here, in Florida at the time. So, the only thing he could do to get the money, was to dispose of me. Dominick was also hired to be my body guard. He—"

This time Kerensa paused because she decided not to tell him about Stone's trickery. She didn't want Vance to know that Stone pretended to be Dr. O'Brian, moving into her father's home and masquerading as her guardian. She didn't want him to know that she fell in love with him too.

"So if this guy is so good, how did you end up kidnapped?"

Kerensa sighed, hating to discuss her own lack of good judgment.

"I wasn't told about the possibility that my dad was murdered, so I gave Stone and his partner, Nate, a really hard time. I even ran away and during that period of time, Stone was shot, and Jonathan along with a couple other guys abducted me."

"How did they find you?"

Kerensa sighed softly.

"I don't know, I never asked about those details. I only know that Stone was injured, actually he was shot but signed out of the hospital and traced me to this deserted warehouse where Jonathan kept me captive. Nate got there first, but he was almost killed by one of the other guys…and well, then Stone just appeared."

She suddenly stopped talking, recalling how he either killed or severely injured anyone in his way. She suddenly looked into Vance's hazel eyes. His brows were furrowed together in a determined frown. She didn't like to see his handsome features so serious. She watched as he ran his fingers through his tan, short hair. Finally, he spoke.

"It sounds like Dominick Stone is your hero."

She gasped.

*Maybe I was goaded into a little hero worship but really, is that all you can think about? Good grief, I was almost killed by a stepbrother I didn't know I had, I was…*

Kerensa took a deep breath, stuffing her wounded emotions away.

"No, it's not like that. Stone may have saved me that day, but that's it…end of story." *Now why in the world are you lying like this! Stop and tell him the truth…*

Vance nodded his head.

"So now Thorne is out on parole already and Stone is worried you may be in danger again. I will handle this, Kerensa; I can make sure that you and Janelle are safe. We don't need any of Stone's help. I realize that it was a serious crime committed against you back then, but Thorne knows he should stay away from you now if he wants to keep his freedom. I won't let anything happen to you, I promise. I think you can tell Stone to go home, if that's alright with you," he added.

"Yes, that's fine with me." Kerensa hoped she sounded more confident than she felt.

"I'll be back later to tell this James Bond wannabe that you don't need him around."

*And I'm going to love doing it.*

Vance leaned over and kissed Kerensa goodbye, then he left.

*James Bond wannabe, hah? You have no clue.*

Kerensa wiped the tears from her eyes and thought about leaving the house before either man came back. Actually she wondered how much time she had to pack everyone a bag and leave the country.

*   *   *

Vance was speeding down the highway, his eyes glued to the road, his thoughts everywhere else. He wasn't even aware of how fast he was traveling, and that was definitely not Vance Robertson's style. He followed the law perfectly, didn't believe in stretching it, or breaking it. There was no gray in Vance Robertson's life, no gray in law and order, just black or white. His thoughts were on Kerensa and this mysterious detective, renegade warrior, a cross between James Bond and Steven Segal all wrapped up in one big precarious package. Who the hell is this guy? Really?

Vance came from a long line of police officers; both his father and his grandfather were retired detectives. He was raised around cops and the law, enforcing justice was built into his entire life. In his career and even as a young adult, he could recall many types of law enforcement officials he encountered. From the brave to the cowards, from the strong with commitment and values to the individuals who didn't want to over extent themselves if justice happened then it happened. He had seen them all, or so he thought.

But this man?

He was all of the above, and none of the above. He'd seen a facsimile of his type before, and he was afraid of very few men, but Dominick Stone was that someone Vance was fearful of. And it pissed him off. *A lot.*

It was the way he walked, the way he carried himself with lethal swiftness and purpose, the lightening flash move he pulled on him without a flicker of an eye, but it was especially the empty, bleak look of darkness in his eyes. Yes, it was that look …and it caught his attention, fast. He had witnessed men like him in the army reserves. It was that reflection in the eyes of burned out solders that had seen or created way too much death and destruction. They were numb, unable to feel anything at all and unable to talk about why. And he knew better than to ever ask. Yet, he wasn't really frightened of them either.

Dominick Stone wasn't just a 'detective' or just a 'sergeant' or just anything. He was a lot of something and Vance was going to find out what that something was.

He pulled into the precinct and slammed his car door with more force and anger that he didn't realize he had. *We'll just see who the hell you really are, you son of a bitch.*

# 4

Kerensa rubbed her temples hoping to force her sudden, out of control headache at bay. She looked up to see Nana enter the room.

"How did Vance take the news?" she asked.

Kerensa shrugged her shoulders.

"He didn't have much to say but I guess he handled it well."

"What happened at the studio?"

She sighed loudly now, deliberately acting theatrical. "Vance tried to punch Stone out, but he was too quick and knocked Vance to the floor. Then to make matters worse, he held him down until I screamed at him to let Vance go. The only thing missing was the camera crew."

Nana tried not to laugh, but Kerensa could see the grin threatening to reach her lips.

"Well, Dominick plans on returning this evening and I just think you need to hear what he has to say," she replied.

"Whatever he suggests I do for protection, Vance is capable of following through with," Kerensa protested back.

"Is Vance coming back too?"

Kerensa scoffed cynically. "What do you think?"

"It sounds like he's got a little competition, that's what I think."

"In what way?"

Nana peered at her from over her glasses. "It's pretty obvious, honey."

"Well if you think he cares about me, you're wrong. He came here because he was hired by Dr. O'Brian again. That man is motivated by money."

Nana didn't answer right away, tugging at the string that she found in the seam of her shirt and pulling it free.

"I know you have issues with him, honey, but I don't see him that way at all."

*Issues, hah? Wanting to strangle him until his head popped off wasn't exactly categorized as an issue.*

Kerensa sighed. She actually didn't see him that way either, but she was allowing her emotions to take over her cognitive thinking. He had a way of doing that to her, scrambling her brain like it deliberately jumped into a frying pan. He wanted to protect her again, afraid that she might be facing danger. It would behoove her to listen; after all, she was almost killed the last time partly because of her stubbornness. This time she had Janelle's welfare to think about. No, she shouldn't respond to him like this was a knee jerk reaction. It was just so frustrating that she had finally decided to move on and now he was back in her life again. Especially now since Vance asked her to marry him. *I'm in love with Vance, so what do I care about any of that?*

She groaned softly beneath her breath. This was becoming more and more complicated by the second.

Kerensa helped Nana with the remainder of dinner and the three of them sat down and ate. The tone was quiet, interrupted occasionally with a question or two from Janelle. Restless, she immediately cleared off the table, and Nana told her not to worry about the dishes, she would do them later on.

"Go sit down with Janelle and relax for a few minutes before our guests arrive," Nana had said.

Guests, Kerensa thought wryly to herself. It was more like Attila the Hun and the Boy Scout with an attitude.

Then, the doorbell rang.

"Let the fights begin," she mumbled sarcastically beneath her breath, attempting to iron her wrinkled blouse with her palms. There was no sense fixing her unruly dark curls into place, they had a mind of their own anyway. She glanced in the hallway mirror before she arrived to the door. Deep, stormy black eyes stared back at her. They were nestled between a straight, little Italian nose and high cheekbones. She always thought her lips were too full for her mouth.

She pulled the door open, expecting to see Dominick, instead it was Vance.

His features appeared much calmer than he was earlier, helping Kerensa to relax a little more. He stepped inside, and then pulled her into his arms.

"I'm sorry I was so abrupt with you before I left," he murmured into her ear. "It's just that there was a lot of information to digest and I needed to get it all straight in my head. It must have been such a horrible ordeal for you. I love you and Janelle, and I'm very concerned about you. But we'll get through this; I just want you to know that I'll do what it takes to make sure you're safe."

*Now that was more like it.*

She nodded her head, grateful that he was thinking more clearly again. But she wasn't so sure if he would stay that way by the end of the night. It was obvious that Stone knew just how to push Vance's buttons. Actually, Stone knew how to push everyone's buttons. They remained in an embrace until Kerensa heard another sound at the door. Looking past Vance, she saw Stone standing there. She quickly pulled herself out of his hold, and opened the door.

Stone acknowledged Vance's presence, noticing how protective his arm was around her shoulders. He also noticed something else; the way Kerensa's smooth skin glowed with an inner light. The way the evening sun filtered through the foyer window and lightly danced across her dark brown curls. The way she filled out those snug little jeans…

*She's killing me.*

"Why don't we go into the living room," Kerensa replied, stepping ahead of both men and leading them there. Stone tried to focus his eyes on something besides the provocative movement of Kerensa's nicely rounded behind.

Nana was already in the living room waiting for them; Janelle sat quietly on her lap. Stone quickly greeted her with a nod of the head and a smile. Then he blew a kiss to Janelle. Kerensa watched Nana and Janelle smile back, and she was aggravated that it was apparent he could be charming with women of all ages. She suddenly wondered if Nana liked him better than Vance. *Now what made that thought pop into your head?* Kerensa sat next to Vance determined that she wasn't going to let any lapses of silence occur in this little, but potentially deadly, rendezvous. The sooner they discussed things, the better she could end it and get rid of both of them. So she decided to speak first.

"Vance and I discussed this situation at great length after you left. We decided that if I should require any protection, Vance is capable of providing this."

Stone's features remained stiff and cold, his eyes focused straight ahead.

"Are you currently employed?" He gruffly asked Vance.

"I am working on a case right now, why?"

"When do you think you're going to find the time to protect both of them?"

"We can work that out," Vance tersely retorted.

"I'm listening," Stone countered. "She's going to need twenty four hour protection, how are you going to work that out?"

Vance hesitated, his eyes flashing in visible anger.

"What makes you think Jonathan Thorne is that dangerous?"

Stone focused directly on Vance. His eyes were like tiny blue marbles.

"He attempted to kill the woman you plan on marrying, Detective Robertson, isn't that validation enough for you?"

Kerensa squirmed in her chair, but was speechless. Stone's remark hit home and Vance was not happy. It was also obvious to Kerensa that Stone was not impressed with Vance's lack of sincerity either. She was right, Stone made up his mind right then and there that Vance did not deserve her.

Nana decided it was time to referee.

"It was quite an ordeal for Kerensa and all of us, Vance. I'm sure that Dominick is trying to prevent any of that from even remotely happening again."

"It's not going to happen again," Vance abruptly retorted. "I will do everything in my power to keep her out of harms way."

"You're damn right you will," Stone retorted bluntly.

Kerensa gasped at his game of playing the biggest bully.

*Are you going to pee against his chair and mark your territory too?*

Stone glanced her way, but continued to speak again, his eyes narrowed to slits of blue black coal. They actually had an eerie glow about them. His tone remained quiet and lethal.

"So, did she tell you how Thorne tormented her? How he bound and gagged her, or how long she stayed in the hospital after he brutally beat her? Did she tell you how my partner found her half dead with Thorne on top of her; how she was almost raped by her own half brother? Did she—"

*I think I'm going to be sick. Shut up! Just shut up!*

She quickly jumped to her feet and ran out of the room. Nana glared at both men, her gaze lingering on Stone. Before she had a chance to get up, Stone was fast on his feet. He shot Vance a look of warning as he strode out of the room after Kerensa.

Kerensa stood stooped over the kitchen sink ready to dry heave her liver out. She was trembling with anger and bitterness. How dare Dominick Stone come back into her life and resurrect old terrifying experiences. How dare he threaten her fiancé like this?

She heard a rustling of footsteps and expecting to see Vance, she looked up at him with tears streaming down her pale face. Instead, it was Stone. She quickly turned away, attempting to wipe her cheeks with her trembling fingertips. Stone stood quietly beside her. *Take a deep breath and don't get sick. Don't get sick. Don't get sick.*

Kerensa could feel her usual spunk returning.

She felt his arm across her shoulders, and shaking him off, she turned and glared into his eyes.

"Don't touch me! You are by far the most heartless and cold blooded man I have ever met. You have no right to tell Vance those horrible things about my past, it was my past, damn you, my past! Then you just waltz back into my life and act like you're my savior, and treat Vance like he's a piece of dirt too. *Breathe, Kerensa, breathe.* Despite the obvious notion that you think you're a real life comic book hero, Vance is more than capable of protecting me!"

Stone cynically scoffed and Kerensa wanted to rip his face off.

"Open your eyes, Kerensa. He's not realizing the extent of your danger, which means he will not protect you the way I will. I know what Jonathan is capable of and I know his mind set. I can predict his movements much better than he can. You're allowing your personal issues between us get in the way."

"My personal issues between us!" Kerensa shrieked, realizing her voice was a little too high; she lowered it to a whisper.

"You deserted me and took advantage of my…" *Don't say the love word!* "Feelings for you, and you turned it into something cheap and dirty. I was young and foolish, and I didn't know any better. There wasn't anything more than that between us. I barely know you, Sergeant Stone. I am in love with Vance and he is qualified to protect me." Kerensa took a deep breath. "And I don't require your services, either."

Stone steadied his own voice, although he could feel the blood in his carotid pounding.

"I didn't come here to certify our relationship. I came to protect you, Kerensa; you have a child to think of too. Do you really believe that he can dedicate himself to protecting your family completely?"

Kerensa glared steadily into Stone's face. There wasn't a flicker of emotion in it. *Doesn't this man have any feelings?*

"Yes, I know he can."

"You are making a mistake, Kerensa."

"No, I'm not," she retorted, deliberately turning her back to him.

Stone reached out, firmly seizing her shoulders and whirling her around to face him. His hands were warm and strong and the heat from them was burning a hole into her heart. She felt weak and lifeless, and unable to breathe in his grasp. *Damn you, you cannot affect me like this again. No, you will not affect me again!*

Slowly she forced her eyes to meet his. Stone's gaze remained locked with Kerensa's for a long time. It was difficult for him to remain focused when her words iced his very soul. Then he spoke again.

"If you really don't have any feelings for me than whatever happened between us is in the past, so let it go." Stone forced himself to continue despite the reflection of emotional pain that just flickered in her eyes. "There's no reason why you shouldn't allow me to protect you until we're sure you aren't in any danger."

She tried to shake his hands from her shoulders.

He didn't move, so she turned her face away.

"I don't require your services, Sergeant Stone."

Stone sighed.

"Kerensa look-I-I never meant to hurt you."

*Hurt me? You emotionally murdered me!*

Kerensa stiffened her shoulders but not before she took a deep, cleansing breath. She wanted to keep her tone as void of emotion as humanly possible.

"Get your hands off me, and please leave, Sergeant Stone. We both know that it's too late for apologies."

He released the grip on her shoulders and took a small step backward. For a long time, he still didn't speak. Kerensa never moved from her position, her body was facing him, but her head was turned away. Finally, he spoke again.

"Good luck, Ms. Fiori, and for future reference, I never once treated you like some cheap whore."

*Yes you did, on the day you disappeared!*

Kerensa took another deep breath, her trembling voice barely above a whisper.

"We are past history, and I stopped thinking about you a long time ago, so don't flatter yourself. Besides that, maybe you should rethink that statement about how you treated me." She paused a moment, her deep breath steadying her tone again. "Women can be bought as cheap as a pound of bologna; didn't you once say that to me, Sergeant Stone?"

*Oh damn.*

Stone paused in his tracks.

"That was a general statement, Kerensa. Maybe I used the term once, I don't remember."

"Maybe you used the term once? She bitterly laughed. "Think again. I bet there are a lot of things you conveniently don't remember."

Stone was as big as life as he silently towered over Kerensa. There was a sudden softness to his features, a smoldering heat to his blue black eyes.

"But there are some things I will never forget, sweetheart."

He cupped her face in one of his big hands. "And it was still good to see you again." He paused briefly as though he wanted to say more, but changed his mind. Then he walked away from her.

She watched his strapping torso stroll right out of the kitchen. Dominick marched directly into the living room and stood in front of Vance. This intimidating action immediately forced Vance to stand up and face him too. There was a look in Stone's eyes that surprised even Nana.

"This family is all yours to protect, Detective Robertson and I trust that you will do so with your own life. If anything happens, anything at all…"

Stone paused, searching for the right words to say without bluntly telling him that he was a dead man.

*Oh, what the hell.*

"You won't live to tell about it."

Vance didn't have the chance to respond, as Stone nodded his head toward Nana and strode right out the door.

And Kerensa puked her guts out.

\* \* \*

*Well that went over like a hot air balloon on an electrical wire.*

He sat in his vehicle for a few minutes before starting up the engine, simply staring at the front window, watching Kerensa slowly walk back into the living room. He realized how difficult this situation was for her, but he could ring her neck for being so stubborn. Yes, he was furious with her, but he also knew the timing was all wrong to prove a point. He would have time to do that soon enough. He would make her think that he accepted her answer and that he headed back to Buffalo. Instead, he wasn't going anywhere except for everywhere she was going to be.

Stone thought about her child and sighed. He knew about her marriage, his friend and partner, Nate, had told him about it. He knew about her divorce too. But he didn't know about Janelle, and unfortunately she was the perfect target for someone as sick as Jonathan Thorne. If Thorne still wanted Kerensa dead to inherit her money, now Janelle was the only one standing in his way. He knew that it wasn't just about the money anymore.

*Retaliation.*

It was a hunting game for sick, demented Jonathan Thorne. The man was a predator, a cold blooded killer, and he knew all about men like that.

*Revenge and retribution.* Money was the frosting on the cake.

Maybe Thorne didn't even realize that yet. But Stone did. He was way ahead of Thorne when it came to hatred.

He considered the situation at hand. There was a lot more at risk now besides Kerensa's safety, and this idiot fiancé of hers didn't have a clue. Stone was still going to take responsibility for her, and her child.

He thought about how he would feel once he saw her again. He had prepared himself to be unemotional, to simply do his job here and then get the hell out of her life, yet laying eyes on her again proved to be even more risky than he ever imagined.

She looked the same as she had almost a decade ago. Her face even more striking than he remembered too. And her body, that dancer hard, yet soft and ever so supple body, always yielding beneath him, a perfect fit. With curves, more curves than he ever remembered. Mature, with hips and thighs rounder, sexier *Geezus, I'm sweating buckets.*

And he wanted to kill that fiancé of hers, jealousy playing the most important part in his desire to cut the man's heart out. Kerensa Fiori would always belong to him and him alone, he tried to forget her hundreds of times, no, probably millions of times, but that beautiful face haunted his dreams, claimed responsibility for many of his nightmares, and disturbed his thoughts time and time again.

*If I had refused to investigate Dr. Fiori's death eight years ago, I would never have met Kerensa Fiori.*

Dominick Stone was a man who did what he had to do, and never liked to consider regrets. Regrets were out of context for him, certainly not the style of a powerful man whose choices and decisions destroyed people's lives. How many times did he ever look back?

What was it about Kerensa that made these buried and sealed feelings from long ago rear their ugly heads to kick him in the ass? He wanted to leave her to the mercy of her fiancé's protection but that simply would not do.

She had a little girl now, and he was obligated to ensure that Janelle would have a chance to grow up. Hopefully, she would never meet a man as treacherous and untrustworthy as he was.

*Sergeant Dominick Stone? Hell, he hadn't used that title in years.*

# 5

Three weeks passed since Stone's visit. Kerensa didn't hear from him again, and figured that he went back to Buffalo. She tried to put all thoughts of him out of her head, but he just kept popping back into her mind like a jack-in-the-box. Vance proved true to his promise, and made sure that he was there whenever she was out and about. Kerensa remained alert and aware at all times. She was scared to death now that Jonathan was free, but she also hoped that his parole officer would have a good handle on his whereabouts. Vance explained to Kerensa that Jonathan would be violating his parole if he left his home state of Ohio, without getting permission first. Vance also called Jonathan's parole officer and apprised him of the situation with Kerensa. Of course, Vance also found out that Stone had already done so. Neither one of them discussed Dominick Stone again. Kerensa was grateful that Vance never asked her any personal questions regarding their relationship. She knew that he wanted to, but he respected her privacy and expected her to tell him when she was ready. She felt a little guilty about that.

Kerensa quickly took a shower and put a sun dress on. It was almost eighty two degrees already, and for some reason, the heat was getting to her today. Her short, lightweight dress was just the right thing.

"Come on Janelle, it's time to go to school," Kerensa called into the other room.

"I don't want to go today, mommy. I want to stay home and play outside."

Kerensa took the little girl into her arms.

"You have a field trip to the zoo today!" she exclaimed. "Are you sure you want to stay home?"

Janelle thought for a brief moment.

"Are the tigers going to be there?"

"Absolutely."

"And bears?"

"Yes."

"Monk-eyes too?"

Kerensa giggled, she knew how much Janelle loved the monkeys. "Yes, honey, lots of monkeys too."

"OK, mommy, I want to go!"

Kerensa laughed again, chasing Janelle and carrying her into the living room.

"What about you, mommy?" Janelle asked.

"I have to go shopping today."

"Will you buy me a toy?"

"I will buy you something special."

Today, Kerensa was in the mood to shop. She only had two months left before she was taking her students to Wildwoods, New Jersey, and she needed to start buying the material for their costumes, sequins, beads, appliqués and lace. There was so much to do yet too. She needed to make arrangements regarding where they were going to stay, and what the final cost would be.

They quickly went to find Nana and located her in the back sun room watching a little television. Kerensa teased her when she walked into the room.

"What are you watching so early in the morning? The soaps aren't on until one o'clock."

Nana laughed, barely glancing up from her program.

"Where are you going?"

"I'm taking Janelle to school, and then I'm going to get some shopping done for our trip."

"Is Vance going to pick you up here?"

"No, he couldn't get away this early. He'll meet me at the mall."

Nana stopped watching television and gave Kerensa her full attention.

"Do you think that's a very good idea?"

Nana sighed; somehow that wasn't reassuring enough for her. Jonathan could be up to no good and still make every parole appointment. Kerensa could tell how uneasy Nana was. She quickly wrapped her arms around her neck and kissed her on the cheek.

"Do you like Vance?" Kerensa suddenly asked.

Nana paused briefly.

"Yes, I think he's a very good man. Now why do you ask?"

"I don't know, I guess because I could tell you really liked Dominick, but I never got the same message when it came to Vance."

Nana hesitated again.

"I think Vance is a wonderful person, Kerensa. I also think that you bring out the best in him."

"Come on, Nana, I know there's more," she prompted.

Nana laughed.

"Kerensa, I don't want to say something that will make you upset with me. It's just that Dominick made me feel as though I would never have to worry about you when you were with him. It's just a 'mom' thing, that's all."

Nana thought another moment. "I like his daring, rather fearless attitude too."

*Fearless attitude? You don't know the half of it.*

"You wouldn't like it on a twenty four-seven basis."

Nana smiled with her eyes.

"I'm serious," she protested. "He's like a mutant Tyrannosaurus Rex and Godzilla when he's on a case. Actually, that's just the way he is."

"Perhaps," Nana mused, shaking her head at Kerensa's unique way with words.

"He's not like other men," Kerensa continued slowly, suddenly laughing out loud. "I know how Hollywood that sounds but he's not average or ordinary. He's, well-a hero, well, kind of. *When he's not being a jerk.* I don't know he's just not the kind of man that settles down with a wife, and children and all that other stuff. A normal life wouldn't be enough for him. He's just different—that's all."

*And that's why we will never be together.*

"Well, Kerensa, I know you don't want to hear this, but even super heroes have to settle down some day. There's something about your relationship with him that clicks."

"How could you say that? You saw me; I'm like a raving maniac around him!"

Nana laughed again.

"Yes, but he makes you come alive. He seems to send these sparks of energy that I can actually feel all around you."

"Well," Kerensa mussed thoughtfully. "He blew it a long time ago so it's too late now, and that's just the way it goes."

Nana didn't respond to that statement. "Please be careful, honey." Then she reached down and gave Janelle a big kiss goodbye.

"Always," Kerensa called out and blew her a kiss too.

Kerensa walked Janelle into the classroom and left. A few minutes later she was on the highway and heading to the mall, thinking about her conversation with Nana. In many ways, she knew that Nana was right. There was a primal chemistry between Stone and her, it was raw and untamed, and if unleashed would definitely be out of control. She had a glimpse of that in the short period of time she shared with him. Yet perhaps this chemistry was purely physical, after all she was a lot younger and that could be why she thought she was in love with him. She certainly didn't want to think about how much he hurt her when he left without any explanations. She didn't think she could ever forgive him for that either.

Kerensa pulled into the parking ramp adjacent to the mall. It was the best place to put her car to protect it from the hot sun. She quickly got out of the car and headed towards the mall entrance, where she agreed to meet Vance. Kerensa waited there for over twenty minutes, but he didn't show up. Annoyed, she called him on the cell phone, but there wasn't an answer. Kerensa glanced at her wrist watch. It was almost ten o'clock already, and she was wasting precious time waiting. Sighing loudly, she tried again. This time, he answered.

"Where are you?" she asked, annoyance reflecting in her tone.

"I'm busy, I can't get there. Call me every hour until you leave so I know you're alright. That's the best I can do, I'm sorry."

Kerensa paused, she didn't want to leave the mall, but she didn't feel safe either. That was when she realized how much Jonathan was already controlling her life. She couldn't let that happen, because her fear would make him the one in charge of everything she did, and that was exactly what he wanted.

"Alright, I'll call you."

Kerensa hung up and quickly scurried away. *Way too much to do, gotta get a move on.*

Three hours later, Kerensa was finished. She briefly sat down in the middle of the mall to take a quick breather. It was one o'clock in the afternoon, but she managed to buy all her material, all the accessories, a new Dora the Explorer outfit for Janelle and a couple new pairs of shorts and shirts for herself. She was dying for something to drink, but she decided to wait until she got home. She needed to pick Janelle up at three thirty. Pulling her tired body forward, Kerensa headed out the front door and in the direction of the parking ramp. The hot, humid air outside slapped her in the face like a wet blanket, and it was only June. She wanted to pull her hair back but her hands were too full with packages. Feeling the heat, reminded her of Stone.

*Why is my brain short-cutting like this?*

Kerensa was almost to her car, when she saw someone in her peripheral vision. She quickly turned her head to look, but she was already too late. He was on top of her in an instant, grabbing her by the hair and yanking her backwards. Kerensa flung her packages behind her, attempting to hit him. It temporarily surprised her assailant and he hesitated long enough for Kerensa to pull away. She ran as fast as she could, and screamed for help, but there wasn't anyone around to hear her. Desperate, Kerensa continued to scream, hoping to catch someone's attention. When her assailant caught up with her again, Kerensa used what she had been taught in self defense. She kicked him hard with the back of her foot. This temporarily rendered him helpless, and Kerensa continued to run. Realizing how hopeless her situation was, she still kept on screaming. Suddenly someone else appeared from behind a parked car. His body was toned and muscular, bare shoulders wide enough to break another man in two. The man instantly kicked her assailant hard in the stomach, and when he doubled over with a low groan, he brutally kicked him again in the head. This time he fell to the ground with a sickening thud. Kerensa recognized the undisputable style of the man who rescued her. She had seen it many times in her last hair raising experience and his fighting was vicious. She stared into the indomitable face of Dominick Stone.

He quickly pulled Kerensa into the safety of his arms.

"Are you alright?" he hissed, his tone husky.

She numbly nodded her head as she trembled. Realizing that she was too shocked to walk, Stone scooped her up and carried her to his vehicle, carefully placing her inside. A small crowd had already gathered, pointing their fingers and talking about both of them. Stone spoke to the mall security. He told them what happened and that they were pressing charges. Another officer brought Kerensa her packages, while the rescue squad responded and took the guy to the hospital. They filed more reports and finally she was cleared to go home.

"We'll leave your car here," Dominick directed. "We can pick it up later."

Kerensa nodded her head in response. "Did you kill him?"

"I should have," Stone replied gruffly, glancing briefly at her.

She sighed warily with emotional exhaustion, not to mention terrified over what could easily be the beginning of a new nightmare.

*An old, new nightmare.*

They didn't say a word to one another all the way home. Dominick silently studied her as he drove. Her emotional health was already taking a bee line straight to hell and this attack wasn't a coincidence. He gritted his teeth with escalating anger towards this so called, *'caring fiancé'* of hers. Forcing himself to control his fury, he pulled into Kerensa's driveway and helped her out of the car.

"Don't worry about the packages, I'll get them."

She nodded her head, as he grabbed them for her. That's when he noticed she was walking with a slight limp. *And a slight limp for a dancer couldn't be a good thing.*

"Did he hurt you?"

"My ankle, I guess it's a little sore. I'll put some ice on it and wrap it. I'm sure it'll be alright."

*Yea, I know you keep trying to protect that brainless man of yours.*

Nana greeted them at the door. She immediately knew something was wrong when she saw Dominick. The color drained completely from her face.

"Holy Mary, what happened?" she quickly asked.

Stone shot Nana a look that could have killed a horse. She instantly knew it wasn't directed towards her, but she wasn't looking forward to the fireworks.

Stone set the packages down on the kitchen table before turning around to face both of them again. Nana in her infinite wisdom decided to pour him a large glass of iced tea.

*It'll take a lot more than a cold glass of sugar and a shot of caffeine to tame this beast Kerensa mussed fretfully.*

Nana handed it to him. "Please Dominick, come into the living room and have a seat."

He acknowledged her with the usual nod of his head, but there was no smile on his face. Kerensa sat on the sofa because she knew it would help her back which was also beginning to ache. Unexpectedly, Stone sat down beside her. He glanced at her slouched position, and her short sundress that barely covered the top part of her thighs. He could tell that she was hurting. This realization made him see red; his true wrath directed again in the direction of the man she claimed to be in love with.

Dominick turned his head away from her; he needed to stop taking this so personally. That was always his greatest liability, and dealing with Kerensa seemed to bring it out in him a little faster. He turned towards Nana who was waiting patiently for an explanation.

"A man tried to attack Kerensa in the parking lot," he responded, his voice still low and menacing.

Nana's face reflected her true fear.

"Oh my God," she whispered. "Where was Vance?"

"Where was Vance?" Stone cynically repeated, his tone now lethal.

Then he simply glared at Kerensa.

She silently met both their gazes. She didn't want to admit that Vance couldn't be there for her, knowing that Stone would cut his heart out. So she decided to blame it on herself.

"I told Vance it was alright if I shopped without him today. I, a-well I promised that I wouldn't be that long, and—" She suddenly stopped talking when she looked into Stone's skeptical features.

"You may be accustomed to lying to me, but don't lie to your Nana," he interrupted softly, an icy chill to his voice. "Besides Kerensa, even if that were true, a good detective should know better."

Kerensa sighed, he was right but she needed to make Dominick realize that the circumstances were unexpected. She opened her mouth to explain the details, but the doorbell rang. Nana quickly rose before Stone could even entertain the thought of meeting Vance first. Her actions caused Kerensa to smile inwardly, grateful that she could still see humor in this situation. She sat upright, attempting to pull her sundress down. Stone leaned forward, his gaze slowly caressing her body as he rested his elbows on his legs.

She quickly turned to face him before they came back into the room.

"It wasn't his fault, please don't do this."

"Do what?"

"Create a problem," she whispered.

He stared into her brown eyes, his gaze penetrating.

"It was his fault, plain and simple. So if you can't handle what's going to happen next, I suggest you leave the room."

There was a deadly edge to his tone, a warning that he wasn't going to go soft.

Kerensa's face turned hot with anger, but before she could respond to him, Vance entered the room followed by a very pale, Nana.

He appeared surprised but infuriated when he saw Stone. Momentarily caught off guard, he recovered and immediately knelt beside Kerensa.

Stone rose to his feet.

"When you didn't call after another hour I panicked," Vance replied, his tone reflecting his concern. "I kept calling you but there wasn't an answer. What's going on here?" Although he was asking Kerensa the question, it was Stone he was expecting the answer from.

"So what made you think she would be home?" Stone crisply asked, ignoring Vance's question.

Vance bristled, deciding he didn't have to put up with Stone's attitude anymore. He tried to deal reasonably with him, but they would never be comrades.

He rose to his feet and turned head on to face Stone. His hands went to his hips, and his legs were apart. Power vs. power, both men faced one another. Through gritted teeth, Vance ground his next words out.

"I didn't know where she was, but I didn't expect her to be with you. Now why are you here?"

"Doing your job," Stone retorted evenly. *You stupid fuck.*

"Look, I couldn't get away, it was totally unexpected."

There was a shroud of darkness that clouded Stone's features.

"That's a piss poor answer, Detective Robertson. You said you could protect them regardless of any unexpected circumstances. You shouldn't have accepted the responsibility of being her body guard, if you couldn't handle the job."

Vance swore vehemently aloud.

*Oh boy, this is bad.*

Kerensa held her breath she had never seen Vance so angry. Nana simply watched as the entire situation deteriorated by the minute. Somehow, Nana knew that Stone would never let it get out of control. Although Nana was right, she didn't know how far Stone would push it. Kerensa knew.

"You know I'm right," Stone declared, his tone menacing.

Suddenly Vance turned on Kerensa.

"So you called and told him I couldn't be there?"

Stone didn't give Kerensa the chance to become involved.

"No, that's not what happened," he interrupted bluntly. "And your issue is with me now, Detective Robertson, not Kerensa. You had one chance, and I warned you, but you failed. She's not yours to protect anymore."

"Like hell, she isn't," Vance furiously retorted. "Kerensa is my fiancé and she has a mind of her own."

He turned briefly toward Kerensa, as if daring her to disagree, then he continued, "Now unless you can give me one good reason why you should protect her instead of me then let's hear it."

Kerensa moaned softly beneath her breath. She knew that Stone was going to set Vance up; it was just a matter of time. She recalled how many times he had done it to her in the early days that she knew him.

*Score one for Stone, none for Vance.*

"Sure, I'll give you an example. While you were too busy at work, a guy tried to jump her in the mall parking lot."

Vance's face looked like a fresh blanket of winter snow. He took a step backwards, and then turned to face Kerensa.

"Is that true?" he foolishly asked.

*Oh God.* "Yes, Vance, but Dominick was there and he, well he-"

She didn't finish her sentence, she didn't need to. Vance knew the rest. She watched in horror as his fists clenched several times. As much as she knew he could hold his own in a fist fight, she also knew that he wouldn't last a round with Dominick Stone. This was the edge that Stone could take even a canonized saint to the tip of. Suddenly Stone took two strides closer to Vance, and in a very low voice, said something to him. Whatever it was, Vance nodded his head, dropping his arms to his sides. Then Stone walked across the room, motioning for Vance to sit beside Kerensa. *Or bring a canonized saint back from?*

For a few moments nothing changed, the only sound that could be heard was the old grandfather clock in the corner of the room, and the silly talking weasel that Janelle was playing with. Thank God she was so oblivious to the inferno in the living room.

Finally, Vance sat down beside Kerensa and put his arms around her.

"I'm really sorry, this happened," he murmured into her ear. "Did he hurt you?"

"No," I'm alright," she answered, already feeling too stiff to get off the couch. "It just scared me to death."

There was silence in the room again. Kerensa knew that Stone was giving Vance the opportunity to take control over the situation. Stone sat there silently, his gaze intent upon Kerensa. It was unsettling for her; like it always was when he looked at her that way. Then, at no surprise to Kerensa, Nana spoke.

"What is the answer to this problem, gentlemen?"

Stone remained silent, *a well planned silence* and it was Vance who answered.

"It's a good possibility that what happened today was no coincidence. Kerensa and Janelle require twenty four hour protection, and that will be difficult for me to provide."

Kerensa sat upright, despite the pain in her lower back.

"What does that mean for me?" she quietly asked.

"It means that Sergeant Stone will be your body guard," Vance replied, through clenched teeth. "But before I allow this to happen, I have some questions of my own." He glared into Stone's face. "Was there ever anything between you two?"

Nana studied Stone's face when Vance asked the question. She knew that Stone would know better than to respond. *Smart man, she thought to herself.*

Kerensa cleared her throat; because she knew that his question was meant for her alone to answer, although it would have been interesting to hear what Stone had to say.

"No, there was never anything between us," she lied, carefully avoiding Stone's gaze.

Vance wasn't so quick to believe Kerensa.

"What's your take on this question, Sergeant Stone?" Vance persisted.

Kerensa could feel the rise of heat to her face. She felt like a fool now that Vance showed a lack of trust in her and it hurt her feelings to think that her past relationship with Stone was the only thing he was concerned about at the moment.

Stone studied Kerensa's face, chuckling to himself. *Boyfriend gets a full ten points for knowing her so well.*

"Kerensa just told you the answer; so my response shouldn't be indicated." His tone held a note of warning as he leaned forward deliberately changing the subject as he spoke again.

"The only way I can properly protect this family is to keep Kerensa with me at all times. That would be easier to do so if I stay here. Is that alright with you, Mrs. Drago?"

"Yes, of course. I will set up the spare bedroom for you."

Stone nodded his head in acknowledgement, automatically assuming that it was alright for Kerensa. She contemplated a refusal, but she knew her little girl and Nana deserved to be protected by the best.

"I still plan on seeing Vance, so I won't need you during the time I'm with him," Kerensa tersely replied.

"He can visit you right here, but that's it."

"That is totally unacceptable to me!"

"It's my terms, and I've already compromised them. I wanted to take you back to Buffalo with me, remember?"

Although Stone's tone was like velvet, his eyes held a warning that she not argue with him.

Vance opened his mouth to speak, but Kerensa quickly stood up despite her stiffness.

"I'd like to see you alone in the kitchen, please," she declared, her voice trembling with anger as she spoke.

Nana appeared surprised and Vance was caught off guard. Stone simply rose to his feet and followed her. Once in the kitchen, Kerensa lashed out.

"Eight years ago I allowed you to call all the shots, and to the best of my recollection you pulled some dirty tricks on me. Even though that was a long time ago, and I was different back then, I know a lot more now…"

Kerensa pocked her finger into his face. "You will take your orders from me, Sergeant Stone, and if you don't agree with my choices, then we will discuss other options."

Stone chuckled softly beneath his breath, it was a low rumble, but she heard it loud as thunder in her ears, echoing off her memories like a hollow drum.

"And furthermore, I don't care if you were hired by Dr. O'Brian this time either, I will be the one in charge."

He wasn't about to tell Kerensa that he came to protect her again on his own accord and that Dr. O'Brian didn't have anything to do with it. He sat down at the kitchen table, and with his chin in his hands he silently studied her. She continued to stand before him, hands on the curve of her hips, and her brown eyes as black as dark chocolate. He didn't appreciate her spirit back then, it got in his way, but he was impetuous and impatient, and a different man back then too. Today, well, he was hoping he could accept variance a little better now. *Although there were no guarantees.*

"Alright Kerensa, let's try another compromise. You can call the shots as long as they don't interfere with your welfare or Janelle's. Otherwise, I take over. Is it a deal?"

"Who decides if it is interfering with our welfare?" She persisted again. This time Stone didn't smile.

"I do," he simply retorted, obviously sending her a message that she not push the point any further. "I don't want this to be a repeat performance of the last time; we're past all that now."

"We are past that, but don't expect me to be agreeable."

"I expect cooperation, Kerensa, anything else I'll consider a bonus."

"I hope you plan on taking along some good reading material. I spend long hours in my studio teaching."

"I once told you that I could spend hours just watching you dance," Stone responded, a guttural tone to his voice. "Or don't you remember?"

Kerensa's eyes met his, and the intensity of his gaze rendered her speechless.

She felt herself drawn towards him, couldn't, or perhaps didn't want to move away. Suddenly Vance entered the kitchen, shattering the moment between them like broken glass. Stone recovered perfectly, Kerensa felt all jumbled up inside. Vance peered suspiciously into her face.

"Are you coming back into the living room?" he tersely asked.

Kerensa was completely back to her usual self now, and she calmly responded, "I didn't mean to exclude you from anything, Vance. I had some issues regarding Sergeant Stone's plans and I didn't want to make a big deal about it in front of Nana."

"So what exactly are these plans?" he asked curtly.

Stone knew that Kerensa should be telling him, but he wanted to make sure that Vance didn't get in the way.

"Sorry but I'll have to accompany you for a while out in public. It doesn't matter here in the house."

Vance scoffed, obviously irate with any of the plans made.

"Look, I don't agree with this, as a matter of fact, I am totally against this. But my opinion doesn't seem to matter right now so I'm going to go along with it only because I love Kerensa, and I don't scare off easily." Vance turned towards Stone, with little space between them; he stared directly into Stone's eyes.

"Man to man, I will tell you that I worked hard to make this lady trust me. Before I came along, she seemed to think that all men lacked conviction and commitment. Somehow, she got that from someone, and I once thought it was her ex-husband. Now, I'm not saying that I believe it could have been you, but I am warning you to stay away from the woman I love. Do your job, and keep your hands off her, or you will answer to me."

Kerensa gawked in awe at Vance.

Stone's gaze was unwavering as he stared into Vance's eyes. Then he nodded his head in respect, and stepped aside for Vance to pass. He kissed her goodbye and walked out the door.

Stone looked up, and saw Nana standing in the doorway.

"The spare room is ready any time you are, Dominick," she quietly replied.

"Thank you, my bags are in the truck."

Then, turning toward Kerensa he replied, "I'll take you to pick up Janelle. I will need you to tell the day care center that she won't be coming back for a little while. Does she have to go there everyday?"

"Well, I send her every day."

"I know that, but does she have to go?"

"No," Nana piped up. "Kerensa takes her there because she doesn't want to take advantage of me. I will be glad to watch her every day until this is over."

"Good, thank you Mrs. Drago. Are you ready to go Kerensa?"

Kerensa bristled, suddenly realizing how close he was behind her when she thought he had left for Buffalo.

"You've been following me this entire time, haven't you?"

Stone didn't respond right away. His face reflected no emotion for several moments. Kerensa knew that she should just leave it at that, but somehow she felt as though he violated her space and had no permission to do so. It reminded her of their last adventure together.

"Well?"

Stone remembered too.

"I did what I had to do. You should know me better than to think I would have simply walked away. I'm not about to discuss something that will only lead to another argument with you. Now let's go pick up your daughter."

Kerensa's mouth dropped open as she watched him turn abruptly around and walk away from her.

She looked at Nana but didn't say a word. She knew that Nana liked the idea that Stone was going to be the one to protect them for as long as it takes.

# 6

Nate Drake kicked at the rocks that lined his driveway with the tip of his steel toed boot. It was seventy two degrees outside, a real heat wave for April 12th in Buffalo, NY. There was a slight chill to the breeze that crackled, tossing about the left over leaves from last fall. And there they lay, in grimy piles of mud and mulch, scattered throughout the front yard, yet another nasty souvenir and further evidence that he was a disgrace to his neighbors. He studied the mess thoughtfully. He figured he could spend some time laboring over his lawn like his boring neighbors to the left of him, or he could do what he really wanted to do.

*Which was nothing. Absolutely nothing at all.*

He glanced at them again; pretending he wasn't watching what was going on over there. His neighbor, Harry, was pushing a wheelbarrow full of debris he had picked up starting at the end of his driveway and about a quarter of a mile down the road too. It was piled high with garbage, and Harry was having trouble maneuvering it into the back yard. Half of it had already fallen off like a trail of bread crumbs behind him. He kept turning around and barking orders to his kids to pick up the runaway junk, as they followed behind him with faces full of miserable boredom.

*Geezus, what a winner*

*Harry* caught his eye anyway and began waving frantically at him. Nate groaned aloud. *Shit.* The last thing he wanted to do was carry on a conversation about the weather and boating, the plans he already had about boating, how he hoped the weather would cooperate with boating. Boating, boating, boating…

The guy never shut up and it was beyond Nate's comprehension to understand why anyone in this area would want to have a hobby as seasonal as boating, but then again, it was just as crazy as snowmobiling. And that was Nate's favorite sport.

He pretended not to see him, and turned his face in the direction of the breeze again.

The crisp breeze that was coming off of Lake Erie was courtesy of the gigantic hunks of ice that kept breaking up and jamming the lake like mini glaciers. The never ending reminder that winter was still not over.

*Forget the lawn work; it'll probably snow again in an hour.*

Somewhere in the distance the mating song of a cardinal echoed through the trees, its familiar *wh-eat.wh-eat* sound gave Nate a sudden boost in his heart. Maybe he was wrong about the snow, at least for today. The Cardinals song was one of the earliest indications that spring was almost here.

It was in the air, too. If he concentrated really hard, he could smell the dankness around him, a blend of old snow, and fresh, new growth.

He strolled over to his lawn mower and stared at it. He could hear Harry's mower now humming in the distance shaming him into doing something productive with his afternoon. He contemplated just cutting the front lawn, but the very thought of dragging that frigging mower out to cut a lawn that would just be covered with snow again was ludicrous.

*Yea, yea, yea, who cares anyway? I'm off today and I plan on enjoying it.*

Nate waltzed back into the house, pulled a brew from the refrigerator and headed to the back porch and away from Harry's scrutinizing gaze. To hell with it, he put his feet up on the side table.

"Ahh yes—now this is better," he replied aloud, leaning his head back and closing his eyes. The sun felt warm on his pale skinned face causing him to instantly think of Stone and wondering how he was making out in Florida.

The fact that it was nearly two weeks and Stone hadn't returned yet was definitely a perk. He figured that he would be back by now bitching up a storm about how stubborn Kerensa was. Hopefully he was there checking into everything, and making that sure she was safe.

As Nate rested, he allowed his thoughts to drift over the events of almost a decade ago and he couldn't believe so many years have passed since he last saw Kerensa. He nearly fell over his own two feet the first time he met her. Drop dead gorgeous, in that sexy white dress, and all that cleavage. She was only five feet tall, and every inch of her was screaming sex. Yes, Kerensa Fiori was hot, and yes, he had fallen hopelessly in love with her. But as much as they were close, it didn't take long for him to realize that he wasn't the one who slipped into her fantasies at night. It was Stone. After they managed to rescue her from Jonathan Thorne that night in the warehouse, it was Nate who stayed by her side. He took care of her after she was discharged from the hospital; he made all the follow-up appointments with the medical doctors, and later on with the counselors. He drove her where she needed to go, held her hand when she didn't know which way to turn, and held her in his arms while she cried on his shoulder. Although Stone was the basis for plenty of her tears, he never accepted responsibility for them. It was Nate who picked up the shattered pieces of her life and helped her glue them back together again. He would be lying if he said he didn't resent Stone for that. But he would never judge him.

Dominick Stone was a warrior, a man who chose to live his life under the most deplorable of circumstances. Involved with a private sector of the government that everyone thinks could exist and everyone just as equally deny. Some days, Stone merely existed himself, his sole purpose to stay alive and eliminate the enemy. His life was about discipline and danger, sacrifice and jeopardy and without mercy for truth or regret.

Nate first met Stone when he was a teenager. They were both sent to the same Karate camp for the summer. Stone was tall but slender, his physique typical of a boy's, but not quite a man's. Stone was quiet, mostly keeping to himself. He wasn't very approachable, and there was this look about him that scared Nate silly. It was later on when Nate would learn that Stone lost his father only a couple weeks before they left for camp. It was years later when Nate realized they shared that first summer together during a time when Stone needed to deal with his new life without his father in it. It was a summer of change, and a summer of growth for both of them.

Nate was raised in a rich subdivision of Buffalo, NY. His parents were both employed by the school system there, his father a sixth grade teacher, and his mother a principal. Born an only child, Nate didn't want for anything in his childhood, his parents doted over him, and his grandparents gave him just about everything he wanted. They loved him unconditionally. Nate often wondered what his mother would say if she knew how precarious his world was now. As smart as she was, she never asked him about the danger. She wasn't the kind of mother that stuck her nose in his affairs; she was so busy living her own life. There were advantages to having a mother who never actually told her child what to do. There were disadvantages too. But he figured that if his mother ever found out about his profession, she would quietly problem solve it away and tell him that she would just hide him from the authorities until the coast was clear. *Unconditional love, yea, you gotta love it.*

Nate grinned quietly to himself, recalling again his first encounter with Stone. Unlike Stone, Nate was several inches shorter, not nearly as quiet, but could still hold his own in a fight. Until one day when Nate was approached by several guys from another school. They were down by the creek fishing and the sun was just beginning to set. The black flies were biting like crazy, but that was about all that was biting. So the rest of the guys decided to head back to the cabin, leaving Nate to shout after them about what 'babies' they were. Annoyed with them, he refused to give up and go back to the cabin early so he sat back down on a rock and cast his rod into the water. When he looked up, he knew they were heading in his direction for a reason. These guys had been cruising for trouble all week, and Nate knew it was only a matter of time before they picked a fight with him. Of all the times to be alone! but then again, wasn't that their plan? There was only one Master instructor left with them, and he was nowhere to be found. Nate recalled how scared to death he was. Feeling pretty outnumbered, he decided to play it cool unless he wasn't given any other alternative. And he had a feeling there wouldn't be.

Josh, the larger one of the group, spoke first.

"Hey, check it out guys, here's one of them rich academy boys."

Nate didn't answer as he gathered up his fishing gear, so Josh stepped in front of him, deliberately blocking his way.

"Is there something you want?" Nate casually asked, swatting at the black flies nibbling behind his ears.

"To kick your ass," Josh responded.

"Yea, well that's not happening, moron."

Josh's face clouded with anger, reminding Nate that he never knew when to shut his mouth.

"Let's just see how well you cream puff girls can fight," Josh retorted, raising his arms in front of his face.

Nate glared into every one of their eyes, giving them his best Steven Segal *'Don't fuck with me'* look, and hoping he looked meaner than he felt.

"I'm not looking for a fight, now leave me alone," Nate growled back.

Josh and the other boys began to laugh.

"That's what I thought; you hotshot academy babies are just pussy's with big mouths."

Nate continued to ignore them, trying his best to practice the beliefs of the Tai-quoin-do teachings, above all discipline first. At least he tried to practice that until Josh threw the first punch and it hurt like hell.

Nate recovered swiftly, whirling around to kick him back in the jaw. But Josh was even quicker, dodging his kick and driving his palm into Nate's nose. Nate staggered backward, his nose squirting blood. Now furious, he lifted his foot again, this time catching Josh's chin with his heel. Josh fell down and didn't get up right away. This created a chain reaction as each boy circled around Nate ready for a fight. Nate counted six of them. He knew he was good, but he also knew he didn't stand a chance against all of them at one time. He was about ready to pee his pants when he spotted a movement off to his right. Thinking it was one of the boys ready to make a move, he reacted only to see Stone standing outside the ring. Each boy turned, and Stone stared them all down. Now that stare down, was first class, prime rib, the best of the best stare down style. Nate knew why these guys were frozen in fear, but he couldn't believe that none of them attempted to fight. One by one, they walked away leaving Nate with his mouth open in surprise, and Stone's mouth curling in a slow, crooked grin.

"Are you O.K?" he asked, wiping his sweaty face off with his tee-shirt. "Man, I hate this heat."

"Yea," Nate responded, squaring his shoulders a little tighter and peering at him through his swollen right eye.

"You did alright," Stone commented approvingly. "How's the nose?"

Nate could taste blood, and he couldn't breathe very well. His lip was split wide open and of course his eyes were about to close completely from the swelling. But he never felt better. He nodded his head and then he began to laugh. Actually they both were laughing as they walked back to the cabin together.

That incident happened over twenty years ago, and they've been in dozens of situations similar to that one ever since. Nate knew exactly what made those boys quiver in fear that day, and he'd seen many men react the same way throughout the years. Countless situations came and went, but one thing remained constant year after year. Stone and Nate were more than buddies; they were brothers, real family. They saved each others lives over and over again. That was why Nate could never judge his unconditional brother.

# 7

In the beginning, the girls simply watched Stone with interest. After a couple days of always seeing him there, they began to ask lots of questions. Kerensa noticed some of the parents observing Stone as he installed safety mirrors, checked the security system and quietly watched all of them from his post in the shadows. Then the parents began to ask questions too. It was morning number three, and Kerensa was trying to get some basic steps perfected in their lyrical number. The girls couldn't get serious; they just had a case of the giggles. Finally, Kerensa called a time out.

"Listen to me, ladies," she shouted above their laughing. "We're going to take a five minute break. When we begin again, I expect full cooperation and you will have worked all that silliness out of your system."

"OK, Miss Kerensa," their little voices promised.

The girls scattered in the studio, some of them getting into private circles to talk and mingle. Kerensa sighed, gazing into the hallway. Several parents had gathered, and they were talking among themselves too. Stone sat in the corner, his eyes intently upon her. She marveled at his ability to do that all day long. He reminded her of the guards in England, statuesque and silent, immobile yet alert. This man was accustomed to darkness. *And that was a creepy thought.*

Kerensa opened the studio door and walked into the hallway. She knew that if she did this, she wouldn't have a moments rest from parents who would be asking all kinds of questions regarding their children. Sure enough, the first mom was approaching her already.

"Will the girls be ready to perform at competitions?" she nervously asked.

Kerensa smiled. This was Madison's mom, Olivia, and she was always worried about something.

"They have a lot of work ahead of them, but I think they are going to do great," she reassured.

Olivia seemed satisfied with that answer and scurried away. Kerensa continued to walk down the corridor toward Stone. She could feel his eyes on her in the dimness of the hallway, and as she approached closer, she could see how his gaze slowly caressed past her low cut leotard top, lingering momentarily on the soft roundness of her breasts before moving downward. She shivered unexpectedly, liquid warmth spreading over her as old feelings quickly stirring within her. Shocked at her emotions, she reminded herself that Vance is in her life now.

"Hi," she quickly replied.

Stone smiled but it didn't quite meet his eyes.

"I think you need to start answering some questions around here."

"They all want to know who you are, right?"

"Pretty much," he slowly responded, "and the one's who don't; want to know if I'll take them to dinner."

Kerensa snickered, instantly reminded of the hypnotic effect he seemed to have on women. *On all women.*

"Did you tell them you're working, and there's no possibility of a day off?" she chided, yet her tone sounded more possessive than light.

"You need to tell them something," he continued, ignoring her glib comment. "I want to have my shoulder harness and my .45 on me as much as possible, and I don't like worrying about someone seeing it and getting scared."

Kerensa nodded, thinking about how dangerous he still was without a weapon.

"Does it have to be on your body all the time?"

Stone didn't answer, his gaze fixed on something behind her. Kerensa turned around to see Vance standing there. Her face lit up, and she reached around his neck and hugged him. Then, she kissed him.

Stone shifted his eyes away; he hated watching Vance kiss the very lips he dreamed about kissing practically every night since he left. Observing their relationship was like experiencing some self inflicted medieval torture.

Kerensa gave Vance another hug.

*Frigging great.*

"I have to get back to my students," she quickly said. "Are you staying for a while?"

Vance glanced at Stone.

"Nope, gotta get back to work."

Kerensa nodded, and then turned to address Stone.

"I will tell them right after class."

As soon as she was back in the studio, Vance spoke to Stone.

"What will she tell them after class?" He tersely asked.

Stone didn't answer, actually, Stone deliberately didn't answer. There were several tense moments between them but Stone wasn't going to offer any information.

It infuriated Vance.

It gave Stone a sick sense of satisfaction.

"So, have there been any new developments?" Vance asked again.

*Persistent, I'll give him that.*

Stone shook his head, no.

"How long do you think this arrangement has to continue?"

"Until I decide she's not in danger anymore."

"Tomorrow night is our one year anniversary; I want to take Kerensa out, alone."

"I don't see it happening," Stone's gaze was hot, and dripping with a challenge that Vance not argue.

Vance refused to take the hint.

Stone wondered why Kerensa never mentioned it.

"Then I want her at my place, I can cook her dinner, and you can sit outside the house."

Stone shook his head '*no*' again.

This time Vance got angry.

"I'm not going to let you interfere with our lives, Stone. I miss my fiancé and I plan on spending quality time with her, alone. That's right, just us, and a box of condoms. If I have to spell it out to you then I will, now stay out of my bedroom."

Stone wanted to kick Vance right in the head. If he had been referring to any other woman maybe he could have tolerated that, but he was talking about Kerensa.

*His Kerensa.*

A smart man would erase the memory of her hot, sultry lips and the motion of those hips as they moved in perfect unison with his. A smart man would totally obliterate from his mind the passion and fire…and a smart man would overlook Vance's statement without emotion.

*But he wasn't being a smart man and no fucking way was Vance going to put his hands on her…*

"Sorry," Stone declared, his gaze penetrating Vance's eyes like a Catena sword. "You'll have to keep it in your pants a little longer."

Vance's temper flared.

"Something's going on with you, Stone. I'm not a fool and I've been checking into your background since you showed up here. I think you should know that." Vance gave Stone another deadly glare before heading out the door without even a second look behind him.

Kerensa was in the middle of a sentence when she watched Vance storm away. She temporarily lost her concentration, pausing with uncertainty. It was obvious to her that Vance was furious and she knew that whatever both men talked about probably had to do with her. As usual, Stone carried a big stick.

Kerensa sighed, trying to concentrate on the lesson she was giving. This was her last class, and she could call it a day.

About a half hour later she finished up and then stuck her head out of the studio door to address the parents.

"Before everyone goes home, I would like to call the parents into the studio for a few minutes."

Once everyone was settled in, Kerensa took a deep breath. She didn't want to appear nervous but explaining Dominick Stone was so difficult for her to do; she really didn't know where to begin or what to say. *Especially since she didn't know who he really was half the time anyway.* She also realized that telling them any element of the truth could scare everyone away. Suddenly she felt a movement beside her. It was Stone. The students giggled at her obvious surprise that he had snuck up on her again. Stone grinned too.

She could tell it was one of his *million dollar I am going to schmooze you silly, smiles.*

Shaking her head, Kerensa turned the class over to him, and then she sat down on the gym floor.

He cleared his throat.

"My name is Dominick Stone and I'm a qualified martial arts instructor. I know some of you have seen me lurking around corners and I want to reassure you that I work with the police department handling some of their security requests. Kerensa has asked me to offer some classes on self defense while I am here. We are still in the process of working that out and I will need to see if there is enough interest for me to teach a class. I would like you to think about this, and let Kerensa know. She is in charge of it, not me."

As Stone continued to speak, Kerensa could see how easy it was for him to command undivided attention. It was unnerving to her.

"I'm also a law enforcement official, therefore you may see a weapon on me. I hope that doesn't frighten anyone."

Stone quickly turned to Kerensa, deliberately ending his dissertation before anyone could object to his weapon.

"Thank you, I'll leave you to finish up."

She nodded, watching him return to the shadows again.

Kerensa smiled at everyone, easily noticing the look of agreement on all their faces. She felt instant relief.

"OK, so if anyone is interested, please let me know."

"Goodbye Miss. Kerensa," the girls called out as each one headed out the door.

"Remember to practice," Kerensa reminded each girl as she waved in return.

When the last girl left, she looked down the hallway in Stone's direction. He stood to his feet, walking in her direction. He wore his usual color, black, a tee shirt that emphasized the ripple of his flesh, and the strength of his chest. He had taken off his jacket, his shoulder harness exposed. Her eyes fixed on the gun in the holster. As perilous as the weapon was, it was the man carrying it who was equally as terrifying. At least that was the word that came to her mind. She suddenly recalled with alarming clarity the night he rescued her. It was the way he barged into that warehouse, furious and determined. His ability obvious by the way he held his gun in his hand as he fought her kidnappers, the brutal commando exterior he had perfected so absolute, so supreme. He was a fighting machine on the outside, but on the inside, he was entirely someone else. She knew how brutal and lethal he could be if necessary, but that tender man who invaded her thoughts through the years was so difficult to forget, and that was precisely the problem. She let go of that man a long time ago, and she couldn't allow him to weaken her again. He may have come back into her life, but it was to protect her, not to love her. She refused to feel the emotional isolation loving him had caused. It was that loneliness which forced her to be pathetic and fragile once upon a time. *Never again.*

"I hope I didn't overstep my bounds," he replied, his tone more like a question than a statement.

"No, I was glad you came to speak with them. I didn't think of saying something, well, any less truthful I guess." She flashed him a smile. "Actually, I didn't know what to say. You know they're going to take you up on that offer."

He chuckled softly.

"I know that."

"Somehow I can't visualize you're teaching style," she quietly chided.

"Are you reminding me that I have very limited patience?"

Kerensa openly laughed.

"Oh yea, most definitely."

*God, that gun is scaring the hell out of me right now.*

"What's the matter?" Stone asked, sensing her hesitancy and noticing that her eyes were glued to his shoulder harness.

She took a deep breath.

"I guess I'm a little intimidated by your weapon," she responded, pointing uncomfortably to the gun strapped to his side.

"Well, I sometimes have that affect on women," he retorted, a smile on his lips that didn't quite reach his eyes.

She wanted to laugh too but somehow a vision of their past lovemaking flashed before her like some neon light. It came from a place deep inside her head, and it made her face flush hot with desire. Her verbal response wasn't necessary; it was quite obvious that her thoughts were transparent.

There was a slight upturn to his lips as he attempted to become serious. "I have my .22 Caliber strapped to my ankle, but I wanted my .45 on my shoulder where I can reach it just in case."

"Two guns, Dominick?" she asked incredulously.

Stone ignored her innocent comment. *Yes, sweetheart, and sometimes a whole lot more.*

"So, why-why do you need so many?" she murmured again.

He deliberately shot her a sizzling smile this time. It made her feel like an inferno inside her belly, instantly forcing her to drop the gun issue. Tiny beads of perspiration collected on her forehead, and she wiped them off with the back of her hand.

*Why am I sweating?*

She realized that seeing his gun again may have invoked past memories. Horrifying past memories.

Or could it be her heightened libido?

When Stone spoke again, his tone was light.

"So, you don't think I have any patience to teach, hah?"

"You have many talents, *as you already pointed out,* but teaching just doesn't seem likely to be one of them."

Stone laughed aloud.

"Point well taken and you could be right. So are you ready to go?"

"Oh, umm," Kerensa stammered, shaking her head to get focused again. "I just have to practice one number, and then I'll be ready to go."

He nodded his head, following her round, sexy bottom with his eyes.

Kerensa found the CD and pushed the button. It was a jazz number, and she needed to dance away her frustrations.

When she began to dance, Stone grunted softly to himself. He'd give his right arm if could be a ballet number; her dancing slow and passionate would have been difficult to watch but still easier than a fast paced dance. His heart began to thump, hard. Watching her move the way she did gave dance a whole new meaning. He remembered the first time he ever saw her dance. She was auditioning for a job at the dance studio in Buffalo, and she managed to give him a hard on in less than twenty seconds. Everything about her screamed of sex appeal, the brisk, erotic movement of her lower body, her hips as she moved them provocatively back and forth, as if she were naked and on top of him… or dancing to the heat beneath him.

Stone couldn't handle it anymore. He slowly turned around, placing his back to the window. He considered taking one of his bullets from his gun and biting on it, hard.

When Kerensa was finished, she turned off the music and searched for Stone. When she saw his back to the window, a stab of pain ripped through her. Somehow she thought he would be watching, enjoying her movements like he used to. She sighed, and pulled on her street clothes, wiggling her bottom into her jeans.

Stone groaned quietly again.

"I'm all set," she replied, grabbing her purse.

"Are you hungry?" he asked.

Kerensa nodded her head and laughed. "I'm famished."

"Well you know the neighborhood better than I do, so you pick the place."

Kerensa took Stone to a little restaurant closer to home. It was small and quiet inside, exactly what she was looking for after her crazy day with the kids. They were seated, and given menus.

Suddenly she caught a small grin on Stone's face. She decided to confront him.

"So what are you smiling at?"

"I just remembered something, that's all."

"What?"

He laughed and shook his head.

"Nothing important, I was simply thinking."

"Don't you dare blow me off like that," she warned. "Fess up, Stone I want to know."

"I just thought about the time we were in that restaurant in Quebec City."

Kerensa thought for a moment, slowly nodding her head in response. "Yea, I remember the waitress."

Stone laughed heartily, and Kerensa had forgotten how sexy it sounded. "You were wrong, you know."

"Wrong about what?" she asked.

Stone didn't answer, forcing Kerensa to think back to that day again.

"I remember we sat down and that waitress was all over you. She was flirting with you and rubbing her body against you and then she gave you her phone number on a napkin, with the check," Kerensa mussed, remaining deep in thought. "You took her number, I watched you do it so don't tell me you didn't!"

He laughed again.

"You're partially right, Kerensa, I did take her number but I threw it in the trash on the way out."

His words gave her a little nudge at the heart.

"You did?"

"Yea, I did," he answered. "Come on, let's order."

Kerensa looked up to see the waitress waiting. She apologized and quickly placed her order, mashed potatoes and vegetarian casserole. Stone ordered the Prime rib, rare. Once the order was given, the moment between them was gone. Instead, *his close but far away* demeanor was back, but she couldn't forget what he said. She remembered how hurt she was when he had taken that phone number, but she never noticed what he did with it. What surprised her most was the fact that he took it so he wouldn't offend the waitress, yet he disposed of it somewhere else. She looked up to see him staring intently at her. She squirmed a bit in her chair, time to talk about something else.

"So, what were you and Vance discussing?"

Stone cleared his throat.

"You're not going to like it."

"Tell me," she responded slowly, the hair on her neck standing on end.

"He asked me if he could be alone with you tomorrow night."

Kerensa could feel a lump in her throat, making it hard to swallow. She swirled her ice tea around in the glass before taking a sip from the straw.

"So, what did you say?"

"You know what I said," he curtly responded, never looking at her as he spoke.

"Why wouldn't you agree? I mean, you know if he's with me I'm protected. Why can't we spend a little time together, alone?"

"I am not taking my eyes off you, Kerensa, not even for a moment."

"You don't trust him, and that's not fair."

"Sorry."

Kerensa tried to control the quick pound of anger in her heart. She was about to argue the point again, when their food came. Instead, they ate in silence.

Stone took a few more bites of his steak and then spoke again.

"What are you celebrating with him tomorrow night?"

She stared into chips of midnight blue eyes.

"What do you mean?"

Stone stared back, those eyes reflecting surprise.

"Vance told me you would be celebrating something tomorrow night. I just wondered what it was."

Suddenly it dawned on Kerensa.

"Oh dear, it's our first year anniversary tomorrow night!"

Stone chuckled softly. *And you forgot it?*

Tears stung her eyes, as she swirled the mashed potatoes around in the gravy like it was a river. He watched her while he finished his dinner. She barely touched the rest of hers.

"Can we leave now?" she whispered.

He nodded his head, realizing that he shouldn't have enjoyed her sudden bout of amnesia as much as he did. He took the check, and led her out of the restaurant.

When they arrived home, Nana was in the kitchen. She looked at both of them, instantly realizing something was wrong with Kerensa. Stone smiled and said hello, then he headed into the living room. Nana sat down at the kitchen table. Kerensa sat down too.

"I forgot my one year anniversary with Vance; I can't believe I would do such a thing."

Nana looked at Kerensa. She noticed how tired she looked, dark eyes that generally sparkled like the forth of July, barely had any sheen at all. She was worried about her.

"There's so much going on with you right now, honey," Nana comforted softly, with one eye on Kerensa and the other one on Stone in the distance. "Please try not to be so hard on yourself, it'll be alright." She rose from the table and gave Kerensa a big hug. "I have to get some groceries bought; Janelle is already in bed. I'll be back in a little while."

Kerensa nodded her head, recalling how Stone gave her quite a bit of money to compensate his stay with them. Although she didn't want it, she learned how hard it was to say *no* to Stone.

Kerensa sighed, thinking about what Nana said. She was right, but that wasn't the only reason why she would forget her own anniversary. She was thinking about Stone far too much again. Falling into the same traps, fantasizing the way she used to about him. She was treading on the most perilous of all grounds, and she had no business being there. Kerensa took a deep breath and rose to her feet. It was time for a heart to heart talk with Dominick. She needed to know how long this arrangement was going to continue.

He briefly looked up from the paper he was reading.

"Where is Nana going?"

"To the grocery store, she'll be back in an hour."

Stone nodded his head, glancing at his wrist watch.

"So, what's on your mind?" he asked, patting the seat beside him.

She hesitated, suddenly recalling how risky it could be to sit next to him.

He chuckled, sensing her hesitation.

"Come on, I already ate dinner, my stomach is full."

Kerensa sighed, hating again how astute to human behavior he was. She sat beside him, smiling briefly before studying his face. Fine lines were barely visible around his full lips and dangerously blue eyes reminding her that he could bottle and sell his anti—aging process. His dark hair with a couple grays at the temples only made him more distinguished and handsome. They also reminded her of how shrewd and cunning he could be. Realizing that he was waiting for an answer, Kerensa quickly looked away.

"I would like to know how long it's going to be until, well, until—"

"…Until you don't have to see me anymore?" he interrupted, finishing her sentence for her.

"Well, not exactly like that," she retorted sharply.

He chuckled beneath his breath.

"You'll know how long as soon as I do."

"It's been four days since the mall incident, so maybe that was just a coincidence."

"It could have been. The man who jumped you had a record, mostly harassment and misdemeanors, but I'm not going to assume that, at least not yet." Stone paused, studying Kerensa's face. "I get the feeling all these questions are because you want to be alone with him tomorrow night. Am I right?"

Kerensa drew a ragged breath. She wasn't sure what she wanted to do anymore.

"Vance is angry that he can't be alone with me. This is a big problem, Dominick. It's really creating an issue between us."

*Oh, I'll bet it is, that horny bastard.* Stone thought cynically, recalling Vance's comment about the bedroom. He really had a sarcastic rhetoric in return but knew better than to say it.

"So you want to get rid of me for the night, right?"

"Well, kind of," she carefully answered.

"And you feel safe with him?"

Kerensa hesitated, hating the fact that she didn't feel one hundred percent safe with anyone except Stone.

"Of course I feel safe with him."

Stone's gaze was sizzling and possessive, quickly noticing her moment of hesitation. "You don't sound very convincing, Kerensa. I want to know if you feel safe enough with that-boyfriend of yours. So don't lie to me, you seem to be doing a lot of that lately."

Kerensa's eyes flashed in anger.

"I'm not lying, and he's my fiancé," she snapped.

"You lied when you told him there was never anything between us."

She felt the hot sting of tears.

"That wasn't a lie; there never was anything between us."

He shot her a skeptical glance.

"The way I remember it, there was plenty."

Kerensa glared at him, hating how cool, calm and collected he was in return.

"If there was anything between us, you would never have disappeared!" She was suddenly shouting at him, hearing her own voice but unable to gain control of her emotions. "You made all kinds of promises you didn't keep. That's the way I remember it."

"Then there was something between us, wasn't there?" he quietly responded.

Kerensa glared at him. *You bastard.*

'"Why are you asking, anyway? You told me to get over it."

"Because I don't believe you're in love with him."

"So what if I'm not, what is it to you?"

"Do you love him, Kerensa?" he asked, ignoring her question.

She took a deep breath.

"Yes, Dominick, I love him very much."

Stone felt the third laser penetrate his heart. This one stayed deep inside, sharp and ragged. He reached over, and in one swift movement pulled her into his arms.

He felt her tremble beneath his touch, just like that night long ago when he held her in his arms as they danced; now he was surprised that she didn't pull away. She felt so soft in his arms, so right. Her hair tickled the tip of his nose as he took a deep breath, enjoying the fresh exotic scent of her shampoo. He wanted to kiss her hard, kiss away any love she had for her fiancé and he wanted to taste her sweetness, lock it inside him like a bowl of honey. He wanted to touch her, everywhere, but instead he spoke to her.

"Then happy anniversary, sweetheart," his tone was smooth, but it had a chilly undertone that was unmistakable. "And tell him to pick you up right here.

If anything seems suspicious, call me and whatever you do, don't let him handle it on his own. I know how Thorne thinks, and what he's capable of. I know I keep reminding you of that, but that fiancé of yours thinks he's hot stuff. Don't make me worry about you, Kerensa, and don't make me look for you, do you understand?"

Kerensa nodded her head, a little annoyed with his demands and his comment about Vance, but she was not about to argue with him. Then he slowly released her, leaving her with a peculiar rather empty feeling.

*Now where did that come from?*

"Is this your way of saying you expect me home by midnight?" she quickly challenged, pushing her other fantasies away.

He chuckled softly again, recalling the rules he had forced her to abide by almost a decade ago.

"A reasonable time, Kerensa, please respect that."

She nodded her head again.

# 8

Kerensa felt strange sitting next to Vance. A little voice inside kept telling her that she was out with the man she loved and Stone wasn't around to bother her.

*I'm in love with Vance Robertson not Dominick Stone.*

"What's the matter, Kerensa, you seem preoccupied tonight," Vance asked his tone slightly tense.

Kerensa leaned over and kissed him on the cheek.

"I'm perfectly fine," she reassured. "I'm just glad to be out with you alone."

"Oh yea, you have no idea how glad I am too," he retorted.

"I don't want to talk about any of that tonight. I just want to enjoy you."

Vance smiled in agreement.

"So, where are we going?" she asked.

"Key West, Nana is watching Janelle tonight, right?"

"Right," Kerensa carefully answered, *Oh my God.* "But Key West is over five hours from here, Vance."

"So we can spend the night there," he retorted.

Kerensa felt a sudden jolt in her heart. She needed to talk him out of this, but she didn't know how without creating a big argument. Before she could open her mouth to speak, Vance beat her to it.

"You're afraid of leaving him that long, aren't you?"

"No, of course not, it's just that he didn't expect us to spend the night."

Vance shook his head in disgust.

"Listen to yourself, Kerensa. You're acting like he can dictate our every move. I'm not going to allow that to happen. I'm a cop for Christ sake; I can protect you and I can protect myself. There's going to be a big confrontation between us, I just know it."

Kerensa sighed.

"I know you're angry, but can't we talk about that after tonight. I don't want to fight; I just want to enjoy myself with you."

"Then call him and tell him we won't be home tonight. End of discussion. If he doesn't like it, I really don't care; he can deal with me when we get back."

Kerensa knew that Vance was deliberately giving Stone a hard time, but she didn't blame him. She knew he was feeling inferior beside Stone.

"I'll call him after we get there," she replied.

They drove all the way to Key West in silence, actually, uncomfortable silence. Kerensa could feel Vance slowly pulling away from her. He was remote, distant, and she knew that he didn't believe she felt safe with him. She resented Stone for the mess he sent her world into, for a second time in her life.

Vance parked the car, and they walked. It was a hot evening, but there was a slight breeze coming off the ocean. When they strolled past Hemmingway's, Vance knew it was her favorite place.

"Want to stop in for a drink?" he asked.

Kerensa thought for a moment.

"No, why don't we get a room for the night, first."

"Let's stop now get a drink and a bite to eat then you can call your James Bond wanna be from here. That way we won't be in such a hurry to leave." He was handing her his cell phone again. So just do it, O.K.?

*Oh God, what to do, what to do?*

"I would rather get the room, relax with you and then call him. After that, we can come back to Hemmingway's."

It must have been the wrong thing to say, because Vance became very quiet again, but he didn't argue. When they checked in, Vance reached for his cell phone.

"Here, now are you ready to call him?"

Kerensa glanced at the time. It was almost eleven o'clock at night. *Oh dear, she thought. I don't want to do this!* When she looked up, Vance was staring at her. Kerensa slowly dialed Stone's cell phone number. When he answered, she felt her voice scatter away, and in its place was a tone barely above a whisper.

"Dominick, its Kerensa. I'm in Key West right now, and Vance and I are going to spend the night."

At first, Stone didn't respond. He couldn't, he was too furious. Somehow he knew this was going to happen, and part of him didn't blame Vance for doing this, either.

"Sounds like you're still good at breaking the rules, Kerensa."

His comment forced her to recall the night she lied to him and then purposely stayed away until early that morning. Except the circumstances were very different then, and she wasn't that same young woman anymore.

"Look, Dominick, I'm more than safe. Please trust Vance, he can handle it."

"Put him on the phone."

Kerensa bristled, she was sick and tired of Stone never saying Vance's name. It was just one more thing that frustrated her to death. She handed the phone to Vance.

"He wants to speak with you."

She observed his lips form a thin, tight line. His tone was gruff as he took the phone.

"Yea, it's Vance."

"I know what you're doing, Detective Robertson, and I can't say that I blame you. However, this wasn't the deal. I'm still responsible for her well being, so you better either take her back to me or do a good job of protecting her. And that means not letting her out of your sight."

*Take her back to me? She doesn't belong to you!*

"Are you threatening me?" Vance asked his tone now low and furious.

"That's right."

He held the phone away from his face.

"I can't believe this asshole," then he spoke to Stone again.

"I don't know who the hell you think you are, but I don't respond to threats."

"So I guess you better follow my orders." Stone retorted, his timbre dripping with acid. "Because I mean every word I say... and I hope you remembered the condoms too."

Stone hung the phone up.

Vance was beyond furious and Kerensa knew their night was already ruined. She wanted to cry.

"Please don't be angry," she coaxed. "I just want to have a good time tonight. Can't we simply forget about this?"

Vance didn't answer her; Stone's comment about the condoms finally put the pieces together for him. He ran his hands through his hair and replied,

"It's time you told me the truth, Kerensa. I know something happened between you two. I accepted your answer the first time, because I couldn't face the truth. This time, I'm ready to. Now, answer my question again. Did you have an affair with him?"

Kerensa could feel herself unravel, slow and methodical, one little thread at a time. If she told him the truth now after denying it the first time, she would still appear like a liar. She heard Nana's voice as it preached to her in the past. *Oh what a tangled web we weave, when we first practice to deceive.*

"Yes, Vance, I had a very brief relationship with him. It didn't last, and I don't care about him anymore."

Vance looked like he had been slapped in the face. Hard.

"You lied to me, Kerensa, and I thought our relationship was built on trust."

She took a deep breath.

"I don't know why I did. I should have told you the truth right then and there. I guess I couldn't bring myself to do it. Please forgive me."

Vance didn't respond, but the disgust in his eyes said it all.

Kerensa began to cry.

"Did you have sex with him?" He asked incredulously, ignoring her tears.

*Oh God, do I have to spell it out for you?*

"Yes."

"So was fucking him just a one time thank you bonus?"

Kerensa gasped.

He grabbed the keys off the dresser.

"Look, I'm sorry, let's just go home. There's no sense wasting any more time here."

She stared in shock at him.

"Please, don't do this. I love you and I want to celebrate our anniversary together, tonight."

"I can't, Kerensa, I'm sorry. I need time to think this out." Vance wouldn't even look Kerensa in the eye, throwing his arms into the air in frustration. "I don't know— it's not like I expected you to be Mother Theresa, hell, you were married and had a child, but—shit you screwed the guy and never even mentioned him in any conversations about our past." His gaze was shifted downward, as though looking at her made him sick to his stomach as he continued, "You almost got killed for Christ sake, and you never even told me about that. I feel like I don't really know you after all, and-." Vance took a deep breath, "and I wonder what else you've never told me about." *There you go, the words were finally out.*

She could feel her heart breaking as a loud sob escaped from her lips.

For a moment Vance paused in his tracks, but then he just pulled the hotel door open for her. She didn't move, couldn't.

"Come on," he quietly replied, "let's go."

Kerensa slowly walked through the door.

They said very little all the way home. She attempted light conversation, but it was obvious that Vance didn't want to talk at all. There was a sense of deep dread in her belly, and it was churning like a siren as each mile went by. Somehow she knew that their relationship was facing a serious change, and she didn't know if it could survive the crisis. She suddenly thought of something else Nana always said. Actually, it was one of the Beatles that said it first. *Life is what happens when you're busy making other plans.* She was fearful of what life now had in store for her.

It was four thirty in the morning when Kerensa finally arrived home. She was praying that Vance would only walk her to the door, and then leave. It was better to discuss their issues surrounded by the fresh morning light, but Vance had something else in mind. Kerensa proceeded into the house with him close on her heels. She was very apprehensive; concerned that Stone may be lurking around any corner. A confrontation with both men would be the frosting on the cake right about now. They entered the living room together, and the voice of experience told Kerensa to check the shadows of the room. Her eyes focused on a dark, still object sitting on the far sofa.

"Oh no," she groaned softly. Somewhere between bad and terrible, something worse happened. *It was the frosting on the cake.*

Vance suddenly stepped forward, strolling purposely toward Stone. Kerensa could see Stone's silhouette as he stood up to face him. She held her breath, not knowing what to expect, especially since she had never seen Vance so angry. Then, Stone spoke first.

"We're civilized men, Robertson. I don't want a confrontation."

"We've been heading in this direction since the first time we met," Vance retorted, his tone full of ice.

*Yea, and I knocked you on your ass once already, remember?*

"But we're not hot headed teenagers, now calm down."

"It's not just about tonight, Stone. It's about you and Kerensa deceiving me. I know the truth about both of you now."

Stone glanced briefly at Kerensa.

"Then you also know that it happened a long time ago, and it's over now."

"Oh really, well that's funny because I don't get the feeling it's over."

Stone turned, the room was dim but there was enough light to see the mask of iciness upon his face. He stared at Kerensa, his features hard and lacking emotion.

"I don't know what Kerensa may have told you, but she was a fling to me and nothing more."

*A fling to me?*

Kerensa felt her face crumble, so did her world. Stone hated himself more than he ever imagined he could. It was a cold hearted lie, but he had to do it. He couldn't even look her in the eyes as he continued, "It was a long time ago, and I took advantage of her. I'm not proud of it." Stone stepped forward even closer to Vance.

"I didn't come here to interfere with your relationship, Robertson. I came back because Dr. O'Brian was concerned for her welfare and I was hired to protect her. She's just another case to me."

*You Bastard! You dirty bastard! Don't react to this. Don't react. Don't react.*

Vance studied Kerensa's face, it was as if he was testing her, observing her response to Stone's statements. Finally, his features softened.

"Maybe I was a little over the top, Kerensa. I need to think about this, I'll call you."

Kerensa simply nodded her head in response. She couldn't do anything else for fear that the screaming in her head would slip out her mouth. *I can't cry, I can't cry, I won't cry...*, but somehow the tears were creeping behind her eyes. He briefly kissed her on the cheek, and then he was gone.

She waited until the door closed securely behind him before she slowly turned around, facing the man who was the true object of her crisis, the real reason why her heart ached with a haunting pain, an eternal pain.

She gritted her teeth to refrain from popping her head off like a boiling kettle too.

"Why didn't you tell me that I was just a fling to you?" How dare you tell Vance but never tell me the truth."

Stone remained silent, his stature considerably larger than hers, looming above her, wanting to crush her taunt sexy body against his, part of him torn between making love to her and shaking her in fury. There was a part of him that wanted to yell back at her, ask her why she would be so quick to believe the hollow words that he told her fiancé for her benefit. He would have reminded her of his love for her now. *If she asked.*

"He needed to hear it," he flatly lied again.

"So did I, but you never said it," she furiously retorted.

Stone remained calm, despite his escalating frustration.

"Kerensa, there were things I couldn't say, but if you can recall the last night we were together—"

"Oh, so this is some kind of riddle. I have to guess what clues you sent to me back then?" Kerensa was only becoming more and more annoyed by the second. She could feel herself falling apart, piece by piece, like the big egg that fell off the brick wall. What made her even angrier was how calm he remained.

Stone wanted to tell her what was really in his heart. He didn't want to be so cruel, even though he could be a son of a bitch, he still wasn't this bad. No, he still wasn't this ruthless. He didn't want to make it hard between her and Vance either, as much as he loved her, he could never give her the kind of life she deserved. The truth, what exactly was the truth anymore? Was he supposed to tell her that he was a CIA operative employed by an elite sector of the government, alright, so maybe he could have said something like that, but then what?

*Oh yea, babe, by the way I'm on my way to a top secret government mission because I follow orders, no, because I kill my enemies for a living. But I should be back in a few months, so don't wait up*

*Piece of cake.*

. Like she was going to understand that? So instead, he just slipped away into the night believing that he had made the best decision for both of them. He kicked himself in the head every day since.

Stone sighed softly, but didn't move away from her. She tried to act aloft, attempted to show him that he couldn't keep affecting her like this. It didn't work though, and he could see the tears streaming down her cheeks in the soft light of daybreak. Recalling how many times in the past his actions caused her to cry suddenly made him disgusted with himself for his lack of sensitivity. He was still doing it.

"Kerensa," he began again, reaching out to touch her.

"No!" she shrieked. "Keep your hands off me."

He dropped his arms to his sides once more.

"I know you don't believe me, but…"

"Please stop, don't say another word!" She cried out like a dam bursting wide open from the pressure. Then she began to sob, her body trembling with emotional pain. Stone folded her into his arms, but she still resisted.

"I hate you!" she cried again, "I really hate you."

"I know, baby," he murmured, pulling her into his arms again. She lashed out, pounding his chest with her fists. She struck him out of anger; she struck him out of hurt and frustration, but most of all she struck him because she hated how vulnerable she still was when it came to him. Kerensa couldn't stop; she continued to beat him with her fists, and pushing him with her palms. Stone just stood there, allowing Kerensa to do whatever she needed to do. Finally he gathered her into his arms, and held her for a long time. She wept bitterly while he comforted her, and his sensitivity made her feel even worse.

"I wish you would have left me alone," she whispered, her voice trembling with attempted bravery. "And I wish you never came back."

"I know, sweetheart," he murmured again. "I know."

# 9

Stone never did go to sleep. He thought about Kerensa from the moment his head hit the pillow. Loving her again was too dangerous for him. It would cloud his head, force him to defocus on the mission at hand. He already made that mistake once before with her. It nearly cost both of them their lives.

Finally realizing that sleep was impossible, he climbed out of bed; put his clothes back on and headed down the hallway. First, he peaked into Janelle's room. She was still sleeping soundly. Kerensa's door was closed.

Perhaps a cup of coffee could provoke his mind into thinking clearly again. As he neared the kitchen, he could already smell the aroma of freshly brewed coffee. Glancing at his wrist watch, he saw that it was almost seven AM.

Nana looked up from the newspaper and smiled at him when he entered the room.

"Good morning, Dominick," she replied.

Stone forced a small grin.

"Do you ever sleep, Mrs. Drago?"

"Sometimes," she answered, "but generally my arthritis is bothering me and it's hard to get comfortable. Anyway, I don't want to talk about my boring arthritis. I have a question to ask you."

"O.K. go ahead and ask," Stone replied sitting down beside her and taking a gulp of his coffee. He noticed she was grinning from ear to ear.

"I want you to teach me to shoot a gun."

Stone nearly choked on his coffee. "Now why in the world do you want me to teach you that?"

Nana giggled softly. "Well, you never know when it could come in handy."

*Come in handy? Sweet Jesus It's not like we're talking about a good lasagna recipe, this is a dangerous weapon.*

"I'll think about it, Mrs. Drago."

Nana had a twinkle in her eye. "You do that, Dominick."

Stone chuckled briefly before thinking about the incident that occurred when Kerensa arrived home. As if Nana was reading his mind, she said, "what happened last night?"

"So we woke you up?" Stone asked, deliberately ignoring her question for the moment.

Nana shrugged her shoulders, still expecting an answer.

*Damn, she's good.*

"Somewhere between my tossing and turning and trying to get comfortable, I did hear quite a ruckus."

Stone looked into Nana's face, his features twisted into a tight frown.

"I'm really sorry about that, and I know you deserve an explanation, *even though I don't want to give you one.* "Kerensa went to Key West with him. She was going to spend the night but it wasn't part of the plans, so I wouldn't agree. I'm not sure what happened between them, but they came home anyway. I never went to bed, so I was on the couch when they returned." Stone smiled at Nana. "There was a confrontation between us, and it got a little out of control."

"Well, fancy that, I can't imagine anything getting out of control with you around, "Nana retorted lightly.

*Hoo-yah, this lady knows the real story.*

"I'm still worried about her safety. I know there hasn't been another incident, but something in my gut tells me to be on guard."

"I trust you, Dominick," Nana responded, "But I'm worried about my Kerensa. This is beginning to take a real toll on her, and I don't want to see her like this." Nana paused, and then finished, "I realize that it's none of my business, but I heard her crying last night."

Stone glanced away from Nana's intense gaze. *Here we go.*

"I'm sorry you heard that," he finally replied.

"Why did it happen?" Nana persisted.

"I'm afraid I said some things that weren't true."

"Then why would you say them?"

Stone cleared his throat.

*Jesus. Having to face this woman makes me prefer to take my chances with the E-Boli virus in an air tight room. How the hell can I go on a covert*

*mission, and crawl on my belly through a jungle with bugs big enough to have
a social security number, yet answering her questions makes me quiver like
a school boy cheating on a frigging Regents test.*

Suddenly Nana spoke.

"I'm sorry, Dominick, I know that I'm putting you on the spot, but
Kerensa is my child, and she is my life."

*Putting me on the spot? Well, that's a polite way of saying, "You will be
toast if you hurt my daughter." Way to go, Mrs. Drago.*

He nodded in understanding, but still didn't say a word.

\*\*\*

Kerensa cried for two hours, sleeping little. But when she awoke, she was
resolved to get a grip on her life again. The memory of Stone holding her
tightly within his arms and comforting her would probably never go away. It
was simple and pure, yet hidden with a desire that could be out of control. She
didn't understand what the truth was between them, but she would remember
that moment forever. She also realized that loving Dominick Stone was an
emotionally unhealthy mistake and she was already engaged to be married.
She crawled out of bed, hesitating briefly at Janelle's room and surprised that
she was still sleeping. Then, she tiptoed away. Perhaps it was still rather
early, probably around seven thirty. A nice strong cup of coffee sounded good
to Kerensa right about now. As she neared the kitchen, she could hear the
faint sound of Nana's voice. There was only one other person she could be
talking to if it wasn't Janelle. Kerensa hesitated briefly, not wanting to deal
with him yet. *This is my house; I should not be avoiding him.* She took a deep
breath, and walked into the room.

Nana stopped talking and looked up at Kerensa.

"Good morning, honey, how do you feel?"

"Exhausted, aggravated, frustrated," she responded, deliberately ignoring
Stone. She walked over to the coffee pot and poured herself a cup, observing
how quiet it became in the room. He glanced at her quickly, instantly noticing
the dark curls piled high on top of her head and the natural pink of her cheeks
and lips before her makeup was on. It reminded him of the way he loved her
the most. Natural, like the gentle breeze of nature, like all those mornings
years ago when they awoke together and sat at the kitchen table sipping their
coffee after a night full of lovemaking. *Oh man, here we go again.*

His reminiscing brought on a tight, burning sensation in his throat. Stone
hastily looked downward, deliberately avoiding Kerensa's gaze too. She

carried her cup over to the table and sat down closest to Nana. For several awkward moments nobody spoke, then, Stone quietly asked.

"When does Janelle wake up?"

Kerensa hesitated briefly in thought.

"She's sleeping a little later than usual this morning." She peered at him over her coffee cup. "Why?"

"I know you don't have any classes to teach today so I thought maybe you would like to take Janelle out for the day."

Kerensa nodded her head, realizing that she should acknowledge his thoughtfulness.

"What do you have in mind?"

Stone shrugged his shoulders.

"We could take her to the beach and bike riding along the boardwalk."

Kerensa smiled, and for Stone it was brighter than the Florida sun.

"She would love that."

"I can pack you a picnic lunch," Nana announced, already pushing away from the table. "By the time I'm finished, Janelle will be waking up."

Kerensa nodded in response to Nana's statement, but her eyes were on Stone.

His gaze was locked with hers too, and she knew he was apologizing for last night. She excused herself, and headed to Janelle's room to wake her up.

An hour later they were driving to Miami Beach. The beach was even more crowded than usual for a hot summer day. As they neared the beach, Kerensa turned off the air conditioning and opened the window. Stone chuckled, and replied.

"We're not exactly there yet."

Kerensa looked over at Stone and laughed.

"I keep forgetting you're used to that cold northern air." She thought another moment and spoke again. "Do you like the heat?"

Stone's respond was swift, causing Kerensa to smile broadly.

"No, it drives me crazy."

"It does take a little getting used to, but I love it."

"I seem to recall that you were either trembling from the cold all the time or complaining that you were freezing," Stone responded. "However you certainly didn't have very warm clothes to wear while you were in Buffalo."

Kerensa sighed inwardly, but managed to smile at him.

"That is true," she agreed, a feeling of bittersweet nostalgia tugging at her heart whenever she thought back to her days with him.

They managed to find a parking place after driving around the block twice. It wasn't too far away from the beach, but since it was across the street, it also meant that she would have to pull out the stroller. She was glad she had brought it along. She reached into the back seat to grab it, when Janelle began to whine.

"No, mommy, I don't want to sit in there!"

"You have to Janelle; mommy isn't going to carry you and it's too dangerous to walk here."

"Nooooo!" Janelle wailed, reaching her arms toward Stone.

"Let me carry her, Kerensa," Stone quietly replied.

Kerensa shook her head no, as she took Janelle out of her car seat. Janelle immediately reached her arms out again for Stone to pick her up. He hesitated, and their eyes met.

"I can carry her," he softly spoke into her ear again.

Kerensa sighed, not knowing how she should feel regarding Janelle's growing attachment to Stone. She took a deep breath and stepped aside allowing Stone to take her into his arms. Janelle clung to him, a satisfied smile on her little face. Kerensa shrugged off the thought of how she wished she were in his arms too.

They walked along, passing the venders and little boutiques that were set up for the tourists to shop for their treasures. When they were ready to cross the street, Janelle began to squirm.

"Put me down," she demanded in her little girl voice.

"No," Stone gently but firmly responded, "I will carry you."

Kerensa expected Janelle to continue to complain, but she didn't. It was suddenly obvious to Kerensa that Stone had a way of commanding authority to even the youngest of those he encountered. She giggled softly to herself.

They continued to walk in silence; the sand was already hot, softly tickling her toes. She studied the horizon as it met the ocean in swirls of cobalt blue and gentian violet. The ocean was a deep ultramarine hue and it was a striking contrast to the color of the sky. It also looked as though it was about to rain.

Stone spoke as if he were reading her thoughts.

"The forecast didn't call for rain today, did it?"

"I don't know, I wasn't really paying attention, but even if it does, it never lasts. The sun comes out and everything is over within a half hour."

Stone smirked at Kerensa. "Show off," he retorted.

She laughed aloud.

"I'm not the one who chose to live in such a cold climate," she reminded him.

"How did we end up discussing this topic all over again?" he chided back, putting Janelle down beside him and taking her hand. Kerensa watched as her little girl shook his hand away.

"No, Mr. ick, I'm a big girl, I can walk by myself."

Stone knelt down beside Janelle and firmly spoke again.

"You must hold my hand, Janelle, or I will have to pick you up again."

He tried to keep a straight face. *Mr. ick?*

Janelle quietly pouted and Stone waited. Slowly she reached out taking his hand in hers again.

"Thank you," he simply responded.

Kerensa liked Stone's firm but gentle approach with Janelle.

"She can't pronounce your name, that's as close as she can get, sorry."

Stone laughed heartily. "Actually, it's a fairly accurate metaphor; I believe there are others who would agree with that nickname."

*Other women perhaps? I wonder if he has a child of his own. Now where did that come from? And why do I care?*

The mere thought of that sent an uncomfortable feeling through her like fingernails on a blackboard. She also wondered what he had been up to the last eight years. Sensing his eyes on her, she shifted her gaze into his face.

"What's the matter?" he softly asked.

At first she shrugged her shoulders, and then she decided to speak her mind. *Should I ask?*

"Do you…" she hesitated, hating the way her timbre softly cracked. "Do you have any children of your own?"

A slow even grin spread across his lips. He didn't answer at first, reaching for the beach blanket and spreading it over the sand. His actions were unnerving and Kerensa felt a pinch of annoyance. Finally, he turned to gaze at her again. There was a strange depth to his eyes, an isolated sadness, disappearing all too soon.

She wondered if she had imagined it.

"You are the only woman I've ever spent any significant time with," he responded softly, "And we never had a child together. So I guess that makes my answer a *no*."

Kerensa stared at him in open shock.

*I remember how incredible the sex was with you. Absolutely mind boggling, head swimming, heart racing, and toe curling unbelievable sex. Yet Mr. Experience has never spent any significant time with anyone but me?*

Suddenly she realized that he was staring at her and her face heated with the memory of her daydreaming.

*He had been thinking about it, and now she was too.*

He grinned at her, a slow even upturn of his lips that almost had her believing he could read her mind. Then he turned his back to her again, quickly pulling his shirt off his shoulders and then over his head. Kerensa moistened her lips, as she stared at him, her thoughts still wandering to the memory of his body moving flawlessly with hers. His physique was well formed and perfect, tight muscles across his chest and abdomen that rippled with power and strength. His hips were narrow and his legs well defined. Virility oozed from this mans pores without even trying. When he moved to the side, she spotted the tattoo on his upper shoulder. One black rose carved in blocks with the name Stone beneath it. *One dangerous rose.*

She recalled the first time she ever saw it. It was the night he finally tracked her down in Montreal when she ran away. Believing that he was her father's killer, she had managed to elude him for over a day. When he found her, she fought him off and attempted to escape. She still didn't know who he really was. Later, she saw him with his shirt off for the first time, and there was the rose tattoo.

Her thoughts continued to linger and she could barely tear her gaze away. It wasn't until she heard him say her name again, that it registered in her head that he was speaking to her.

"I'm sorry, what did you say?"

"I asked you if you were alright."

"I'm fine," she quickly retorted.

Feeling foolish, Kerensa reached for Janelle's arm, slipping her sundress over her hips and exposing her little pink bathing suit.

"Come on, mommy, let's go!" Janelle impatiently exclaimed, tugging at Kerensa's hand.

Stone detected her hesitation.

"Aren't you going to swim?" he asked.

She didn't respond to Stone, her gaze intently staring past his head. Stone slowly turned around to see what had captured her attention, easily noting the look of uncertainty in her eyes. He observed a man of medium height with blond spiked hair and an earring in his left ear. He looked a little bit like a middle age back street boy with his twelve year old sister, except she was clinging to his arm like a dog in heat. The man had a smug grin on his face as he approached closer, but the woman with him wasn't smiling at all. Actually, she was openly glaring. Kerensa quickly reached for Janelle, and tugged her towards Stone.

"Please pick her up and hold her," she whispered to Stone.

He immediately responded, a strange feeling of possessiveness washing over him. The man stopped several feet away from Kerensa.

"Well, hello Kerensa. How have you been?" He asked her.

She shivered in the morning sun, hoping that neither man could detect her uneasiness.

"Fine," she retorted curtly.

There were several moments of uncomfortable silence. It was obvious to Stone that Kerensa had no intention of introducing him to this man, nor did she want him to linger with light conversation. Unfortunately, the unknown man didn't get the hint. Or did he?

"This is Virginia," he said to Kerensa. Turning towards Virginia, he replied, "And this is my ex-wife, Kerensa."

Neither women shook hands, they just nodded crisply in acknowledgement.

Stone studied the little girl he held tightly in his arms. There was no element of recognition, no visible awareness that the man standing before her was her father. Stone stared directly into Connor's eyes. He didn't like what he saw.

*I refuse to introduce Dominick to Connor; I absolutely will not. Oh damn…*

Kerensa cleared her throat and sighed, "This is Dominick Stone."

He reached over and shook Stone's hand.

"Hello, I'm Connor"

Connor looked at Kerensa again, a small sarcastic smirk on his face.

"So, where's the fiancé, or did you decide to spice up your life a little more?"

Kerensa froze but only for a brief moment before looking directly into his eyes.

*Don't mess with me buster, I can run circles around your words.*

"Is your newest girlfriend skipping school today, Connor?"

Stone suddenly chuckled aloud, forcing all of them to focus on him. He didn't care; he was still observing how Janelle didn't bother with him at all.

Now there was another moment of awkward silence and Connor suddenly reached over to Janelle and touched her hand.

*Silence means 'leave' you fool.*

"Hi sweetheart," he replied, his tone much too animated. "Are you going to swim in the ocean today?"

Janelle turned away from Connor, squirming uninterested in Stone's arms.

"I guess we should be going," Connor finally said. It was quite obvious that Janelle's behavior was embarrassing to him.

"Yea right," Kerensa responded, quickly turning away to take her shorts off.

*Go ahead, run away, isn't that what you do best? Isn't that what all men do best?*

Stone watched as they walked further and further away. Finally he turned toward Kerensa, full of questions. He was ready to ask them except the vision of her in a white bikini totally blind sighted him. Attempting to recuperate as quickly as possible, he placed Janelle back on the sandy ground.

*Holy shit she's freaking killing me.*

"He's Janelle's father, isn't he?"

"Yes, he is."

"Why doesn't she know her own father?" Stone persisted.

"He never wanted her," Kerensa retorted, reaching out to rub some lotion on her arm.

Stone studied Kerensa. He knew her well enough to read through that blasé attitude.

"Doesn't he visit her?" he persisted.

"No."

"Ever?"

"No."

"Why not?"

Kerensa hesitated; she didn't want to share this painful part of her life with him. In some ways she actually blamed Stone for her interest in an older man to begin with.

"How old do you think that woman who was with him is?" she asked, deliberately changing the subject.

"She looks under twenty one to me," Stone retorted. *Actually she looks a few years older than Janelle, and with a name like Virginia, how perfect.*

"Exactly," she responded bitterly. "He likes his women very young; they boost his ego, he never wanted a child, it reminds him of his own mortality."

*Sounds more like a pedophile to me.*

She turned toward him and handed him the suntan lotion. "Here do you need some?"

Stone nodded.

"Turn around," he directed.

Realizing that he wanted to put some on her, she complied.

Stone was ready to ask another question until he spotted the tattoo at the small of her back. It was a red rose with swirls of green leaves that encircled it in the shape of a small heart. At the tip of the heart was a thorn with a tiny drop of blood suspended from it.

His throat suddenly felt tight and dry, he swallowed quickly, overcoming his shock.

*The tattoo surprised me more than the ex-husband did.*

Kerensa suddenly called out to Janelle who was wandering a little too far away. As soon as Janelle came back, Kerensa turned around and peered suspiciously at Stone as if to say, *what are you waiting for?*

Stone stared directly into Kerensa's eyes, an uncharacteristic look on his face and she instantly remembered her tattoo. *Damn! I keep forgetting that stupid thing is back there. Please don't ask me about my brainless moment.*

As if he could read her mind, he placed his hands on her shoulders, gently turning her around again. Kerensa took a deep grateful breath that was short lived. His rugged hand felt incredibly arousing on the soft skin of her shoulders, and it became nearly impossible for her to concentrate. Recognizing that she needed to focus on something else, she continued to talk about Connor again.

"When he found out I was pregnant, he wanted me to have an abortion. I refused, and two months after Janelle was born, I left him."

"He wanted you to have an abortion?" Stone repeated, his tone more perplexed than questioning. *What a self absorbed asshole.*

She nodded her head.

"So he never visits her?" Stone asked again.

"Not really. His sister picks her up once in a while for her grandparents to visit with her. That's about all."

"He pays child support, right?"

"Like clockwork."

"What does he do for a living?"

"He's an attorney," she answered, gratefully taking the suntan lotion away from him before she did something really stupid.

"How old is he?"

She sighed. "Connor is forty three years old."

Stone watched as she put a little more on Janelle.

"Are we ready to go into the water?" she asked.

"Yes, of course. So why were you attracted to him?"

She bit down on her lower lip to refrain from reacting to his question.

*I was still in love with you; I was foolish enough to think I could replace you, and stupid enough to get a tattoo to remember you by.*

"I don't know, I never thought about it."

Stone didn't respond, and Kerensa knew better than to look at him. She knew that he didn't believe a word she said.

"Do you still care about him?" He asked again.

She quickly stopped walking and whirled around to face him. "Are you kidding me?"

Stone shook his head, *no.*

"I never loved him," she finally retorted.

*As if I know anything about love.*

\*\*\*

It was nearly nine o'clock in the evening before they headed toward home. The setting sun was glorious, with shades of orange, crimson and magenta dissipating into burnt reds and golden hues at the horizon. There was a gentle breeze that cooled the beach, making it very comfortable. Janelle was in Stone's arms again, this time fast asleep. They walked hand in hand down the deserted shore, tiny granules of sand slipping inside her sandals and tickling her toes every now and again.

Kerensa suddenly let go of Stone's hand and darted ahead of him. He observed her as she ran back and forth stooping down to pick something up and throwing it into the ocean. After several minutes, she came running toward him, out of breath.

"What are you doing?" he asked softly.

Her hair was pulled back in a high pony tail, her face translucent with color beneath the dim light of a street lamp. And she was animated, her energy just sparking all around her. "I'm throwing the starfish back into the ocean. They'll die if they stay out here on the beach."

*Starfish dying in the sand.*

Stone suddenly felt the full force of the differences between them. She saved Starfish. She probably couldn't kill a bug either. And she was a vegetarian.

He deleted his enemy, the nicer version of saying that *He killed people.*

When they arrived to her car, Stone easily shifted Janelle around in his arms, and buckled her into her car seat, still chuckling when his gentle jostling didn't cause her to stir at all. Standing upright beside Kerensa, he observed her yawning as she opened the driver's side of the vehicle.

"I can drive," he replied.

She paused, flashing back to the days when he told her what to do.

"No, it's alright, I'm fine."

Stone sighed. "Kerensa, don't argue with me. I know you're tired, and I don't mind driving."

Kerensa began to giggle.

"Some things never change about a person, do they?"

Stone pretended to be insulted.

"That's not true, Kerensa. In the past I would have bodily removed you from the vehicle if I had to."

This time she openly laughed.

"I believe you did bodily remove me from a vehicle!"

They laughed together for several moments, before she became very serious, a strange reflection in her eyes. She thought back to that incident, recalling how Jonathan Thorne attempted to manipulate her into his vehicle with the hope of kidnapping her that night. As angry at Stone as she was, thank God he was there, furious that she had disobeyed his orders and chose to leave with Jonathan instead of him at the end of the award ceremony. Determined that she remained with him, Stone slammed Thorne up against the vehicle and carried her away as though she were a rag doll. *And saved her life that night.*

Realizing how much she was living in the past again, she focused on Stone's face. He was intently studying her, and she felt really stupid. Stepping aside she gestured for him to get behind the wheel.

Stone grinned, and realizing that he was blocking the way for her to move to the other side, he guided her past him. But he didn't want to let go of her, and his grip gently tightened around her waist. Captured within his strong arms, held against muscles that felt more like a concrete wall than a man, her legs felt as unsteady as liquid jell-O.

She gazed upward, allowing his eyes to hold her equally as captive. There was little space between them as Stone drew her tighter against his hard body, his hands now hotter than the Florida sun. She wondered if he could feel her heart pounding while it hammered unevenly in her chest. She allowed him to move his hand to the curve of her chin as he gently caressed her face. When his lips brushed against hers, her breath caught in her throat. *How glorious it would feel to kiss him again, those soft, incredibly sexy lips that always tasted like coffee with a lump of testosterone. Actually, a big lump of testosterone… the strength of his hands when they were… Oh God, you cannot do this!* Her conscience screamed like a five alarm fire.

"No Dominick let me go."

He loosened his hold, allowing ample space between them, but still did not step away.

She wouldn't look at him as she replied, "we can't do this. We both know it's the physical attraction that draws us together. But I'm engaged to a man who loves me, a man who can promise me a future. What about you, Dominick? I woke up one morning, and you were gone. Sorry I keep bringing that up, but it's a rather important piece to remember in a relationship. You know it's the part where you commit to a person, instead of disappear. Then, just yesterday, you said I was a fling to you and nothing more, you do recall that, right?"

Her words instantly hit home, and he abruptly released her. Although Stone was an expert when it came to hiding his emotions, he wasn't able to do so quickly enough. Kerensa was shocked when she witnessed the emotional pain that reflected briefly on his face.

*Oh my God, why did I just say all that?*

"I'm sorry," she murmured. "I shouldn't have said that."

Stone didn't answer; he simply reached into the car and adjusted the seat. Then, he stepped inside and closed the door. Kerensa slipped into the passenger side, hating herself for being so honest. They drove in silence for several miles. Finally Stone spoke first.

"I apologize for what happened back there. I wasn't trying to-"

Stone's voice trailed off. He didn't know what he was trying to do.

Kerensa took advantage of his hesitation. "I shouldn't have said all those things, I'm sorry too. I guess hearing you tell Vance that you never cared about me was, well…" she took a deep breath; she hated how her voice always gave her true emotions away. Before she could continue, he interrupted her.

"I thought you knew me better than to believe the words I told Vance."

She studied his face in the opaque darkness.

"What are you trying to say?"

Stone didn't respond he simply stared at the road ahead. Kerensa thought about his question.

"Are you trying to tell me that you deliberately lied to Vance?"

Stone cleared his throat before indirectly answering her.

"I asked you if you were in love with Vance, and you told me *yes.* I didn't want the situation to become any more escalated than it already was."

Kerensa lapsed into silence.

*What is that supposed to mean? Why won't you tell me what's really going on inside? You keep shutting me out…*

*Damn you, Dominick Stone.*

\* \* \*

The following morning Kerensa was back at the dance studio.

She was in a crabby mood, and she could tell she was driving the girls much too hard, but it wasn't until Madison wiped her tears with the back of her hand that Kerensa realized how hard. She felt terrible. Walking over to her CD player, she hit the stop button. Then she stood there in silence just studying all the sad faces. Kerensa smiled at the girls.

"I have an idea," she replied cheerfully. "Why don't we get Mr. Dominick, and see if he will come with us across the street to the ice cream store, and I will treat everyone?"

The girls began to scream with glee, and Kerensa placed her hands to her ears in feigned distress. She turned around to see if Stone was in his usual corner of the hallway, but was alarmed to see that his chair was empty. Walking over to the doorway she peered into the corridor. When the students began laughing, Kerensa whirled around to see what was going on. There, right behind her stood Stone.

"How in the world do you do that?" she exclaimed, recalling again how many times in the past he managed to quietly sneak up on her.

"Really, how do you do that?"

Stone smiled, jiggling the change in his pocket.

"Alright girls, let's form a single line and I'll lead the way."

The girls fell into place, and Stone walked behind them. There were only a few moms in the studio, and Kerensa invited them along too.

Soon, everyone was eating ice cream and socializing. Kerensa noticed how much happier the girls were, and she noticed something else too. The mom's wanted to be anywhere Stone was. She watched how they rallied around him, enjoying every movement he made, or every word he said. She chuckled at how charismatic he was with women, and she was a little envious of the attention they were receiving too.

She tried to shrug it off; she even tried to rationalize it. After all, Vance hadn't called her since their anniversary night and she was becoming more and more depressed. She also wondered how long Stone was going to continue this bodyguard plan. Grateful that nothing else had happened, she decided that she really wasn't in any more danger.

Stone suddenly glanced in Kerensa's direction, almost as though he could feel her thoughts. She smiled wanly at him, and looked away. When she looked again, he had excused himself from his fans and was heading her way. Kerensa popped the last of her cone into her mouth and licked her lips.

Stone's gaze immediately went to those lips, watching her sweet, pink tongue move slowly across the softness of her mouth. *Oh Ke-rist.* He felt twenty degrees warmer.

"Are you ready to go back to the studio?" He asked, wiping his forehead with the back of his hand.

"Yea, I think I redeemed myself enough," she retorted, laughing.

Stone chuckled, raising one eyebrow.

"You were a little harder than usual on them," he declared.

Kerensa sighed.

"So you noticed, hah? I'm just a little crabby today, I guess."

Stone nodded. "Does any of that have to do with the man?"

"Maybe so, I haven't heard from him."

"He said he doesn't scare away that easily, Kerensa. Remember?"

She nodded her head, deep in thought.

"Yea, but a two headed Cyclops would be afraid of you."

Stone laughed heartily.

"Come on, let's get everyone back."

"I see you didn't deny that statement," she retorted again.

Once back at the Studio, the girls were in much better spirits. Kerensa was trying to set the music up again, when she noticed that the students had instantly quieted down. Kerensa stopped what she was doing, and decided to pay attention to what was going on. Stone stood in the middle of the studio, with the parents and students all around him. Two of the girls were facing one another and he was diligently using them while teaching everyone else the art of self defense. She watched him, long solid biceps flexing as he reached outward to position one of the girls while showing the other girl what to do in a forward attack. His tone was even and precise, his movements like liquid music, fluid and defined. *There should be a law against a man with a body that gorgeous.* Kerensa was equally as mesmerized with his commanding presence as his audience was.

When he was finished, it was apparent to Kerensa that he had the beginnings of something big. Everyone, both mother's and students, wanted to sign up for the self defense course. Stone turned over the details to Kerensa.

After they left, Kerensa was too tired to practice her own dance. She turned out the lights, and located Stone in his usual post. He immediately challenged her decision not to practice.

"Haven't you forgotten something?" he asked.

"I don't feel like it today, I'm a little tired."

"Not a good reason," he retorted bluntly.

Kerensa nervously giggled.

"Is there anything that you don't do well?" she asked, attempting to change the subject to reflect on his Karate class earlier.

Stone ignored her question, reaching into the doorway of the studio and turning the lights back on. He left Kerensa standing there as he walked into the room and flipped on one of her slow dance tunes. Then he motioned for her to come over. She complied, feeling a tingling sensation right down to her toes. She knew he wanted to dance, and Kerensa wasn't sure if she could handle this without feeling feeble at the knees. He gently embraced her, reminding her of the last time they danced together.

"You didn't answer my question," she murmured softly.

"Law enforcement is what I know," he whispered into her ear.

"But why don't I know more about you?"

"Like what, Kerensa?

"I would like to know something more about you, about your life. I mean, even something as simple as where did you learn to dance this well?"

Stone chuckled softly and then he replied, "My mother."

"Come on," she coaxed.

Stone chuckled again. "I was born and raised in Buffalo, NY. When I was eighteen I joined the Marines, Special forces…"

"I know all about that," she interrupted. "That's standard talk, like you've rehearsed it a thousand times before. I want to know about Dominick, the man."

She felt him stiffen, and she giggled softly.

"That's a lot harder to do, isn't it?"

He remained silent for a long time; finally he sighed and with an even, balanced tone, he began to speak.

"My mother still lives in Buffalo, but my dad died when I was a teenager. I didn't…take it well, so after I graduated from high school I decided to join the Military. I guess I was running away. My mother and I had a good relationship, but I think she could tell that I was sort of-I don't know, lost I guess and reckless too. Joining the Marines was impulsive, but it worked for me; they taught me what I know."

"Which is?"

Stone sighed again, his tone quiet without a hint of brag in his voice.

"I can pretty much use any kind of weapon, any kind of explosive device, I can blow up any type of structure, and get any bad guy out there. Chances are if you're hiding out and thinking you've outsmarted the law, you didn't outsmart me because I will find you..." He paused, taking a deep breath. "And well, that's all there is."

*Well, that's more than enough to remind me that you don't play nice.*

Pulling herself together, Kerensa hoped she didn't show her sudden discomfort over his mini dissertation. It was the 'find you and—part' that really gave her the cold prickles.

"I'm sorry about your dad, was it an accident?" she was hoping the change of subject would steady her pounding heart. *Like the subject had anything to do with her out of control heart!*

Stone took another deep breath.

"No, not really, he had a heart attack."

"Oh my God, how sad, he was a young man, right?"

Stone just nodded his head, *yes,* hoping that Kerensa would get the drift that he didn't want to talk about his father's death. He never talked about that just like he never discussed his missions. His father was dead, and nothing would ever change that. But he knew she would want to dissect it apart, detail by detail like the very few women he ever told it to. Of course, he was right.

"Were you close to your dad?"

"Yes, yes I was."

"So tell me the story, I mean, how did it happen?"

*Oh shit, here we go.*

"I don't talk about that, Kerensa, I never have."

Stone felt her body stiffen beneath his touch.

"Then you never recovered from his death," she softly responded. "I'm so sorry."

Stone felt his chest constrict and his throat go dry. What was it about this woman who could see inside his soul?

Several minutes of silence went by.

He opened his mouth, he actually wanted to tell her, but he couldn't.

"It's alright, Dominick, I understand," she murmured.

She understood? Did she also understand what a jerk he was? What a secretive, coldhearted asshole he could be? *Geezus, talk to her!*

"It was a hot summer day, and my father and I were building a small woodshed behind the house. He was always complaining that he wanted to get rid of the clutter from the garage. He was a neat freak, I guess, always believing that everything had its own place." Stone paused swallowing past the lump in his throat. "Things like my bike, various toys, stuff we didn't really use anymore. So anyway, he was sawing a piece of wood and I remember how pale and sweaty he looked, but I didn't know—" Stone paused again, this time he didn't continue.

Kerensa held her breath, but she didn't speak either.

Stone kept his tone steady as a rock.

"He finished with the wood he was sawing and he carried it into the garage. I picked up the other end and carried it over to the shed, and I heard a sound, it was-not good." Stone paused again. "So I ran into the garage and I saw him leaning against the wall, slowly slipping onto the floor. I grabbed him and lowered him to the floor and by then he wasn't breathing anymore. They couldn't revive him."

Kerensa felt too choked up to speak. She wasn't sure if her strong feelings were because of the tragedy of the situation with his father, or because he finally told her something straight from the heart. She was moved beyond words.

*His father died in his arms!*

"Thank you for telling me," she finally responded.

*Is that all I can say about an experience that obviously ripped a boys heart out? I need to say something more, to acknowledge what a tragedy it was. How do you recover from that?*

Stone silently thanked her. He thanked her for not coddling him with sappy words of sympathy. He thanked her for not making him feel like a blubbering idiot. He was grateful that she accepted his story for what it was.

For a while, they simply danced in silence. As each moment went by, Kerensa felt like she was loosing what little control she had. Her thoughts began to linger on tearing his clothes off and making love to him right there on her studio floor. The more she thought about how he finally trusted her enough to share a piece of his past, made her desire intensify, until she thought of Vance. Wasn't that what she was going to do with Vance?

*I have to get these fantasies out of my head. Talk about something else.*

"So don't you ever get tired of…?" Kerensa paused, not really sure how to word her next question. "-Of doing all kinds of, you know, top secret things?"

Stone snickered.

"What, your interrogation isn't over with me yet?" Instead of allowing Kerensa to answer, he spoke again. "That's not what you really wanted to know though, is it Kerensa?"

When she didn't respond, he continued, "No, I think you wanted to ask me if I actually like the danger, or if I ever get sick of –well, of doing what you still don't really know what I do, right?"

Kerensa sighed. *What a thin line you walk. That line between right and wrong, good and evil, who are you?*

She slowly nodded, and for several moments nobody spoke.

"I guess I don't understand how you can drift from job to job and place to place and not get lonely." She finally responded, eager to tweak the subject a little.

Stone didn't respond, and many more moments passed. Kerensa was beginning to think he wasn't going to answer when suddenly he spoke again.

"I'm not sure how I gave you the impression that I don't get lonely."

"Well, maybe because you really don't act like you need anyone in your life."

This time Stone remained silent.

Kerensa thought about what he once said to her. "I realize you know where to find company when you need it but…"

Stone sighed, interrupting her. "Did I tell you that?'

She giggled. "Yea, you did."

"I'm beginning to realize I said a lot of inappropriate things to you once. I'm sorry for that."

"So, let's forget about what you said or didn't say once upon a time. I'm interested in knowing if you ever get tired of living your life with so much…uncertainty. She tried hard not to sound so probing. *What exactly do I mean by that question?*

Stone laughed softly.

"Do you ever get tired of dancing?"

"It's hardly the same thing!"

"It's still a choice you made."

Kerensa thought a moment.

"Then you're happy with what you do?"

"I didn't say that."

"Are you sorry about anything, Dominick?"

"I don't know what you mean by that question, Kerensa."

"Regrets, do you have any?"

Stone took a deep breath; he wanted to tell her that his life was full of regrets, full of demons that visited him in his sleep at night, full of 'what if's' and used to be's, he wanted to tell her that he had to look over his shoulder because he never knew who was really out to get him or if he would live to see tomorrow. But he couldn't say all that, he didn't even want to admit it, not even to himself.

And his greatest regret was in his arms right now, holding this angel who was willing to accept him without truly knowing anything about him. Grateful to embrace the least little bit of information, but he still shared more than he ever should have, ventured too far out on that limb. Any knowledge she could have about his past could be held against her someday.

He didn't answer her; instead, he simply pulled her closer to him, even though his mind was screaming something else.

*Don't get close, don't loose focus. You need to let her go.*

Kerensa didn't know how long she melted in his arms, but when Stone's body stiffened, she realized that something was wrong. In a split second, he pushed her behind him and drew his gun.

She looked up to see Vance standing in the doorway.

# 10

For a moment, nobody said a word. Kerensa felt an instant migraine piercing her forehead and blurring her vision, making Vance look all the more angry. However his fury wasn't directed toward Kerensa. She knew Vance well enough to see that he was now over the edge, beyond thinking with his cognitive brain instead of his emotions. It was a deadly situation. Stone took several steps away from Kerensa, and she knew that he was posturing himself for a possible fight. Stone slowly reached around his side, tucking his weapon away.

"This isn't what you think," he flatly replied.

"And you must really think I'm a first class fool," Vance retorted through gritted teeth.

"There's nothing between us, I told you that already."

"Oh yea, this really looks like you're just her bodyguard." Vance stepped closer, a flash in his eyes that spelled out danger.

Kerensa gasped, she knew that a fist fight was inevitable but she just couldn't believe it was going to happen. She attempted to stop Vance from striking first.

"It is true, Vance. Please believe me, I still love you."

"No, Kerensa, you don't know who or what you love anymore."

Vance took another step closer to Stone.

"But where I come from, we stand up for what we believe in. We fight for our women, and I plan on fighting for mine."

Stone shook his head.

"You don't have to fight for her, she's already yours."

Kerensa's mouth was open in shock. She felt like she existed in a time warp, a past dimension that was set in the middle ages. All they were missing was a coat of armor and a couple of smelly white horses.

Suddenly Stone turned on his heels and walked away from both of them. "I've told you before, you can have her," he bluntly stated.

Stone's typical dismissive attitude was the fuel Vance needed to fan his furious flames. He lunged forward, momentarily throwing Stone off guard. Stone swung around, catching Vance's first punch squarely in the mouth. When Vance attempted to swing again, he was surprised how quickly Stone recovered. Stone's movements were so swift, Kerensa had no idea how Vance ended up on the floor with Stone's knee at his throat. But he did.

"I keep telling you that I won't fight you," Stone snarled viciously. "But you just don't want to listen. Now get up and walk away."

His words and the determined look on his features sent a powerful message to Vance. Although Vance didn't want to admit it to himself, he could never stand a chance against Stone. Slowly he nodded his head, and Stone released some pressure against his throat.

"Get out of my way," Vance croaked.

Stone complied, reaching his hand out to assist him. Vance angrily refused, and once he was standing upright, he cleared his throat and turned to face Kerensa.

"I ran a background check on this guy, Kerensa, and I couldn't find any verification that he even exists. There is no Sergeant Dominick Stone in the New York State Police Department, and there is no such name in Buffalo either. This guy is a big fake, his ID is phony and he's hiding something. Dominick Stone is a very treacherous man, Kerensa. I can't begin to tell you how dangerous he really is, but I can tell you that he will slit someone's throat so fast they won't even know they're dead yet. You have no business being around a man like that, Kerensa, and you're not safe with him." Vance took a deep breath, as if he thought he needed to talk fast before Stone attacked him. "Now come home with me."

Kerensa stared into the unwavering faces of both men. Her heart began to thump wildly, and she felt like her head was going to explode. *Holy Mary, what am I going to do now? What if it's true! He's so secretive, always in the darkness...* She opened her mouth to speak, but no words would come out. Her throat felt as dry as the desert sand. She studied Stone's behavior. He never moved or reacted to Vance's accusations, he didn't deny them either.

Kerensa took a deep breath, but her voice trembled as she spoke,

"Dominick Stone is a police officer, Vance, why can't you work with him?"

"You know the answer to that, Kerensa, it's because he won't work with me. Men like Stone only work alone, they can be in the same room with you, and you won't even know they're there. You've learned that first hand yourself.

They can move so fast, if you blink, you missed them and the next thing you know, someone's dead on the floor and you can't even describe the attacker. Why can't you understand this, Kerensa? You have no idea how treacherous a man he is."

"Vance, you're scaring me," Kerensa finally choked out.

"I'm scaring you?" he shouted incredulously, poking his finger at Stone's face. "This is the guy that should be scaring you!"

"I've seen his identification, Vance; he is who he says he is."

"Jesus Christ, how could you be so naïve, Kerensa? We have such high tech equipment now to falsify credentials. You don't know this guy at all."

Kerensa studied Stone with uncertainty. Vance had a point there.

Stone watched as Kerensa's eyes began to cloud with suspicion. He figured everything was under control as long as Kerensa believed him instead of Vance. Unfortunately, the table was doing a proverbial turn, and he was ending up the guy under it. Stone cleared his throat; it was time to speak up.

"Kerensa I can explain why I'm not so easy to find. You just have to trust me."

*Trust me? But do I truly trust you?*

"Then explain it to me."

Stone cleared his throat again.

"I will tell you in confidence." He turned toward Vance.

"Go home Detective Robertson, I assure you that your fiancé is safe with me, if I wanted to do something to her, I would have done it by now."

"I can't," Vance quietly replied.

She observed Stone's response. She recognized that look in his eyes all too well. Stone's patience had finally grown thin. His eyes narrowed into small hard pebbles of blue-black coal. He turned his attention to Kerensa. His tone was hushed and solid as steel.

"Tell your fiancé to go home Kerensa, before he gets hurt."

She nodded her head, praying that her decision to trust Stone was the correct one. She quickly thought back to the last time she didn't trust who he said he was. *He lied to you back then. But he still saved your life…*

"Just don't hurt him," she whispered beneath her breath to Stone, then, turning toward Vance she softly replied, "please leave, I'll call you later."

"Kerensa if you send me away, I'll never be back," he murmured quietly.

Tears instantly sprang into her eyes, quickly slipping down her cheeks. She could feel her muscles beginning to tremble.

"Please don't make me choose," she whispered back.

Several moments passed with Kerensa and Vance just staring at one another. Stone knew there was no turning back for them, and this was the moment of truth. Stone could kick himself for interfering with something he had no business destroying. As much as he loved her, Vance could give her the stability he could never give. Vance did nothing as the tears continued to slip down her cheeks. Stone could feel his pulse quicken, and his anger mount. His thoughts about Vance were becoming more and more despicable by the minute. *Brainless, egotistical nimrod...*

Finally, he addressed Vance.

"This woman loves you, but frankly I don't think you deserve her. You're a fool, Robertson." Stone looked at Kerensa as he said this. There was an understanding that tangled between them. Vance noticed it too, and it only made him angrier.

"I'll be outside waiting for you, Kerensa."

With that, Stone walked right out the door.

He stood outside hoping he did the right thing. He was still keeping so many secrets from Kerensa. He didn't like Vance, not because he was the man she planned on marrying, but because he didn't truly appreciate all that she was. It was as though history was determined to come around full circle and kick him in the pants. Stone kept his eyes glued to the studio door wiping the sweat off his forehead with the back of his hand. He cursed beneath his breath at the humid, hot air that still hung in the atmosphere like a thick cloud of boiling water. *And that wasn't the only thing boiling.*

*** 

Kerensa buried her face in her hands. Why didn't he understand how difficult this was for her? Stone's words were ringing true in her head. She knew that Vance was angry because Stone won another round. It was all about the competitiveness between these two men, not necessarily about her. That hurt most of all. Realizing this, she took a shaky breath, and spoke again.

"I can't make you believe how I feel about you anymore. I guess I don't blame you one bit. I'm only asking you to give me a little time..."

"I've given you more than enough time, and you know it."

"That's not true," Kerensa defended. "You've been very considerate despite how sudden this situation came about, but you still haven't given me enough time to see it through."

"I've seen just about all I care to see, Kerensa. Sorry."

She couldn't believe this was really happening. He was breaking off their engagement, telling her that it was over between them. Her lower lip trembled, her eyes full of tears. When she gazed into Vance's eyes, she didn't see a flicker of emotion in there.

"I can't compete with a man like Dominick Stone, Kerensa. He's in a class all his own. He may be every woman's bad boy dream, but there's no sincerity in a man like that. He won't ride the storm and stay with you like I would have. He's in your life today, but that's about all. He'll come and go like a ghost in the night, using you over and over again. Go ahead, and take your chances. You don't have to admit it, but you still love him. Face it honey; you're in way over your head already."

*'Would have' done, what's that supposed to mean?*

Kerensa turned away. She wasn't going to beg, and she certainly didn't want to hear his version of her fragile heart.

Unfortunately, Vance read her non verbal cue as a message of farewell.

"Before you go, I would like my ring back."

*Your ring back?*

Vance saw the look of hurt that immediately flickered across her face.

"Well, you know why, Kerensa. You know it's an heirloom diamond from my great grandmother."

This time, Kerensa couldn't hold her tears back any longer. They fell freely down her inflamed cheeks.

*God, did you think I was going to toss it overboard like on the Titanic too?*

She whirled around to face him, furiously yanking the ring off her finger. Then, she simply plopped it into his hand and kept on walking.

She headed right out the door of her studio and ran across the street. She didn't want anything to do with either man.

***

The sight was aimed perfectly at her head. That pretty little head with all those dark curls. He didn't know she was so beautiful; hell, maybe he should kill him first, and have a little fun with her before finishing the deal. Slowly he moved the sight again, this time following the back of his head… "Come on now, a little slower and turn around, face me you son of a bitch, I want to see your eyes."

He inched a little closer to the cement railing and crouching as low as possible, he brought the AK 47 up to his face and peered through the scope again.

"Just fractions of an inch to the right, you bastard, come on!"

*Let me see your eyes.*

He was overheated and tired, having been hiding there for over two hours just waiting. He was impatient now, pissed off that it wasn't going as smoothly as planned. He kept away from the camera overhead, knowing just how far he had to crouch so that he wouldn't be seen.

*Come on you bastard, turn around and look at me… Yes, just like that. Let me see your eyes…*

*Oh yea, this one's for you little brother…*

He smiled, and pulled the trigger.

***

It only took a moment for Stone to spot Kerensa. He instantly knew what had happened. "Fucking idiot," he muttered beneath his breath, then cussed violently a few more times as he ran across the street to catch up with her.

"Kerensa, wait!"

She wouldn't turn around.

*Son of a bitch!*

"Leave me alone!"

Stone was about ten feet away when he suddenly saw something else. A tiny red laser light smack in the middle of Kerensa's head. He turned around and looked upward, and he knew he had to act fast. In one split second of time, Stone yanked Kerensa backwards, slamming her body ruthlessly into his. It knocked the wind right out of her as she struggled against the horrible feeling of strangulation. Stone pinned her beneath him on the sidewalk, his hard body shielding her frame with his. A loud, crisp popping sound instantly filled the air. He continued to hold her against him and then rolled her half-crushing, half-protecting, to safety behind the closest building.

Kerensa knew that sound, it penetrated her memory like an eternity of broken dreams reminding her how eight years ago could suddenly become eight seconds in the scope of time. She gasped for air, attempting to refill her lungs with the precious element she needed to breathe. He shifted his weight, allowing her to lean up against the warm brick of the building to catch her breath.

"Don't move," he ordered harshly.

*As though he really thought she could.*

Kerensa nodded her head in response, her eyes still tearing from the lack of oxygen. Suddenly she caught a movement across the street and she strained to identify who it was. She realized that it was Vance, weapon drawn, and crawling in their direction. The street was fairly deserted at the time of the gunshot, but someone had called the police. She could hear the sounds of sirens in the distance slowly getting louder and louder.

*But where was the shooter?*

"What's happening now?" she gasped, attempting to whisper into the back of Stone's head.

Stone turned and put a finger to his lips to silence her.

She nodded, realizing that she had to take slow deep breaths so she wouldn't be panting so loudly. Her heart was just roaring in her ears and she felt like fainting from the hyperventilation.

She watched Stone as he sent some hand signals to Vance and he disappeared behind another building. Kerensa looked upward into the direction that Stone was staring. She couldn't see anything.

Several police cars suddenly arrived onto the scene. At least six cops jumped out of the vehicles.

"We might as well forget it now," Stone muttered beneath his breath. Turning toward Kerensa, he gently grasped her by the shoulders. She stared into his face, noticing that his skin was moistened with perspiration.

"Are you alright?" he asked his tone agitated.

She numbly nodded her head.

"Sorry I knocked the wind out of you, but at least you're alive. Stay right here, and I'll be right back."

*At least I'm alive? Yes, sweet Jesus, at least I'm alive!*

"Where are you going?" she hysterically whispered.

"To see where Vance is."

Kerensa suddenly felt remiss for not really thinking about that.

She nodded her head again, but it was obvious to him that she was a few fries short of a happy meal. He began to wonder if she was in shock. Pausing briefly, he wasn't sure if he should leave her alone. All of a sudden, they weren't alone anymore as several police officers were rushing toward Kerensa. Stone stepped aside; actually he took that opportunity to simply vanish into thin air. He headed around the building toward the area where the shooting came from.

There were several large buildings parallel to each other, a Laundromat, the ice cream parlor where they took the girls to the other day, and a Chinese restaurant. But there was no Vance. Not that Stone actually wanted to find

Vance. It was the sniper he really wanted to snag. Stone tipped his head back, looking up as far as possible.

*Shit.*

That sniper was so gone; he was probably ordering his dinner by now.

*Fuck.*

Then he caught a movement in the distance and he squinted to see who it was, except he still couldn't tell. Stone moved quickly and quietly, his operative training along with his military training was the perfect combination to make him move swiftly and efficiently. This was like a stroll in the park for him. Stone came up behind Vance and he nearly laughed aloud when Vance released a little squeal that sounded more like it was part pony and part man.

"Sorry, man, I didn't mean to-"*Geezus, I don't want to piss this guy off any more than he is already.*

It was too late; the look on Vance's face was enough to stop a nuclear holocaust.

"Where the hell did you come from?" Vance asked furiously.

Stone didn't answer his question. "Did you see anything suspicious?"

"No," Vance paused, taking a deep breath. "I don't think the guy is here anymore."

*No shit, Sherlock.*

Stone didn't answer, he simply turned on his heals and headed back to Kerensa. He was gone less than a minute, and that was time enough to be without her.

There was a sick feeling just grinding his gut out. This attack was different from the last time when Thorne and his goons were hunting them. Whoever shot that gun was a professional, a real expert.

Someone hired to kill Kerensa.

# 11

Kerensa sat in her living room in a catatonic state of mind. She could see Stone sitting across from her, Vance on the other couch with the chief of police, and Nana was beside her with Janelle cuddled quietly in her arms. Yet Kerensa wasn't really there at all. She felt separated from her body, their voices sounding like a dull cannon just shooting words into her brain. She tried to comprehend what they were saying, but it just wouldn't compute. Only her beautiful, sleeping child beside her made any sense at all.

She didn't realize that she was crying until Nana reached out to hold her in her arms too.

"My poor Kerensa," she crooned, "don't worry, everything will be alright."

Kerensa slowly tilted her head sideways to look at Nana. Although her words and touch were soothing enough, the look on her face was enough to stop a runaway train. Nana was terrified.

She suddenly focused on a question the chief of police asked Stone.

"So what exactly do you do?"

*This should be interesting.*

Stone cleared his throat.

"I'm a private investigator."

"And I also heard that you were a Sergeant in the New York State police department?" The chief of police retorted as he suspiciously regarded Stone.

"I'm retired as a police officer."

Chief Donovan shot a look at Vance.

"Detective Robertson told me that he couldn't find any background check on you. Frankly, Mr. Stone, I did some research myself and you don't exist."

Kerensa held her breath and studied Stone. He never even flinched. It was as though his facial features were carved from a two hundred year old brick slab.

*How can he pull that off so perfectly?*

Stone chuckled; it was a throaty, self confident sound.

"Chief Donovan I can assure you that I am very much alive, and obviously I do exist. You can rest assured that my identification and my qualifications are registered with the United States government for whom I serve. Now I am not at liberty to discuss anything further than that, but I can give you some references if you still question my identity."

Donovan was silent.

Vance sat upright.

Kerensa was very much aware of her surroundings now.

Nana's eyes doubled in size.

Stone bulldozed on, directing his question to the chief of police.

"I need to know exactly what your department plans regarding the incident that occurred today. Although I am certain that my qualifications are of interest to you, they are not the priority in this situation. Kerensa's safety is."

Chief Donovan nodded his head in agreement.

"Unfortunately, I don't have the manpower to spare any individual protection for Ms. Fiori," Donovan finished.

*Perfect.*

Stone blew out a sigh of relief very slowly and efficiently. This was exactly what he was hoping to hear. He knew there wasn't anyone who could protect Kerensa as well as he could.

"I expect that your department will be available if I should need them," Stone clearly defined.

"Oh now wait a minute," Donovan bluntly retorted, "I never said you can protect Ms. Fiori. I simply stated that I cannot give her individual protection."

This time Stone's features hardened and his eyes narrowed. Kerensa knew that look all too well. She braced herself for the touch down hurricane and hoped the damages wouldn't be too difficult to repair.

Stone leaned forward, placing his arms across the tops of his legs and pausing briefly before he spoke.

"I don't think you understand my intentions, Chief Donovan, so let me rephrase them. I will be protecting Kerensa and that issue isn't up for debate, by you or anyone else," he added glancing briefly at Vance. "However I may require your department for emergency services. That is all I am requesting of you."

Chief Donovan stared at Stone with that same expression on his face that

Kerensa had seen on a hundred other faces. Then his cheeks flushed bright red, his face resembling a boiled ham.

"I don't require you to spell anything out for me, Mr. Stone. I am perfectly capable of following the details myself. However, I'm in charge of this investigation and I still don't know who you really are."

Stone was irritated a mille-second before he calmly spoke again.

"Kerensa stays with me, and there is no other alternative. Frankly, Chief Donovan I don't care if you don't know me, nor do I care what your rank is. I was hired to protect Kerensa and I am in charge of this case, you, sir, are only in charge of the incident that happened today."

If Donovan was angry before, this time he was furious. He didn't hide it very well either. He rose to his feet and stood in front of Stone. He was an older gentleman of medium height, his body was lean but out of shape. He wasn't afraid of Stone and he wanted him to know it. Any other man would take an action like that as a challenge to fight. Not Stone. His eyes narrowed, and a muscle twitched in his jaw. He reached around to his cell phone and dialed a number, before anyone answered the phone, he ended the call. Then he handed the phone to Donovan. "Push the send button," he instructed, "You can check out the number I called later, but you can speak to the person there now."

Donovan took the phone from him, a bewildered expression across his features.

Kerensa observed Chief Donovan as he sat back down, briefly identified himself to the phantom person on the other end, and asked for information. There were several moments of silence as Donovan just listened to his answer. Donovan then gave the person on the other line his fax number. When he hung the phone up his face was a translucent shade of pea green.

"My department will be glad to provide you with any assistance you may require, sir."

Kerensa's mouth dropped open. Vance simply gaped in shock. *What just happened here?*

"Who do you think that was on the phone?" Nana leaned over and whispered into Kerensa's ear.

She shrugged her shoulders. *Probably the President of the United States.*

Chief Donovan spontaneously rose to his feet, an indication that their conversation was over. He said goodbye to Nana, and reached out to grasp Kerensa's hand. She cautiously shook his.

"You're a lucky young lady, Ms. Fiori. Sergeant Stone not only saved your life this evening, but he will be providing protection for you until this problem is resolved. I suggest you follow his directives."

*Oh, so now it's Sergeant Stone.*

If the situation wasn't so serious, it would have been hysterically funny to see how Chief Donovan suddenly became the leader of the Dominick Stone fan club.

Kerensa numbly nodded her head, but her eyes were on Vance. He was looking downward choosing not to make eye contact at all. The sickening feeling she felt deep down in her gut earlier that evening came flooding back.

*Vance doesn't think he can compete with Stone. He doesn't want me anymore…*

Chief Donovan nodded his head one last time, his cheeks back to their normal color again. Kerensa kept her gaze on Vance, determined to catch his eye if he chose to send a glance her way. He didn't.

She heard a few choice words escape Stone's clenched teeth. They weren't pretty.

When the door closed, Kerensa felt as if someone found the switch to her body and turned it off. Her muscles felt like silly putty, her legs had no structure.

The last two hours finally took over. She was worn out and fatigued, well past the point of exhaustion. She blinked several times, but everything looked really fuzzy; at least until it all went black.

***

When she awoke she was staring into several sets of eyes, and Janelle was crying at the top of her lungs. She could hear Nana's futile attempts to comfort her. Poor Nana, she had one eye on Kerensa and the other on her screaming grandchild.

She attempted to sit upright.

"Relax, Kerensa," Stone instructed his tone firm. "Try to calm down."

"I'm alright now, just give me my baby."

Stone nodded his head to Nana, giving her the permission to take Janelle over.

Kerensa sat forward at the same time that Stone steadied her in his powerful arms. Then, he took Janelle from Nana and placed her on her mama's lap.

Janelle instantly quieted down, burying her little face into Kerensa's bosom. She rocked her baby, placing her head on top of hers and whispering soothing words of comfort into Janelle's ear. It only took a few minutes for Janelle's eyes to close.

Stone gently lifted Janelle from Kerensa's arms as easily as he would have lifted a piece of paper. Her eyes popped open for a brief moment, until they focused on Stone. Then, her eyes fluttered closed and she settled into his arms. He immediately carried her down the hallway into her room, a strange tightness in his chest as he gazed into her tear streaked face. When he came back, he noticed that Kerensa was dozing off to sleep too. He leaned downward and lifted her into his arms as effortlessly as he held Janelle. She stirred too, and gazing into his eyes she felt herself drowning in their oceans of blue. She leaned her head against his taunt bicep and closed her eyes momentarily again. She briefly opened them when she felt the comfort of her own bed beneath her exhausted limbs but when she felt him leave her side; she reached out and whimpered, halting him in his tracks.

"What's the matter, sweetheart?" He asked, realizing it was too late to take back his term of endearment.

She peered at him through partially closed lids, her long eyelashes covering her eyes like shades. He felt a surge of heat as he suddenly had a flashback of the first time he ever passionately held her in his arms. She had been sleeping but was awoken by a terrible nightmare. He recalled how frightened she was, clinging desperately to him and asking him to hold her. He knew that if he did, he would never be able to control his actions. That night was the first time he ever intimately touched her, but he stopped himself when she confessed that he would be her first. He recalled with instant clarity how cold and snowy that night in Toronto was, he also remembered the inferno within him. *The heat. The passion. His obsession for her. Always his obsession for her...*

*His hesitation, and the reason he couldn't continue...*

Gazing into her beautiful face now, made his body ache to feel her just one more time like that again.

She opened her eyes, as though she sensed him staring at her.

"Please Dominick, don't leave me."

His breath caught in his throat. He suddenly felt overheated just like that night eight years ago... But his mind screamed something else. *One more chance to hold you again, but then what? Haven't I destroyed enough of your life already?*

"Sleep, Kerensa, I promise everything will be alright."

"No, please..."

He swallowed hard.

"Please, what?" he softly asked.

"Hold me, just like you used to."

*Hold me. That was a simple request. No commitment, no complications. No way he could hurt her again, right?*

Stone took a step in her direction, but when her gaze locked with his, the intensity of emotion in her eyes was too much for him to bear.

He took a deep breath.

"I don't think that's a very good idea, Kerensa."

Her eyes filled with tears.

*Damn!*

Stone was a man who could stay in control, it wasn't just what he did, but it defined who he was. But this shouldn't be about his control; it was about her needs, right?

He paused a brief moment longer, then silently slipped into the bed with Kerensa.

He was so quiet, so absolute, that she never felt him there until he pulled her softly into his arms.

Kerensa gasped, shocked at her bodies reaction to his tender touch. Memories fast and furious quickly flew to the surface. They were crushing and amazing all at the same time. She wasn't in the least bit tired anymore. At first, she didn't know how to react. Her initial thought wasn't actually a thought at all. It was instinctual, a sensation of pure heat with a desire for him so strong that it stole her breath away. His warmth mixed with the scent of his masculinity was intoxicating. She struggled to sit upright. In the split second it took for Kerensa to do that, Stone was already very much aware of her reaction. Suddenly he pulled her toward him again, and she felt the warmth of his breath on her cheek his tone thick with desire.

"I thought you wanted this."

Realizing that Stone thought she was reacting to any wayward intentions on his behalf, she felt her heart race even faster. *If only you knew, I trust you; it's my own desires now that are in question...but I must be crazy to love you again. I must be crazy to think we could be together. Love shouldn't be like a cyclone, it should be calm, not this blinding mix of passion and commotion and gut wrenching pain...*

She relaxed her arms, allowing him to tuck her snuggly by his side. She sighed, wishing now more than ever before that she had the strength to fight these intense feelings that kept washing over her like a poisonous chemical. *God, please don't let me love him again...I can't do this again!*

Somewhere in between her prayers about love, and Stone and all that other stuff, Vance's face popped into her head.

***

Jonathan Thorne gulped down his JD and water in one long swallow. He needed money bad, but tonight he was celebrating. Glancing at his wrist watch, he began to laugh aloud. She was about to die, or maybe she was dead already and in a couple days he would make his next move. His only remorse was that she wouldn't be alive to see her little girl kidnapped and sold. He wanted her to suffer, to feel the same hideous torture that he felt as a child. He wanted her to experience what it was like to be abandoned, emotionally and physically executed. That was what his mother did to him. That was what his father, no-her father, did to him too. But not to her, not to perfect little Kerensa. Oh no, she lived in luxury and wealth, had everything she ever wanted just handed to her. *Daddy this, and daddy that…*

Soon he would have the money he deserved, money that was meant to be his from the very time of his birth. Soon, he would win the game and show that son of a bitch, Stone, how cunning he really is. After all, his father was a doctor. It didn't matter anymore that his mother was a stupid, sick bitch who physically abused him. She was dead, and he was about to live his life like a king.

He was going to get even with that fucking guard at Elmira Prison too. That son of a bitch never did follow through with his promise. He was a dead man too now. Thorne knew exactly when and where to strike, he had enough connections to never get his own hands dirty again. He was above all that now. It would be down the line though, when nobody could put it all together. Then, he would kill Sammy Jackson.

He was in charge of himself, hell; he was in charge of the world. He could con anyone; make them believe what he was capable of just about anything. Yea, he was superior, and he was brilliant!

"Is this seat taken?" She asked, interrupting his precious thoughts.

Thorne's face instantly clouded over with rage, but the moment fled quickly away, replaced by a sexy rise of the eyebrows and a slight upturn of his lips.

"It was waiting for you," he drawled.

She smiled softly, quickly turning her face away.

"What's your name?" He asked, noticing that she had dark, curly hair.

"Maya."

"Nice name, so Maya, what are you drinking?"

She smiled, and he also noticed the dimples in her cheeks.

"Just a coke, I'm the designated driver for tonight."

"Oh, what a bummer," he retorted.

She laughed, reminding him of someone else. Someone he despised. He signaled the bartender and ordered her a coke.

"So what's your name?" she asked.

"Jonathan."

"You don't look like a Jonathan," she mussed thoughtfully.

He raised his eyebrows again. "Oh really, why is that?"

"I don't know," she answered, long, polished red nails reaching into her pack of cigarettes and pulling one out. "You just look like a guy with a tougher name than that."

He stared into her brown eyes, realizing how much he hated women with brown eyes too.

*You want tough, I'll give you tough. Oh yea, bitch. I'll give you a night you'll never forget.*

"Do you like tough men?"

"No, I'm not into the 'big bad wolf' thing."

"Well, you needn't worry; I'm as gentle as a teddy bear."

Then, he smiled, all teeth.

# 12

When Kerensa awoke Stone wasn't by her side anymore. Frightened and disoriented, her eyes darted to the bold red letters of her alarm clock to give her a clue what time it was. Grateful that it was only six o'clock in the evening, she was relieved to see that she only slept for two hours. Suddenly she panicked again. Where was Janelle? Surely she should be awake by now."

Kerensa swung her legs around the edge of the bed and sat upright. She could hear Nana's voice, Stone's rich timbre responding, and little Janelle singing her ABC's at the top of her lungs

She smiled wryly, time to get up and join the living. Time to face whatever plan Stone had concocted. And she was sure he had a plan.

She quietly walked down the hall and Janelle spotted her first.

"Mommy, mommy!" She shouted with glee, wrapping her little arms around Kerensa's legs.

Kerensa began to laugh when she saw what Janelle was wearing. Draped over her own clothes was Stone's black muscle shirt. She could tell that Janelle had a little help strategically strapping it into place by using her Care Bears belt. Her hair was pulled back into a pony tail and she was wearing Stone's watch on the top of her arm, completing the ensemble.

"Hey, my Nellie, have you been playing dress up again?"

Janelle put her hands above her head and slowly twirled around, forcing Stone to laugh aloud. Kerensa shook her head at her little daughter showing off. Nana smiled, and Kerensa could almost feel the love mixed with fear in Nana's face when she gazed at both of them. Suddenly a feeling of doom washed over Kerensa. Her eyes filled with tears, causing her to quickly turn her back on all of them. She stooped down and wrapped Janelle into her arms. She pulled herself together, and faced them again. She knew Nana would recognize the watery gaze in her granddaughter's eyes but would Stone realize how fragile her emotions were?

Almost in answer to her own thoughts, Stone slowly rose to his feet and walked toward Kerensa. He softly touched her arm, immediately thinking about how supple she felt when he held her and how hard it was to keep his hands off her. As soon as she fell asleep, he had slipped away from her, damning his body and the uncomfortable erection he was stuck with. *Freaking great.*

He cleared his throat.

"I know a lot has happened to you today, but we need to talk right now."

Kerensa nodded her head, wondering when Stone had become so thoughtful. Her memory floated back to the numerous times in her past experience with him. The 'other' Stone would have forced her to discuss this 'plan of action' immediately. He would never have carried her off to bed and allowed her to rest first. She made a mental note to comment about that later.

*Or maybe his ulterior plan hadn't been revealed yet?*

Realizing that he was watching her, she set Janelle down and followed him to the sofa. Janelle immediately climbed onto Stone's lap.

"Janelle, come sit by Nana."

It was the first time Nana had said a word.

Janelle refused, planting her little bottom firmly on Stone's upper leg.

"It's alright, I don't mind" he replied, placing his hand on Janelle's shoulder to steady her.

This time Kerensa thought about Vance. She suddenly had trouble recalling if Janelle ever chose his lap instead of hers or Nana's to sit upon. Appalled with herself for having such fragmented thoughts, she attempted to focus on what Stone was already saying.

"…I don't have to tell you that what happened today is proof your life is in danger. This isn't like the other time, Kerensa." Stone paused, choosing his words carefully. "This time it's, well, it's different."

*No kidding, thanks a lot, captain obvious.*

Kerensa felt the blood shoot straight to her head. It wasn't the words Stone was using that disturbed her, it was the obvious way he was tip toeing around the truth that really annoyed her. She wasn't about to let him get away with that. She turned her body slightly to the right, facing him squarely.

"Don't *candy coat* this situation to patronize me, Dominick. You hid the truth from me the first time and I won't allow you to do it again. I may not be some hot shot government official," Kerensa sarcastically emphasized that phrase before continuing, "but I do know when someone is trying to kill me."

Stone's eyes narrowed and a slight twitch on the side of his jaw was the only tell-tale sign that he was annoyed with her. Kerensa didn't care. She waited for him to speak, her dark eyes resembling a black abyss.

Stone sat upright, changing Janelle to the knee furthest from Kerensa.

*You don't want to hear the cold, hard truth, sweetheart. You could never handle it. But I'll give you my cleaned up version.*

Focusing on his large, strong hands, her thoughts drifted again. This time they were downright dangerous.

*This is crazy, why am I panicked one minute, and horny the next?*

When he spoke, she shifted her gaze to his face. It was ice cold, and so were his eyes.

"If you want me to give it to you straight, then I will." He suddenly glanced over at Nana as if to apologize for his callousness.

"Whoever shot at you today was a professional. It wasn't Jonathan, or even any of his derelict friends. It was someone hired to kill you with one shot, and one bullet. You were lucky; actually you should be dead right now. Fortunately, the assassin missed, but that doesn't mean any of this is over. It's only the beginning and he isn't going to stop, Kerensa, the job isn't done until the mark is retired."

Kerensa's breath caught in her throat. *Oh, sweet Jesus, I'm the mark! Stay calm, stay focused. You told him to tell it to you straight, so you can handle this. But what about Janelle! How much danger is she in?*

She felt lightheaded again, her heart stuck in her throat before pounding out of control in her chest.

*Air, I need air.*

"Kerensa, are you alright?" Nana asked, breaking her trance.

She nodded her head, trying hard to breathe in through her nose and out her mouth in long, deep breaths.

She stared directly into Stone's eyes as she finally whispered, "he's going to kill me, isn't he?"

Stone did not hesitate, his features twisted into a mask of pure vengeance.

"Oh no sweetheart, he's a dead man already."

*And Thorne is next, that fucking dirt bag.*

It was at that exact moment Nana truly realized how treacherous Stone was and she studied him as though she met him for the very first time. She saw a very powerful man, an enigma, mysterious; strong and hard-edged, capable of murder without remorse if justice warranted it. One large hand held little Janelle protectively against his chest, gentle and tender, no one would ever guess the ferocity of the man beneath. It was obvious to Nana that Dominick Stone was distinctive, even exclusive in who he was. She also realized that she should be afraid of him, but she wasn't. She felt safe and sheltered, like cotton wool.

Poor Vance, he must feel so incomparable against him.

She also noticed that Kerensa wasn't wearing her engagement ring anymore. But Nana didn't care about that. Her concern was Kerensa and Janelle, and she knew that Stone would never let anyone hurt them.

*I thank you dear God for sending this guardian to protect us.*

There was a sudden clap of thunder; it was as though God heard Nana's prayer.

Janelle squealed in fear, and Kerensa jumped about ten feet in the air. Janelle wrapped her arms so tightly around Stone's neck that he needed to pry her hands away.

It was rather comical despite the surprise change in the weather.

"Whoa, princess, don't be scared. It's going to be alright." he reassured, a small grin turning the corner of his mouth.

"I'm a-scared of the thunder," she responded, her brown eyes as big as saucers.

"Didn't mommy ever tell you it's the angels playing games in heaven?" Janelle thought for a moment.

"Tell mommy what you said, cause' she's a-scared of the thunder too."

This time Stone couldn't control his laughter. He gazed at Kerensa, easily noting that her eyes were about the same size as Janelle's. He couldn't help but notice how beautiful yet vulnerable she looked too. It made his chest ache at the opportunity to hold her and make love to her again.

Then suddenly, as if the thunder and lightening had something to do with his cognitive thoughts, he realized something so complete, so obvious that it sucked the life right out of him.

*What the hell am I doing? Here I am standing in this house like it's my own, holding this little girl like she's my child and admiring the only woman I ever loved as though I'm part of this family. I can never have this kind of life and I know better. I was taught to eliminate my emotions the same way I was taught to eliminate the enemy. Kerensa is a case to protect. This feeling will end right now.*

Stone abruptly handed Janelle to Kerensa despite her loud protests. Stone stepped away from both of them and Kerensa noticed the instant change that came over him. His features transformed right before her eyes and he was suddenly all business.

A moment later the wind began to howl, and the palm trees bowed to the force of the storm. Nana quickly closed the patio door and the door leading into the breezeway.

"Does anyone know what the weather channel is reporting?" Stone asked his gaze still on Janelle's death grip around her mama's neck now.

"They have been predicting a small tropical storm; I imagine that it's here." Nana answered calmly, wiping her rain soaked hands on her shirt.

"How long does this sort of thing last?" Stone asked again.

Nana smiled.

"It depends, but I don't think it will be very long tonight."

"Is there anything I need to do to help you?" Stone asked again, winking at Janelle as he spoke.

"This house held up during Hurricane Andrew in the early nineteen ninety's so I'm sure we'll be fine tonight."

Stone nodded, thinking to himself how he would rather put up with a good old fashioned Buffalo blizzard instead of being airborne and landing on the wicked witch of the west. Noticing how both Kerensa and Nana were watching him, he spoke again.

"I phoned Nate earlier today and I told him the newest development. He's taking the first flight into Miami and he's due to arrive around midnight."

*Nate Drake!*

Anxiety mixed with nostalgia rippled through her veins again. Nate was her friend. Kind, caring and thoughtful he was everything Stone was not back then. He was her salvation after she was rescued from the warehouse. He stayed by her side despite the fact that he confessed his love for her and she couldn't reciprocate. Hopelessly in love with Stone, Nate still remained her confidant even after Stone disappeared into oblivion. She remembered how Nate agreed that Buffalo just wasn't the right place for her to live. He understood when she asked him to take her to the airport and when he kissed her goodbye he told her to move on and forget about Stone. Hurt and exhausted she vowed to keep in touch. For a while she did. Days became months and then years; it had to be at least five years since they had any contact with one another.

Nate and Stone were partners; comrades. She always believed that Nate knew the real story behind Stone, the man. She never put him on the spot though; she knew he wasn't at liberty to tell.

Now, he was. coming to her home town.
*Back into her life*
She took a deep breath.
"Why did you call him?"
He looked sharply at her, as though she had just taken a stupid pill.
"Because there are people out there that must be stopped before they kill you and you also need someone to stay here and protect you."
If Stone wasn't thinking about candy coating his words anymore, he was doing a damn good job. She shivered involuntarily.
"Will you be going to the airport to get him?"
Stone shook his head. "No, he'll be here."
"Doe's he know where here is?"
Stone slowly looked at Kerensa. He observed smooth skin, dark mysterious eyes, a full kissable mouth, oh yes, the kind of mouth he could only imagine what he could to do with…He blinked, forcing that vision out of his head. When he opened his eyes again, he saw a young woman who needed protection.
"He's a big boy, Kerensa he'll figure it out."
Kerensa stared incredulously at Stone. *Something has definitely changed. Why was he acting like such a bastard?*
She raised her eyebrows as if to ask him that question. Except there were no words tumbling from her lips. Instead, she simply sighed and turned away. Something was definitely eating away at him, but she was too mentally exhausted to explore the notion.
"Whatever you say," she finally murmured, shifting Janelle to her other hip.
Stone switched his gaze to Nana completely ignoring Kerensa.
"I realize that it would be too much to ask…" he began, "but…"
Nana quickly interrupted Stone, shaking her head from side to side.
"It's no trouble for Nate to stay here, Dominick. As a matter of fact, I insist upon it. I'll figure out how to make enough room, and besides I think it would make more sense to keep everyone together."
Kerensa smiled at Nana. She knew what Nana was really thinking, she was onto her sneaky little ways. Nana would allow an army to stay in her house right now, as long as the army carried big sticks and fast machine guns.
Stone nodded his head in agreement, and Kerensa could see the slightest of a smirk that turned up the corners of his mouth. She knew that Stone was thinking the same thing. She watched him as he strolled over to the window.
Gazing into the twilight, he was relieved to see that the palm trees were

standing upright again, and the wind was already beginning to die down. The rain was diminishing into a little more than just a dull roar and hopefully Nate's flight would arrive on time.

Lord knows how much he needed Nate right about now. Yet it wasn't because he required assistance in protecting Kerensa, it was mostly because Nate knew how to make the most out of Stone's brusque and rudimentary mannerisms. He needed Nate's talent when it came to dealing with Kerensa too. It was time for Stone to take a few steps backwards, he must remind himself that he didn't bring Kerensa into his life again because he loved her. She was someone who needed his help.

It was too bad that her relationship with Vance had deteriorated, but he wasn't going to loose sleep thinking it was his fault. He had a lot more important things on his mind besides Kerensa's emotional well being and her love life.

Besides, she always related better to Nate anyway.

He felt a slight movement beside him, and glancing downward, he saw Janelle gazing back at him.

"Pick me up, Mr. ick," she requested, in her cutest little girl voice.

He remained motionless, just observing her small arms outstretched to him. He sighed, shuddering at the realization that Janelle was already so deep inside his heart.

"Come here, princess," he murmured, pulling her up and swinging her into his arms.

She cried out in delight, burying her face into his chest. He sighed deeply again, glancing around the room as if he suddenly noticed that he wasn't alone in his thoughts. Kerensa was only a few feet away from him, and she was studying him intently. Nana had left the room, and he had no idea when she may have done that. *Damn, I need to focus!*

He abruptly turned toward Kerensa and handed Janelle back to her for the second time that night.

"You should get some rest, although the night is still young, you've had a very trying day."

Kerensa didn't answer him; she simply stared into his face like he was an alien coming and going inside Stone's body. Stone knew that his sudden change of behavior was very puzzling to her.

"What's bothering you, Dominick?" She asked, her voice carrying an ever so slight tremor of uncertainty.

Stone hesitated, before responding, "I'm just concentrating on the gravity of this situation," he lied. "I don't want to frighten you, Kerensa, but you must listen to everything I instruct you to do. When Nate arrives we will construct a plan and than all of us will discuss the details."

She numbly nodded her head, and he could tell that she was only half listening. He imagined the other half of her mind was still screaming in terror.

"I will not let any harm come to you, Janelle or Nana. I promise you that."

Kerensa slowly nodded her head again, and then took a deep breath.

*I must ask him this next question, although I know what he's going to tell me.*

"Who are you, really, Dominick?"

Stone simply stared. It wasn't the first time she had bluntly asked him that. He suddenly recalled with vivid clarity the night they were together at a restaurant in Buffalo. They were in the parking lot and from out of nowhere they were jumped by two men. They would have abducted her if it wasn't for his fast thinking and even faster leg work. Afterwards, she stared up at him with her terrified eyes and she asked him who he really was.

"It's rather complicated, you know that," he finally replied. "Tonight is not the night to discuss it."

"It's never the right night, the right time or the right place. You have avoided that question from the beginning, Dominick. There will always be an excuse, so please stop treating me like I'm a brainless idiot and talk to me."

Stone's eyes flashed anger. Kerensa could witness this even in the dimming light of the evening and the bleakness of the storm outside.

She didn't care. She wanted the truth.

She continued to stare directly into his eyes for several moments until she bent down and stood Janelle upright on her feet again.

"Janelle, go find Nana, and she will fix you a snack before bedtime."

Janelle ran off without her usual argument about bedtime.

It was as if she was plotting against him too.

Kerensa's gaze found his again. *You will not intimidate me, you will not intimidate me…* She quietly waited.

Stone cursed several times beneath his breath before he finally spoke again.

"I work for the government, Kerensa. I'm sure you've figured that out already. Why do you have to know more than that?"

His tone was crude, and forceful. There was a tight glare that narrowed his eyes to a dangerous slit, warning her to cease the questioning immediately.

She tried to cover the expression of surprise mixed with hurt that flickered across her features, but she wasn't going to allow him to bully her into silence. Taking a deep breath, she spoke again.

"You keep asking me to trust you, but you won't be honest with me. It works both ways and frankly I'm tired of cooperating with you despite your lies. So what's it gonna be, 'detective'? No, wait—I mean 'sergeant', or is it 'private investigator?'—Hmm…, maybe it's some secret agent government official, or are you Spiderman, in disguise?'"

Kerensa knew that her sarcasm would push him over the edge. She was right. This time, he didn't hide his rage. But instead of speaking, he reached out and pulled her roughly against his muscled body. Startled, she tried to take a step backwards, but Stone would not let her go, his hand like steel on the small of her back. He ground her harder into his body, forcing her to be still against him. With his leg wedged intimately between hers and his chest pressed tightly against her breasts, he whispered huskily into her ear. His words were crude and harsh.

"Stop being so fucking naive, Kerensa. Deep down inside you know exactly what I am, and that should be enough. Don't ever ask me again, do you understand?"

She wanted to say something, but she didn't trust her voice. She did all she could not to let him see her cry. He ultimately did intimidate her, just like he did all those years ago. She was suddenly scared to death of him. When she didn't respond, he withdrew slightly. He could feel her tender body trembling in his arms, forcing him to realize that he had shocked her enough. But it still wasn't enough; he needed to scare her beyond ever questioning him again. He needed to make her angry enough to stop caring about him. He needed to make her hate him…again. He would have to walk away from her when this was over and he wanted to make sure she would never be vulnerable or at risk. He remained unrelenting, despising himself for his cruelty, and expecting an answer from her.

"Do you understand?" He repeated gruffly.

She barely nodded her head up and down.

Reaching downward, he tilted her chin so she would look at him. As uncertain as she was, she faced him with strength. He saw the tears threatening to spill from behind her eyes, and he wiped a small tear from the corner of her eye with his thumb. It was as if he could read her mind when he spoke again. This time his tone was thick with an emotion she couldn't identify.

"I will protect you and your family, Kerensa, I promise. I will do that with my life, but you must accept me without issue again."

He abruptly released her, turned on his heels and walked out of the room.

# 13

The house was quiet, almost too quiet. The entire family had gone to bed. Although it was past midnight, Stone was still a little surprised that Kerensa decided to retire for the night. *Of course she ignored him the remainder of the night anyway.* Breathing a sigh of relief that he wouldn't have to debrief Nate with an entourage to distract him, he tried to relax a bit before Nate was scheduled to arrive.

His thoughts drifted to Kerensa, again. It was as if these cognitive thoughts were separated from his brain and they had a mind of their own. He tried to block the memory of Kerensa's face when he coldheartedly cautioned her not to question his identity again. He deliberately intimidated her, and he hated himself for it, but her lack of knowledge regarding his choice of professions kept her a lot safer. His mind wandered over the details of his last mission. Caught up in a government assignment of trickery and deception, he wasn't sure if he would make it out alive. It was a bitter reminder of the life style he had chosen to live. No, not live in; merely to co—exist in. A life full of lies, danger and the horror of looking into the mirror everyday and wondering if the choices he made could have been different, better. Questioning himself if he could have saved a life instead of snuffed it out, appalled that sometimes he was too numb to care. His world was an existence of not really being alive, but not being dead either. It was a dark and sinister world, and he wanted to fill it with the soft, gentle sound of a little girls laughter; the caress of a woman's silken hands on his body, the heat of her when he was deep inside, and he wanted that woman to be Kerensa. He suddenly ached for that kind of life, felt his soul parched and dry, yearning for the chance to fill his heart with hydration like a man who was dying of thirst.

But maybe she didn't love him anymore. *Or if she did, would she still love him if she knew what kind of a monster he really was?*

The glare of headlights into the front window brought Stone to his senses, and to his feet. He waited until he heard the car door slam shut and knew it was his life long friend, before he opened the door.

His abrupt action startled Nate.

"I'm honored that you're so eager to see me again," Nate chortled.

"Shuu…"Stone hushed, "I don't want Janelle to wake up."

Nate peered at Stone through narrowed eyes. *Who the hell is Janelle?*

Once inside, Nate set his luggage down and folded his tall, lean frame into the sofa beside him. He studied Stone again as he double bolted the door, and left the room for a few moments. He returned carrying two cups of coffee and handed one to Nate. *Oh boy, that's not a very good sign; we're in for a long night.*

Nate reached out and took the coffee, and waited until Stone settled on the sofa beside him before he spoke again.

"I get the feeling there's a lot of conversation ahead of me."

"Yea," Stone murmured, "you might say that."

Nate nodded his head. *Freaking great.*

"Well, why don't you start by telling me who Janelle is?"

"She's Kerensa's daughter."

Nate paused in surprise. He sat forward, resting his elbows on his long legs.

"Wow, that one slipped by me. How old is she?"

"Three."

"That certainly changes the climate of the situation. Are you afraid that Janelle may be Thorne's newest target?"

"I don't think he knows about her. I think he would have targeted her by now."

"I see. So how many attempts have been made on Kerensa's life?"

"Two, the first one was just a guy who jumped her in the parking lot. It could have been unrelated, but I don't think so. The cops interrogated him, but he wouldn't talk. The second attempt was the reason I called you." Stone paused a moment before continuing, "someone shot at her yesterday."

Nate whistled softly beneath his breath.

"Oh, man. That's bad. Are you sure he wasn't aiming at you?"

Stone suddenly grinned at his friend's dry sense of humor.

"I may have a lot of enemies, but that red dot was on the back of her head, not mine."

Nate's mouth twisted into a sarcastic smirk, showing the dimples in both his cheeks.

"I just wanted to make sure, partner. I know some people think of you as the devil incarnate. So where were you when it happened?"

"It was right outside her dance studio, and in broad daylight."

Nate suddenly felt a pang of apprehension. He didn't like how dangerous this situation had become.

"The guy's a professional, isn't he?"

"Oh yea, this time Thorne hired someone to do his dirty work for him."

"Is Thorne still living in Ohio?"

"I've been checking up on him as much as twice a day and I'm told he hasn't left his front porch except to see his probation officer."

Nate rubbed his eyes in exhaustion.

"Like I'm going to believe that one, so where do you think he got the money to hire a merc?"

Stone shook his head. "I don't know, but that's one question I plan on getting an answer to. Now that you're here, I can start doing some real investigating."

Nate's head shot sideways, his face contorted into a deep frown.

"You mean, I'll do the investigating and you will continue to protect Kerensa."

"No," Stone retorted, lifting his cup to his lips and draining the rest of the coffee. "I want you to stay with Kerensa."

Nate studied his friend.

"Why do I get the feeling there's something about the two of you that you don't want to tell me."

Stone shot Nate his best 'don't mess with me' look, and he knew that look all too well.

*But he always ignored it.*

"Fess up, Stone. What's going on?"

Stone didn't answer; instead he took both cups and disappeared into the kitchen. He returned shortly after with two fresh cups of coffee, handing one to Nate. Nate was thinking about how the last cup already had his heart valves doing calisthenics in his chest. He accepted it anyway, and set it on the table beside him.

"How the hell can you drink so much of this stuff?" he thought aloud.

Stone shrugged his shoulders, taking a deep gulp.

"Well, anyway, don't think I'm gonna let you off the hook that easy. You owe me some answers, Stone. I'm not too crazy about being Kerensa's bodyguard right now; I think you are much more qualified to do so."

"You'll be fine. I'm not allowing her to leave this house until we catch this guy anyway."

Nate thought about Kerensa's nature. Somehow he didn't think her being secluded or isolated was going to be a suitable solution for any length of time.

"And how does she feel about this?"

Stone's head shot upward, his eyes meeting Nate's.

"She doesn't know about it yet. She doesn't have a choice in the matter either."

Nate laughed a little too loudly before realizing it. He lowered his voice and replied, "Some things never change, do they?"

Stone bristled. He wanted to tell Nate how much he already compromised since he met up with Kerensa again, but it wasn't relevant. Besides, it was going to end. Tonight.

"I can't properly protect her unless she's isolated. That's just the way it has to be. I'll find this guy; just give me twenty four hours."

"Why so long?" Nate chuckled. "Just try to refrain from killing him until after we make him talk." He thought a few moments before speaking again.

"Anything else I need to know about?"

Stone ground his teeth, hating to bring up the next subject.

"Up until today, she was engaged to be married to a guy named Vance Robertson. *Actually an idiot named Vance.* He broke their engagement because he has several issues regarding this situation."

Nate whistled softly beneath his breath again, but didn't say a word. After many moments of silence, Nate replied. "These issues that you're talking about, do they all have to do with you, or just the majority of them?"

Stone glared at Nate, hating to feed into his all knowing, sarcastic comments.

"He had his own-issues."

"Yea, right, I'll bet he did. You threatened him, didn't you?"

"I did what I had to do. Listen, none of that is relevant, I just thought you should know that she was engaged to this guy-OK?" Stone hesitated a brief moment. "He's a cop, too."

Nate just shook his head from side to side. *I don't want to know anymore, I can pretty much figure out the rest myself.*

"Alright, so is there anything else?"

"No," Stone answered, disappearing into the kitchen and returning with another cup of coffee.

"Damn, Stone, that stuff will rot your gut out. Besides, how the hell can you sleep when you have enough caffeine in your system to raise a cemetery?"

Stone grunted in reply, taking another long gulp of the black liquid.

"You have the back bedroom, I'll help you with your bags and I'll show you the way."

Nate yawned and looked at his watch. It was already two o'clock in the morning. He wiped his forehead with the back of his hand. Even though there was air conditioning, the air felt thick and muggy. Stone noticed Nate's gesture.

"It's damn hot around here. I can't wait for some good old fashioned cold weather."

Nate chuckled. "Yea, man, you never did like the heat."

Stone grumbled a reply and became silent. After several moments of silence, Nate let out a small, appreciative breath before speaking softly again.

"So is she still beautiful?"

Stone's eyes focused sharply on Nate's smooth features. *Geezus.*

"More," he curtly answered, *if that's even possible.*

Nate nodded his head, and as if reading his partners mind he replied, "So here we are again, hah, Stone?"

Stone didn't answer. He didn't look at him either.

Nate sighed. "We both love the same woman; you can't ignore that truth like it doesn't exist."

Stone's gaze finally turned toward Nate. His face was like a granite slab, but his eyes held oceans of pain in them.

"It was a long time ago and it doesn't mean a thing anymore. If you still have feelings for her, then tell her. The fiancé dumped her, so she's ready for someone to show her that she's still… desirable. Do you really love her, or do you just want to know what it's like to fuck her?"

*I know I can be a real son of a bitch.*

Nate glared in fury at Stone for several moments. Stone was certain that he had pushed enough buttons to get Nate really pissed off at him.

And he did.

Nate wanted to put his hands around Stone's neck and squeeze, hard enough to make his head pop off. *You fucking dirt bag.* It took a lot to piss off Nate.

He processed for a few moments knowing full well what he could say that would stop Stone dead in his tracks. Words were still better than hauling off and decking him right about now.

"I don't really know what I feel, but if I wanted to know what it was like to just fuck her, I'd ask you about that, right?"

The room lingered in dead silence. *Bingo.*

Stone's gaze remained unwavering as he stared into Nate's angry brown eyes. He deserved that statement and he knew that, but it infuriated the hell out of him to think that Nate could even be contemplating his feelings regarding her.

*Kerensa deserved the best, and if he wasn't capable of giving it to her, he expected that Nate was a better man than him. He didn't want to hear otherwise.*

"I'm sorry I brought the subject up," Nate replied quietly. "It's really late, time to call it a night."

When their gazes met, there was a silent truce, a hushed understanding that didn't need any further exploration.

Yawning, he rose from the sofa and grabbed two bags. Stone took the remainder and he quietly escorted Nate to his bedroom. He walked past Janelle's room and glanced in quietly. She was sound asleep.

He pulled the door halfway closed but not until Nate peered into the room to see her.

"Cute kid," he replied.

Stone didn't respond, he simply pointed to the next room and told Nate that it was Kerensa's. He brought him to the other side of the house to show him where Nana's room was.

"Wow, this is a big house. How many bedrooms are there?"

"There are four; you'll be staying in the room I was in. I decided to sleep on the couch."

"I feel honored again."

"Yea, well you better get some sleep; it's going to be busy when Janelle wakes up."

Nate chuckled softly to himself. *Stone babysitting, hmm... This is going to be very interesting.*

"Oh I'll make sure I get up early to watch the show," Nate chuckled as he spoke.

As usual, Stone didn't appreciate Nate's sarcastic sense of humor.

*I liked you better a moment ago when you were pissed off at me.*

"Goodnight," he growled.

\*\*\*

*She was running as fast as she could, but she wasn't going anywhere.*

*Her feet felt heavy and wet as she sloshed through the murky swamp. Her face stung as the small, thin branches slapped against her sensitive skin and she closed her eyes so they wouldn't get poked. There was a putrid stench of rotten water in her nostrils, making her want to gag. Her breathing was labored as she pushed her body onward, but she just couldn't go fast enough.*

*"No!" she screamed, "someone please help me."*

*But there wasn't anyone there to help her, only the cold, dark night. She knew she was in danger but she didn't know why her heart was heavy with dread. Suddenly she heard him behind her, his feet echoing off the wet, boggy ground. She was being chased, was that why she was so terrified?*

*"Someone help me!" she desperately cried out again.*

*Yet it was hopeless, and she felt his hands grip her shoulders, pulling her backwards. She was falling into the swamp, and when she stared into the face of her attacker, it was her father's death mask staring back at her.*

*"Danger, my child," he whispered. "Run for your life."*

Kerensa awoke with a start. She was covered with perspiration and her heart was pounding like a bongo drum in fast forward. She swiped the tears away with the back of her trembling hand as they trickled down her face. Then, she swung her legs over the side of the bed, and tried to stand up. Her legs were still weak, and so she sat back down again.

*It was that dream again. I haven't dreamt of my father in years. Not since he first died and Thorne was trying to kill me. Oh good grief, what does this mean?*

*Is my father trying to send me a message from the grave again?*

Kerensa rubbed her forehead with her fingertips. She took a deep breath, and attempted to stand to her feet for the second time. Although her legs were still like wet clay, she was able to slowly stand up and take a few more steps. She glanced at her alarm clock; it was 3:00 in the morning. She suddenly wondered if Nate had arrived in Florida, and if he was in her house. She walked quietly across the room, and pushed open the door. Venturing down the hallway, she paused briefly at Janelle's room and peaked inside. Breathing a sigh of relief, she continued on.

When she reached the sun room, she tiptoed over to the window and gazed outside. It stopped raining, there was a little puddle on the patio chairs and the level of the pool was nearly overflowing, this was the only proof that there was any kind of rain storm earlier in the evening. Sighing softly, Kerensa unlocked the patio door and slipped outside into the warm, muggy night. The humidity was unusually high for this time of year, but it felt like a comfortable quilt wrapping its warm arms around her. She tilted her face upward, staring into the vast darkness of the star glittered sky.

Kerensa felt his warm breath on her neck before she realized that someone was behind her. She released a startled cry as she whirled around to face him.

He was shrouded in darkness; only inches from her. There was a slight sliver beam from the underground pool lights to indicate that there was a man there. Yet she could sense him, feel him coursing through her veins, she could see his eyes piercing the obscurity of the night like a wild predator a wolf perhaps?

A night wolf.

In a split second his arms went around her, and his body pressed hard against hers as he shielded her in protection.

"What the hell are you doing, testing the snipers night vision?" he harshly murmured into her ear. "Get back into the house, right now."

*He might as well tell me I'm a blazing idiot, for Christ sake. What was I thinking?*

She allowed Dominick to protect her body as he pushed her back into the security of the enclosed patio. Once inside, he released his arms from around her rather abruptly, as if holding her too long was suddenly going to give him cooties.

"How did you know I was outside?" she asked, deliberately trying to act as if she hadn't noticed her stupidity or his cootie moment.

He didn't answer her, at least not immediately. He stood there glaring into her face, as though she just murdered the neighbors and buried them beneath her pool.

He was naked from the waist up, his large shoulders honed and fit, muscles rippling with every small movement he made.

"I would have thought you knew better than to stick a big bull's eye on your backside," he retorted, obviously not willing to let her moment of poor judgment pass without a marathon discussion.

She quickly bristled, narrowing her eyes to glare steadily back at him.

*You're acting like an asshole.*

"I didn't think I could be shot at in the dark, OK?"

Stone suddenly snorted out loud. It was a sarcastic and crude sound, deliberately meant to insult her, instantly reminding her of the past.

"Did you ever stop to consider there's equipment so sensitive that a fly could be shot off the tip of your nose in the middle of the goddamn night?"

*Oh yea, he's definitely hung up about something. Less than twelve hours ago he carried me to bed and held me in his arms while I slept. Now he's treating me like I'm an absolute idiot.* Suddenly she realized the truth. He had only done that because he felt sorry for her. It was pity, and nothing more. *How could I still be such a stupid fool?* She felt her entire breath whoosh out of her lungs. She quickly turned her back on him, hoping he didn't notice her legs threatening to buckle beneath her.

Her voice was barely above a whisper and with a forced steadiness she spoke again.

"I get the point, alright?"

Silence.

Kerensa could feel a recurrent bitterness seeping into her heart. She tried not to lash out at him, but his crude attitude put her in a really foul mood.

"I certainly don't want to be your first casualty on the job," she found herself crisply snapping again.

Stone winced at her incorrect critique of the situation.

"Actually you wouldn't be the first, but that isn't the point."

She furiously whirled around to face him.

"So much for the promises you made about protecting us, huh?"

Stone's eyes dangerously glowed.

"I never break my promises," he slowly responded, a deadly curl to his quiet tone. "It's not about that, Kerensa. I need you to stay focused, and I expect you to make common sense decisions."

Kerensa's thoughts drifted once again to the last time she was running for her life. They were in the hotel in Montreal and Stone had specifically instructed her not to open the door for anyone after he left the room. She didn't follow his orders and was dragged down the corridor by a man who was trying to kidnap her. Stone arrived just in time to rescue her. Once inside the room, he lashed out, chastising her for disobeying his orders. He was doing the same thing now, only she was seeing his more charming side.

*At least, for now.*

She stood there staring at him, half her mind still in yesterday. Embarrassed and angry, she cleared her throat.

"So are you trying to say that I'm stuck inside this house indefinitely?"

Stone leveled his gaze on her and nodded his head, *yes.*

"What am I on, house arrest? If that's what you're thinking then it's totally unacceptable to me."

Stone barely controlled the wrath that boiled to the surface.

*Damn straight you're on house arrest, Ki-riest someone is out there trying to kill you!*

"This wasn't a request, and I wasn't asking," he replied, his eyes sending her a warning that she was past his negotiation point.

"Now go back to bed and stay away from the goddamn window."

Kerensa watched him in shock as he stalked out of the room.

# 14

It was shortly before five o'clock in the morning when Stone slipped away. He never did fall asleep. But he was used to being sleep deprived for several days, so this didn't even affect him. Besides, he knew that the earlier he got away, the better the plan to find Kerensa's hired killer, the quicker he could put Thorne away for good, and the faster he could get back to his own life again.

*Well, his pathetic existence of a life.*

Although getting back was essential, he also knew that there was still another reason nagging at his barely conscience level.

He didn't want to watch Kerensa and Nate when they saw each other again. It bothered him a little-well OK, maybe it bothered him a lot, and they would probably have the reunion of the decade, hugs, kisses, and the whole nine yards. A far cry from the hello he received a month ago, or rather the goodbye she gave him a month ago, but it didn't matter anyway. He needed to be one hundred and ten percent focused, which had never been an issue unless Kerensa was around.

He was pissed off at himself, too. He practically gave Nate his best wishes along with his blessings if he wanted to try getting Kerensa to fall for him again. Hell, he even told Nate to take her to bed and have sex with her too.

Compliments of his inability to get in touch with anything that remotely made him have feelings or emotions. *Geezus*, he really did have some major issues and he was pretty fucked up. Oh well, he reminded himself to be the hard ass he always was and to focus on the situation at hand. Whoever this sniper was, he had to be stopped, eliminated, and then Thorne would be next.

Stone turned the corner and slowed his vehicle down. He pulled alongside the curb and parked the truck. As he exited the vehicle, he quickly assessed his surroundings. The street was fairly deserted, giving him the opportunity to accurately study the details of yesterday. He walked onto the sidewalk and turned his body in the exact position that he was when he spotted the red laser light on the back of Kerensa's head. Measuring with his hand the precise height she was to him, he measured the distance with his eyes from the angle where she was standing yesterday. Then he looked upward on either side of the street. His gaze rested on a building approximately ten stories high.

*Bingo.*

Stone headed across the street in the direction of what he now knew was the snipers location. He waltzed into the lobby as though he owned the place. There was a security booth to his right, but there wasn't a soul sitting there.

*Perfect.*

Stone walked right into the elevator, doors already open as though they had a premonition he was on his way.

*Perfect again.*

Stone took the elevator to the tenth floor and stepped out. There was new carpeting on the floor, and the hallway was newly decorated too. It looked like the building had been remodeled for elite business offices.

Stone looked for the stairs. He located them at the very end of the hall across from a hideous purple vase with large tropical flowers in it.

*These colors were almost as bad as the security was.*

He read the *do not enter* sign on the door in bold print, q*ualified Personnel only.*

*Well, he has been considered as qualified personnel, right?*

He checked for any alarm boxes. There weren't any. He checked for any sensors. There weren't any. He checked for any cameras and surprise, there weren't any; so much for good solid security after the 9/ll incident.

He pulled the door open and headed up the stairs. Once he reached the roof, he checked everything out. It was a small roof, with one area completely open. On the opposite side, the side facing Kerensa's studio, there were several large brick stacks, perfect for hiding behind. Stone headed that way and looked down into the street below. Oh yea, it was the ideal location for that fucker to point a gun at Kerensa's head.

Stone could feel the surge of angry adrenalin choking him again. He stooped to his knees and examined the area by his feet. There was nothing unusual, no evidence of anyone or any weapons at the site. He was certain this was the location.

Stone looked at the stacks again. His eyes followed a thin, metal pole all the way upward. What do ya know, there was a tiny camera attached to the top of that pole pointing back down at him.

Stone nearly laughed aloud. Actually he did laugh aloud. With any luck at all, that sniper just had his picture taken. Except now, he was on candid camera too.

"Put your hands in the air, and slowly turn around."

Her voice was strong, but he detected the ever so slight tremor of fear.

Stone did what he was told, and came face to face with a young woman dressed in security attire. She wore her very blonde hair up in a pony tail away from her face. She had a starched white shirt on, perfectly pressed black pants and black polished shoes. *Security doll Barbie.*

Stone grinned.

"What are you doing up here, sir?" she asked, the gun still pointing at him.

"Seeing how long it would take for you to find me," Stone retorted.

"Excuse me?"

"Yea, I'm with the FBI and we're running a security check with all the buildings on this block. So far, you're flunking big time."

She barely flinched.

"I don't believe you, so you better start talking real fast before I call for backup."

Stone chuckled. *Not bad.*

"My guess is you don't have backup. But if you'll let me take my arms down, I can show you some ID."

She took a couple steps backwards. "Move real slow, and with one hand only."

Stone reached downward with his right hand into his back pocket. He pulled his wallet out and held out his badge that was attached to it. She reached her arm out and took it from him, still keeping the gun pointed at his head.

Glancing downward, she checked the badge out.

"Not enough," she crisply replied, "I need a picture ID with your name on it."

Stone sighed; this was starting to get old. "Alright, then flip open the wallet, you'll find what you want."

She flipped through the wallet, but every other second her eyes were back on his face. She had trouble juggling the wallet in one hand, and holding the gun with the other, so she dropped the wallet.

*It was better than dropping the gun.*

Stone sighed with edginess, worried that her slight problem with clumsiness may extend to a premature click of the trigger.

"Look, Jade," he continued, reading her name off her ID badge. "I'm really harmless. Put the gun away and…"

"Don't get any ideas," she warned, noticing how Stone was stepping toward her.

It was only a matter of time before Stone was going to get impatient. *Son—of—a—Bitch!*

"Put the damn weapon down. If I wanted to do something I would have done it already and you would be lying unconscious on the ground by now. Now, get that gun out of my face."

She bristled, but somehow his bluntness struck a truce. She lowered her weapon, and than put it away, but she still held his ID in her hands.

"My name is Agent Dominick Stone, and I really am a government official. *'Agent' was close enough to the truth.*

But I did lie to you about why I'm up here sneaking around on the roof." She peered at him through glasses that were much too big for her face. "Why are you here then?"

"Did you hear about the shooting yesterday?"

Her eyebrows shot up. "Sure did, it was all over the news."

"Yea, I know." Stone was suddenly glad Kerensa hadn't watched the news. After he had searched the area and returned to her he managed to whisk her away from Donovan and threatened the reporters with their lives if they as much as mentioned Kerensa's name on TV.

He decided to get a little closer to the truth with this young woman who looked as though she would pee her pants if he moved any closer to her. *Take it slow and she'll help you.*

"I was the one the shooter was aiming at. I believe he was in this building and on this roof at the time of the shooting."

Her eyes got big as saucers.

"Why do you say that?"

"I say that because of the angle of the gunshot, the angle of the laser, and the fact that your security sucks. No offense."

She glared at him.

"Here's your ID," she replied, handing it back to him. "Now kindly leave my building."

"You know it's true," Stone continued, "I strolled right in, took the elevator to ten and then the stairs onto the roof. Where were you?"

"Doing my rounds on another floor," she retorted, stepping as far away from him as possible. "My partner had an emergency so he had to leave; they're sending me a replacement soon."

*Yea, right.*

Stone nodded his head, pointing at the camera.

"I think you may have gotten a '*say cheese*' shot of this guy. Can we check on that?"

She bristled again, but he could tell that she was already feeling a little more comfortable with him.

"I can check it out, but not with you."

"Oh come on," Stone grinned, shooting her his sexiest smile. "Give me a break. What time do you punch out?"

She glanced at her watch.

"Another hour and a half, why?

*Jesus Christ, does this girl need everything spelled out for her?*

"Because I was hoping we could go back to the security post and check out yesterday's tape."

"That camera doesn't work right."

Stone sighed, waiting for a further explanation. He should have known she wouldn't give it.

"What's wrong with it?"

"It doesn't always scan, sometimes it cuts the film off or it's blurry. It's a really old camera."

*No shit.*

"Well that's alright, you should see what I can do with a non functioning piece of equipment."

She peered at him above those ridiculous glasses again, no doubt trying to figure out if he was joking or serious.

Stone remained silent now, deciding what plan B was going to be if she still refused to help him out.

He didn't have to plan it. She suddenly smiled, and motioned for him to leave the roof first. Stone listened and quickly exited down the stairs and into the elevator before she could change her mind.

Once in the security office, Stone checked out the equipment. It was pretty antiquated. Actually that was a really nice word. It was pitiful. But pitiful worked, as long as there was some kind of a video tape he could burn onto a DVD and let technology do the work. Stone checked out the surveillance screens, there were four of them. He shook his head in disgust. There were ten floors to this building; it was newly remodeled with brand new furniture and a coffee bar in the corner. One of the screens was located in the gym. A workout gym that was loaded with state of the art equipment, a hot tub, pool, and sauna room, game room and tanning beds, but there were only four frigging cameras in the entire building.

*What a fucking joke.*

Now all he had to do was talk her into giving him the video, or a copy of it. Piece of cake.

She was about to find out that Dominick Stone could be a very persuasive man.

\*\*\*

It was some kind of furry brown thing that looked as if it had been dead for a year. The fir was matted, and what was left of it was up his nose and making him want to sneeze. Of course his eyesight was still blurry with sleep. It was talking to him too, but he couldn't make out a word it was saying. Geezus, *what the hell is this?*

Nate struggled to sit upright. Then he heard a child giggle softly.

"Janelle Rose, where are you?"

Damn, how he missed Kerensa's voice.

Nate sat upright perfectly awake now. He put his finger to his lips and motioned for Janelle to come and sit beside him. To his surprise, she did.

He sat her on his lap and she giggled again. Shuu, Nate whispered, but it was too late. Kerensa followed her little girls giggle right up to the bed they were sitting on. Then Kerensa let out a surprised squeal followed by a piercing scream, wrapping her arms around Nate in an instant. And he loved every bit of it too, as he pulled her onto the bed and nearly on top of both of them. Janelle squealed with delight her brown eyes dancing with laughter.

Kerensa gave Nate one final squeeze before struggling to stand upright again. That wasn't enough for Nate. He jumped to his feet too, wrapping his arms tightly around her and lifting her off her feet twirling her around. She laughed aloud.

"You're such a dog!" She exclaimed.

Nate pretended to be offended, but Kerensa didn't feed into it one bit. He laughed again as he knelt down and held his hand out to Janelle who suddenly decided to get shy. She was hiding behind her mommy.

"I bet I know what your name is?" Nate teased.

Janelle cocked her little head to one side, like she didn't believe him.

"It's Janelle Rose, right?"

Janelle paused, then solemnly shook her head, no.

Kerensa and Nate laughed again.

"Good girl," Kerensa replied. "Never say yes to a stranger."

"A stranger, hah? Well we'll just have to change that, won't we?"

Nate slipped his arm between Kerensa and gently tickled Janelle until she giggled. "You're a smart little girl for knowing I'm a stranger," he praised.

Then Nate turned toward Kerensa and in one second flat his eyes sucked in every inch of her gentle curves. Dressed in jogging shorts, and a yellow tee shirt, her curls tousled and tangled in every possible way and with no make up on, he still couldn't get his eyes off her.

*Damn, drop dead gorgeous.*

"So, babe, how have you been?" he asked, his tone tight with sentiment.

It was as though that was all Kerensa had to hear. There was always chemistry between them, a connection that made Kerensa love him like he was her brother, but that was a really sore subject for Nate.

Kerensa's eyes instantly filled with tears, and all that bottled up stress was ready to pop the cork right off. She put her arm around her little girl.

"Go find Nana, honey, tell her to put some breakfast on the table for Mr. Nate."

Janelle eagerly ran off to find Nana.

Kerensa took a deep breath hoping to stop the tears from spilling from her eyes, but they had a mind of their own and they fell down her cheeks like buckets full of water. Before she knew it she was back in Nate's arms again sobbing her little heart out. Nate held her for a long time, stroking her forehead and murmuring words of encouragement in her ear. Didn't life have a way of coming full circle?

"I'm so sorry…" she hiccoughed, "I feel like such a ba-aby."

Nate held her tighter. "You've gone through a lot, cut yourself some slack, Kerensa."

"It's just been a never ending, stressful month. "I…" She shook her head sadly, too choked up to say another word.

"You know it's going to be alright," Nate whispered. We'll make sure everyone is safe and you'll have your life back together again. This is just a temporary thing.

She nodded her head.

"I know, but it's-well, it's more complicated."

"It doesn't have to be, Kerensa."

She pulled away slightly, just enough to look into his eyes.

"You sound as though you know more than I think you do."

"I know a little," Nate admitted. "I know that you're engaged, well, you were engaged. Jesus, I'm sorry! I didn't mean to…"

Kerensa managed a weak laugh. "No, it's OK. You're right, I'm not engaged anymore. He broke off our engagement yesterday. He just plain dumped me. You know, I guess I should feel sad, I don't know, I should be heart broken or something like that-I mean, I was really upset yesterday, but now, well-I'm not." She took a deep breath and sighed. "I'm... not."

This time Nate pulled her away from him, studying her thoughtfully.

He knew that look in her eyes all too well.

"Oh God, Kerensa, you went and fell for him all over again, didn't you?"

Her eyes filled with tears again.

"Damn-it, Kerensa, you did!"

She nodded her head.

"Oh babe, what am I going to do with you?" Nate shook his head back and forth, recalling his conversation with Stone just a few hours ago. He suddenly found himself wanting to kick his ass all over again. He made a mental note that he was going to tell Stone to keep his goddamn hands off Kerensa or he would have to answer to him. She didn't need to be more confused than she already was. *And that was bad enough.*

"Kerensa, are you into self mutilating behavior, or what?"

"Why don't you just shoot me now and put me out of my misery?" she moaned, wiping her eyes with the back of her hands.

"Get yourself some Kleenex, babe," Nate sighed, releasing her. He paused in thought, recalling how much she cried after her last experience eight years ago. "Geeze you should probably buy some stock in the company."

Kerensa slowly stood to her feet, shooting Nate a dirty look.

"I hate you," she retorted.

"Yea, well you should love me. I keep telling you that, but no, you insist on doing detrimental things to your well being... where the hell is he, anyway?"

Kerensa shrugged her shoulders. "I woke up at seven and he was gone already, I thought you were with him."

"Oh, well then I have an idea what he's up to."

"He couldn't wait to pawn me off on you, could he?"

Nate chuckled. "No, it wasn't like that. He just couldn't wait to break someone's neck that's all."

*And never make a sound doing it.*

Kerensa's eyes got wide.

"Figuratively speaking, of course," Nate quickly added.

Kerensa sighed.

"I don't care what you say; I know he wanted to get rid of me as fast as possible. He's been in an especially foul mood since yesterday evening."

Nate chuckled again. "Yea, well, he gets that way when he hasn't been able to beat the shit—I mean, tar, out of someone for over twenty four hours. He's a testosterone junkie. So, what's for breakfast, I'm starved. And it better not be cold since you had to blubber all over me for a half hour."

Kerensa shook her head incredulously at him, and slapped his shoulder. She'd forgotten about his sarcastic sense of humor. But how could she have? It once saved her.

\*\*\*

Stone managed to get a copy of the last forty eight hours of surveillance digital tape, along with a cup of coffee and a promise that he would return the copy within an hour. *Duck soup.* Since she wouldn't let him stay there, he decided not to push his luck so now he was heading for the local library. Yea, that's right, a library. Stone hadn't been inside one of them since, God knows when. He glanced at his wrist watch, it was only 8AM. Seems a little early for a library to be open. *Shit.* Was there any such thing as a twenty four hour all night emergency library service?

Well, he didn't think so, but it was the computer he needed.

Now where was he going to get a computer? He could go back to Kerensa's but somehow that seemed more complicated than what he was in the mood for.

*Get a grip, you coward.*

Stone sighed. He really needed to go back to Kerensa's but somehow begging security doll Barbie to let him use her computer seemed like a better option. Yea, he would rather beg. Granted, he could utilize his position to professionally persuade her to work with him. He just didn't want to give her the wrong impression, she was already looking at him as though he wore a red cape and had a big 'S' on his chest. That expression started right after they had the conversation about what it was like to be an FBI agent. Stone didn't exactly tell her he wasn't technically FBI; so anyway, she told him how her "life long dream" was to be an operative. Maybe all Stone really had to do was tell her she could watch him work. *Oh boy.*

He headed into the building. This time she was in the security office. She peered at him from above those massive glasses, but she had a shy smile on her face too. *Damn, Stone knew that look. He'd seen it on hundreds of new recruits scheduled to be with him in the past.* Stone decided that the professional approach would get him into the least amount of trouble.

"Listen, Jade, I can't find another computer this early in the morning. I promise I'll be out of here before change of shift, hell maybe I can show you a trick or two while I'm at it."

She didn't say a word. That was alright though, he was beginning to realize that it took this girl a few extra seconds to process words after the rest of the world did.

"I guess that'll be alright," she responded, unlocking the security door.

Stone quickly stepped in before she changed her mind again. He sat down quickly too, and popped the digital cassette into the computer.

"Let's see what kind of equipment you have here," Stone murmured aloud.

He began quickly scanning the tape to see if he could catch a glimpse of anyone there.

He was going so quickly, that Jade suddenly replied, "I can't even tell what you're looking at."

Stone chuckled. "There's a little trick to scanning, it takes some practice to allow your eyes to encompass the entire screen in one glance."

Stone could see Jade in his peripheral vision. It was really quite comical to note the skeptical look on her face as she was trying to keep up with him.

"I still don't think you're going to see anything, scanning that fast. I mean, everything is just a big blur to me."

Her words were no sooner out of her mouth when Stone spotted a small object on the right side of the screen. He quickly stopped the tape, slowly scanning it frame by frame.

"Do you see that small movement right there?" Stone asked, pointing with his pencil to a minuscule object in the frame."

Jade squinted. "Yea, I see it, but what is it?"

"Watch this," Stone instructed, as he enlarged the object over and over again until he could get a clear image.

She watched in awe as Stone verified what it is.

"Wow," she exclaimed, excitement peaking through her voice. "That looks like the top view and forehead of someone."

"Yea, it is. Is it anyone you recognize?"

She sarcastically scoffed. "Do you really think I can recognize someone with just a dot on the screen?"

Stone bristled, his tone tight, as though he were speaking to a small child.

"Concentrate, Jade, and there's no telling what you can discover."

She glared at him, but his statement forced her to study it closer.

"Wait a minute, there's a mark on his forehead, do you see it?"

Stone nodded, already zooming in closer. It was still too blurry, but he had another idea. He cut that corner out of the screen and pasted it separately on a cleaner background. Then he zoomed closer and closer again.

*Bingo!*

"Do you see that?" he asked her again.

"Oh my God, it looks like the head of a serpent, or something like eyes."

"It's a tattoo," Stone replied, "and it's right across this guy's forehead."

*Fucking idiot, He may as well have tattooed his name and social security number on his forehead too.*

"Anyone you know?" Stone asked her again.

She looked at him shocked, and then nodded her head *no*

Stone chuckled to himself.

He printed the picture and deleted everything. Next, he signed on line and went into the FBI files. Then he turned to Jade again.

"Shouldn't you be going on your last set of rounds?" he asked.

She grinned at him. "You want to get rid of me now, don't you?"

*Well glory hallelujah, she does have both ores in the water when she wants to.*

"Yes, actually I do."

She nodded, copping her little attitude again. "I can't believe I'm even letting you sit here. I could loose my job if my replacement decides to come in early."

"Five more minutes, that's all I'm asking for," Stone coaxed, recalling how she lied about her replacement on the way almost an hour ago.

"I'll step out, but I'm not going on my rounds."

"Fair enough," he responded with one of his killer smiles.

It was enough to melt Jade's already *'falling in love with him'* heart.

Stone waited until she stepped out and quickly went to work. He typed in his password and went to the lineup page. Then he typed in the details that could narrow down his search. He narrowed it down even more by typing in *"serpent tattoo on forehead."* He found twenty four hits. Stone then narrowed it down again by guessing that the guy had recently been paroled or was in prison at one time.

*Eureka!*

He had his man. His name was Muhammad Ruger, originally from the Bronx in New York, incarcerated for ten years on a convicted charge of armed robbery, assault in the second degree and possession of drugs, turned

Muslim while in jail. Paroled three months ago, and ironically, he was in the same prison as Thorne was. Stone couldn't wait to get his hands on this low life moron.

Stone signed off, and left the security office. Jade was standing guard by the door, obviously scared to death that her replacement would be there any minute.

Stone smiled, she was going to be a hell of a law enforcement officer some day. He walked up to her, and extended his hand.

"Thank you, Jade. You were a big help."

She smiled a little girl with a big crush, smile.

"Did you find your man?"

"Nope," he lied, "but I got some leads."

She gave him that skeptical look again, and he laughed.

*This girl already knows me.*

"So, I guess that's it then, hah?" she asked.

He slowly nodded his head. "You really handled this situation well. I know some male officers who would have been scared to approach me on that roof. You did what you had to do and I admire that."

Jade nervously laughed. "Then you have no idea how petrified I really was. I just kept thinking, oh my God, this guy is going to kill me."

"Yea, but you could have run for your life, instead, you pointed a gun in my face, not bad."

"Actually," she confessed softly, "I was more afraid of you after I met you than I was initially of confronting you."

This time, Stone roared with laughter. "I've heard that one before." He confirmed. "Take care of yourself."

She nodded, and watched his gorgeous body until he disappeared from her sight. *Nice ass too, she thought to herself.*

***

Stone headed directly to the address he memorized. He could feel his heart pumping overtime already and his endorphins speeding ahead into overdrive. He couldn't wait to get his hands on this guy; the address was in a section of town that made the definition of run down, sound like a million dollar mansion. It was dirty, with illegal activity almost everywhere he looked. So he made it a point not to look. He was along the shore of the ocean, but that was deceiving because it certainly wasn't prime oceanfront property here. He slowed down, pulling alongside a small building with a sign on it that read, "Luxury Apartments at an affordable price." Stone nearly laughed aloud. The building looked dirty and practically deserted, but it matched the address he memorized.

Stone quickly exited the vehicle and slipped inside the building. Wow, that was easy too. It seemed as though doors were just opening up for him all morning.

But it was too bad the windows weren't open. The heat inside the hallway was stifling. It had to be over one hundred degrees in there. Yes, the heat was bothering him terribly until something else happened, and it bothered him even more. The smell, actually, the stench; it was comprised of decaying flesh and by his calculation; it seemed more than twenty four hours worth of rotting flesh.

*Jesus Christ.*

Stone took the steps two at a time until he reached the top. There were three metal doors. Each one of them was heavily dented with graffiti scribbled all over them, but this time his luck had run out. They were all locked.

Stone dropped to his knees and sniffed beneath the first door. It didn't have any identifiable increase in stench. He stood up and checked out the next door, dropping to his knees again. He sniffed in a deep breath. Suddenly the door wasn't there anymore, and in its place were a pair of badly scuffed sneakers. Of course the sneakers were attached to a pair of feet too. Stone paused for a brief second, and then his arm snaked out. He grasped the man's legs, pulling them right out from under him. The guy let out a startled scream, but it sounded more like a squeak since Stone's body was already on top of him, snuffing out his voice box.

"Who are you?" Stone growled into the guy's ear.

"I-I don't know what's going on man, but I ain't tryin' to hurt nobody."

"Who are you?" Stone repeated, tightening his hold on the guy's neck.

"The name's Dexter, man, and I can't breathe."

Stone released his grip, and in one fluid motion pulled himself and Dexter to his feet. Dexter stumbled for a moment, and finally steadied himself.

"Sorry man," Stone replied, flashing his badge.

"Shit," Dexter replied, attempting to smooth his dirty clothes into place. "It's about time a cop came by to check this stink out." Dexter was flailing his arms about as he said this, pointing in the direction of door number three.

"So you already notified the cops about this?"

"Shit yea, I sure did. They ain't even botherin' with my complaints, till' you come along."

Stone stared at the door. He needed to get inside as soon as possible, even though he knew what was in there waiting for him.

"Is there a landlord around?" Stone asked again.

Dexter snickered. "Yea, right, do ya really think someone would live in this hole if they owned it?"

Stone didn't answer.

"So when did you first notice the smell?"

"I don't know, man, but it smelled really bad about six o'clock this morning. I woke up and I said holy shit, it smells like something died in this place. So I knocked on this guy's door," Dexter motioned toward door number one, "and he didn't answer. I figured he was either still out or out cold since the guy never crawls out of his vodka bottle. So anyway, I decided to call the cops."

Stone nodded, staring at the door again.

*I might as well get this over with.*

He pulled out his cell phone and called the local precinct. Then he called Chief Donovan and his sidekick, Vance.

Stone studied the mess in the hallway and wondered what made people tick.

"So, do ya wanna come in for a cup of coffee or something?" Dexter asked.

Stone peered past Dexter into his apartment. There wasn't a spot there that didn't have an article of useless clutter. Garbage was strewn everywhere, white shopping bags thrown about with nothing but more bags in them. Dexter was probably some sort of homeless guy you saw on the streets pushing a shopping cart loaded with nothing but junk in it, thank God Dexter still had a home to settle his junk in.

*At least for now.*

Stone sighed; it was going to be a long day after all.

# 15

Stone could hear the sirens in the distance. It gave him the excuse to politely refuse Dexter's hospitality. Dexter appeared genuinely disappointed and Stone promised him a rain check. He was beginning to like the guy. Dexter was strange in a rather eclectic kind of way and he was pretty sharp too. They remained standing in the hallway and Stone took the opportunity to ask him more questions.

"So, do you know the guy that lives in that apartment?" Stone asked, pointing to door number three.

"Naw, he moved in only bout' a month or so ago. He don't talk much, not too sociable, if ya know what I mean?"

Stone nodded, but didn't speak, allowing Dexter to continue.

"So I stop him one day, and I say, hey guy, that's some tattoo ya got there. The guy just stares at me like I got two heads, ya know? And I think to myself, I ain't the funny lookin' guy with the dumb snake tattoo all over my head, man, you are. So I told him I was sorry to be botherin' him and I just minded my own business ever since. If ya know what I mean?"

"Have you ever noticed any kind of strange activity coming from there?"
Dexter thought a minute.

"Naw, not really. He ain't home that often, 'cept for that one night."
Stone raised his eyebrows.

"Yea, that one night bout a week ago, I heard all kinds of commotion' comin' from that apartment."

"Were they male voices or female?"

"It was the guy who lives there and another man's voice. They was yellin' a lot. Woke me right up, and that ain't easy. If ya know what I mean?" Dexter flashed a toothless smile. "Anyways, I yelled shut the hell up and a few minutes later the arguin' stopped. I ain't heard a sound from there since."

Stone could hear the pounding of feet as several men began to ascend the stairs.

"Thanks a lot, Dexter. You've been really helpful. *It's any wonder why they didn't kill you too.* Sorry I tackled you a few minutes ago. Safety reasons, do you know what I mean?"

*Geezus, I'm beginning to sound like him.*

"Yea, man, I get it. No problem."

Stone shook Dexter's hand just as Vance Robertson appeared in front of him. He quickly assessed the scene before him, and directed his attention back to Stone.

He looked tired, and in a bad mood. His hair was rumpled, as though he rolled out of bed and threw his pants on.

*Hey asshole, having trouble sleeping since you dumped the best thing that ever happened to you in your whole life? Just ask me, I can tell you.*

He fanned the air, as if he could actually clear the stench. Then he glared into Stone's face.

"So what's going on?" he asked, deliberately not addressing Stone by name.

Stone chuckled. "You look like shit, Robertson. But we won't discuss that. I have reason to believe that the guy who shot at Kerensa yesterday is dead inside this apartment today so we need to get inside."

Suddenly there were several other officers rallying around them, but no Chief Donovan.

"How do you know that?" Vance asked.

*Great, you're going to give me a hard time, just like I thought you would.*

Stone counted to ten in his head. It didn't matter; he was still getting really pissed. He could probably count forever, and it wouldn't help.

"Look, Robertson, I'll share all my toys with you later. Right now, just trust my judgment, and get a locksmith, or find the goddamn landlord. I don't care; we just need to get inside as soon as possible."

Vance must have suddenly received a wave of good judgment, and forgot the grudge against him. He straightened up, and turned to one of the locals asking him to find the landlord. In the meantime, another officer called back to dispatch and asked for a locksmith as soon as possible.

Ten minutes later, the landlord showed up. He looked like Dexter's brother with a few more teeth. He pulled out a key chain that must have had a hundred keys attached to it. After fumbling for a few minutes, he finally found the right key. As soon as the door opened slightly, Stone nudged the landlord aside, and took control of the door. He could see Robertson out of the corner of his eye, and he knew he was pissed. Stone didn't care; he had the right to pull rank.

He pushed the door open slightly, and the odor just oozed out of the apartment like toxic waste. It was enough to gag a Tasmanian Devil, which was surprising, based on the fact that the body could only be dead about twenty four hours. And suddenly Stone knew the answer to that too. He drew his gun, and stepped to the side. So did the rest of the officers. Then, Stone pushed the door open, and it hit the wall with a bang. The stench hit them with a bang too.

Stone heard groans and comments from the other officers as he carefully crept into the apartment.

The place was small, only a couple rooms. There was a card table with two chairs in the middle of the apartment, but no other furniture in the room. On top of the table was a glass with some juice left in it. Beside the glass sat an empty bowl and a quart of rancid milk with flies all over it. It was still open and it was the snipers last meal.

Stone continued on into the next room, wondering what Nate and Kerensa were up to, while the rest of the officers were concentrating on what kind of horrors they may find. Sadly enough Stone was immune to that.

\*\*\*

Janelle was out of control. Kerensa had never seen her so wound up and it was all Nate's fault. He had been chasing her around for nearly a half hour now and every time he caught up with her it was another pony ride. Janelle was in her glory.

"Alright, children, that's enough," Kerensa shouted. "It's time for lunch."

Nate stood upright, pulling Janelle over his shoulders. He walked into the dining room with Janelle's head almost touching the ceiling. She couldn't stop giggling.

"Well, I know she isn't afraid of heights," Kerensa remarked.

Nate leaned forward over the chair, gently depositing Janelle into it. Then he sat down too.

After a mouthful of scrambled eggs and mushroom soufflé, Nate moaned in dietary bliss.

"This tastes wonderful, Mrs. Drago," he drawled.

Nana laughed at Nate's sound effects. "Thank you," she answered, just shaking her head at him.

He looked over at Kerensa and she smiled at him.

*Why couldn't I fall in love with you? You're intelligent, brave and very nice looking. Maybe there really is some kind of self destructive mode built inside of me.*

"What's on your mind, Kerensa?" Nate asked.

She gazed back at him, amused that he could still read her so well. She shrugged her shoulders. "I was just thinking, about some things, that's all."

"What kind of things?" he asked, deliberately cocking his head to one side like he was a curious little dog.

She laughed aloud. "I was wondering what Dominick is up to and if he's, you know—if he's alright."

*Oh boy.*

"Yea, Kerensa, I'm sure he's just fine. If I were you, I'd be worried about the sniper right about now."

This time Nana laughed aloud, nearly choking on her water.

"I'm with Nate on that one," she retorted, shaking her head again.

Kerensa giggled too, realizing how foolish she must sound to the both of them.

She glanced from Janelle to Nate, recognizing that his gaze was still intently resting on her face.

"Now what?" she asked.

Nate shook his head. "Nothing, I'm just admiring how beautiful you are."

She shot him a skeptical look, and feeling uncomfortable, decided to change the subject.

"So what have you been up to the last few years?"

"Oh nothing much, you know the usual thing. Chasing bad guys, dodging bullets, nothing compared to what you've been up to," Nate winked at Janelle as he spoke.

Kerensa followed Nate's train of thought immediately. "I'm sorry I never caught up with you, I know you tried to contact me a couple times but I didn't call you back. Things just became…crazy I guess."

There was a strange look that crossed Nate's features. It was partly mixed with understanding and emotional hurt. It was strong enough to make Kerensa glance away with embarrassment.

Nate wasn't the type of man to carry a grudge. At least not with someone he cared about as much as Kerensa.

"I'm offended you didn't ask me to marry you," he bluntly said.

Kerensa looked sideways at Nate, attempting to figure out if he was kidding or not. When he gave her that dimpled grin, she knew he was pulling her leg again.

"Maybe I still will," she teased back.

"Be still, my pounding heart," Nate retorted, his right hand across his chest. "You heard her, Mrs. Drago; I may need you as my witness some day."

"That could be a little complicated," Nana responded, laughing too.

"Traitor," Nate moaned.

When they finished up their meal, Nate pushed himself away from the table and thanked Nana again for the hospitality. Kerensa could see that Nana was beaming over the compliments Nate had showered upon her. She cleaned Janelle up, and told her to play in the sun room, but she had other ideas.

"Mommy, I want to go swimming."

"Not right now, you can in a little while."

Janelle seemed satisfied with that, but Nate wasn't happy. Kerensa immediately caught the look he shot her.

"What's the matter?" she asked.

Nate sat down on the sofa, and patted the seat beside him. She joined him, a sick feeling inside her gut.

"I really am on 'house arrest', aren't I?"

"Well, I hate to call it that, but you're right. We can't leave this house or even go outside until that sniper is out of commission. That's why I'm here, Kerensa. My job is protecting you while Stone is out stalking the stalker. Sorry."

Kerensa nodded, her thoughts a flurry of ideas whizzing by her. What do I tell my students? What about New Jersey? What about the future of my Studio?

She took a deep cleansing breath.

Nate slipped an arm around her trembling shoulders. "It's not going to be that long. You know how Stone is. He'll find out what's going on and he'll report back to us." *After he kills the guy.*

"What do I tell my students?"

"That they have a day off. That's all. You don't have to get into any lengthy conversations, Kerensa. Stop trying to complicate things."

She bristled. "I'm not trying to complicate things, are you kidding me? I'm trying to think ahead."

"You don't have to think ahead until the ahead is here. Trust me, OK?"

Kerensa sighed again. She trusted Nate with her life, and she trusted Stone in a way that she could never admit to herself. She rose to her feet. "I better start calling my students."

Nate watched as Kerensa walked out of the room. It broke his heart to see her so upset again. It was bad enough that her life was in imminent danger, she had a toad for a fiancé, or ex fiancé or whatever the hell he was, and she was still in love with a prince charming that had the potential of turning into a toad at any time. And he felt like the lily pad they were all sitting on.

Life certainly was no fairy tale.

# 16

Stone could barely control his fury. He took several deep breaths in through his nose and out his mouth in an attempt to calm down. He could hear the displaced laughter from the coroner and a couple of detectives on the scene but there was nothing funny about the situation they were in. There was a decomposing, very dead body in the bedroom of this incredibly stinking apartment, and it was a woman. Stone was hoping to hit the jackpot, but instead he found himself in a bigger maze. It was a maze that made him almost nauseous when he began to put two and two together.

The dead body wasn't the number one bad guy on his hit list; actually, it was a woman who had an uncanny resemblance to Kerensa. She had been dead a whole lot longer than twenty four hours too. The terrible part, was watching Vance and the rest of the boys take their turns throwing up. He suspected this wasn't their first stiff, but the gruesomeness of the killing along with the extent of decay was enough to turn any seasoned detective. The man who killed her knew how to use a knife. One deep cut, on the side of the neck directly across the jugular. There was blood, now blackened with age and peppered with maggots everywhere. Stone studied the body carefully. Then, he stepped back and studied the scene. Something just wasn't right. True, her body was mutilated, but there didn't seem to be enough blood to substantiate the extent of the neck wound. Something just didn't fit.

Stone had seen plenty of death in his line of work, and some were women. Yet he could never view a dead woman the same way as a man. He avoided killing a woman, never liked to see any violence associated with even women who had an agenda of eliminating him in return. It was his one and only *soft spot.* His superiors warned him it was the one thing that made him human enough to be killed. He was glad that there was still something human about him.

Yet this woman wasn't an assassin, she wasn't a spy out to hurt or murder innocent people. She was a victim; her only mistake was looking like someone else.

Stone watched as several more cops had trouble holding down what they had eaten for lunch. Of course Vance was watching Stone every second of the time too, and no doubt he detected all kinds of emotions on Stone's face more than just once. He was probably hoping that Stone didn't see him puking his guts out when he went outside behind the building either. But Stone was watching Vance watch him. Despite the seriousness of the situation, it really was quite comical.

He was getting ready to leave, when Commissioner Donovan arrived. He avoided everyone and marched straight up to Stone. He had this *do not pass go, do not collect two hundred dollars* look on his face.

"Hello, Sergeant Stone."

Stone nodded his head in response.

Donovan paused a moment, probably giving him the opportunity to explain himself. When that didn't happen, he sighed loudly and spoke again.

"So what's going on here?"

Stone moaned softly to himself. He could see Vance in the background, an expression of anger and surprise written all over his face.

*Ask your boy, he's the one in charge of this case.*

"Commissioner Donovan, we have a problem."

Donovan scratched his head, momentarily studying Stone before responding to his obvious conclusion.

"What have you got, Stone?"

"I have reason to believe that the sniper who shot at Kerensa was living in this apartment. The dead girl was a warning."

"A warning why is that?"

Stone hesitated a split second hoping that Donovan didn't notice. He didn't want to spill all the beans with him, at least, not yet.

"You'll know the answer to that as soon as you view the body. I'll give you a little hint, though. It's a woman who's been dead a lot longer than twenty four hours and she resembles Kerensa Fiori."

Donovan swore softly beneath his breath and slowly nodded his head.

"Was she sexually assaulted?"

"Undetermined at this point, but she's completely naked. Once we get an ID on the victim, we can go from there. So let me know, alright?" Stone was still talking as he walked away. He was hoping that he could distract Donovan enough to slip out the door. That was really wishful thinking.

Donovan was much smarter than that.

"Hold it right there, Sergeant Stone. What were you doing at my crime scene?"

Stone shrugged his shoulders, a slight grin on his lips that didn't quite reach his eyes. He stared at Donovan, but didn't offer any explanation as he slowly walked away again.

"You got two hours to come down to the station and explain yourself to me, Stone. I expect answers."

Stone nodded his head, but never turned around.

"I mean it Stone, two hours."

He continued down the stairs and out of the building. He thought about stopping for a moment to speak with Vance, but decided he didn't care enough to try and patch things up. There was no fixing the real reason why both men hated one another. Stone headed in the direction of his pickup but stopped short when he spotted a group of teens eyeing his vehicle. His hesitation was short lived when he decided that although he was in no mood to kick some ass maybe that was exactly what he needed to get some of this simmering adrenalin out of his system. Stone was a few feet from his vehicle when he told the tallest of the group to step aside so he could open his door.

The kid snickered.

*Freaking great.*

He narrowed the distance between them considerably. He was only about five inches from the kid's nose. His breath smelled of stale tobacco and alcohol.

"I said get out of my way."

He still didn't move, and his friends moved in closer.

"I said get the fuck out of my way and I'm not saying it again."

That's when the guy to the right of Stone showed him his knife.

Stone burst into laughter. In a few short moves he quickly managed to take the knife out of the kid's hand forcing him to the ground moaning in pain.

"What else have you got?" He quietly growled to the rest of them.

They all shook their heads and moved aside. Stone opened his door, and glanced at the kid on the ground. "A little ice should do the trick," he told him.

Stone closed the knife and slipped it into his jeans pocket.

"Thanks, you boys shouldn't be playing with knives."

He stepped into his vehicle and sped away. "Damn," he said aloud, "I was hoping for a little more action than that."

Yet perhaps he needed to be careful what he wished for, after all, he was on his way back to Kerensa's and she was capable of giving him a real run for his money. He didn't want to return yet, but he had some down time and he needed to get an ID on the dead woman at the apartment first, before finding the whereabouts of his sniper friend. He concentrated a moment to sort out the facts. First, he knew that there was a link between Jonathan Thorne and the sniper; they were incarcerated at the same prison. They probably planned the details of Kerensa's death perfectly, but for what price? Thorne had a public defender, so he was obviously broke. Thorne, and Ruger, were two monstrous men with an evil plan, but both men wanted something in return. He knew what Thorne wanted, but what did Ruger want? And who was this mystery dead woman, and how did she fit into the puzzle?

Still too many questions and Stone wanted the answers, yesterday.

He pulled into Kerensa's driveway, assessing everything in his immediate surroundings. Nate's rental truck was parked near the garage and the door was closed. Kerensa's vehicle wasn't visible and Stone figured it was in the garage. Everything else looked normal enough. He swore beneath his breath when he thought about how difficult it was going to be to keep his wits about him with Kerensa while Nate was around. He parked his truck dead center in the driveway.

He tried the front door and it was locked up tight. Good going, so far. He went around the back of the house and tried the gate. It was latched tight and so was the side door. Good enough for him.

Stone went back to the front door and let himself in. The first person he saw was little Janelle. She squealed at the top of her lungs, her voice piercing the air like a siren.

"Holy cow!" Nate exclaimed, holding onto his ears.

"This little girl can hit some decibels."

Janelle ran over to Stone, tugging at his jeans and yelling, "Mr. Ick, pick me up, pick me up!"

Stone chuckled; leave it to Janelle to make him feel wanted. He tried hard not to smile too wide. He reached down swooping Janelle into his arms as she gave his neck one of those big bear hugs. Stone grinned some more.

He located Nate in the corner of the living room quietly observing him. Kerensa wasn't anywhere around.

Stone shrugged his shoulders, staring at Nate. "What are you looking at?"

"Mr.Ick?" He asked, fighting back a smirk.

"Yea," Stone countered, walking over to the sofa and sitting down with

Janelle. "So did anything out of the ordinary happen today?" he asked.

Nate shook his head *no*. "What kind of trouble did you get into?"

Stone remained quiet for a few moments. Finally he shook his head too, and sighed. "I didn't get to the sniper in time. He was already gone."

"Gone as in dead or gone as in escaped?" Nate sardonically replied.

"Who was already gone?" Kerensa asked, marching into the room and taking Janelle right out of Stone's arms. His grip tightened on the child momentarily, before letting her mother take her.

Kerensa felt his resistance and she glared at him briefly. Janelle wasn't too happy. She howled at the top of her lungs that she wanted to stay with Stone.

Kerensa kissed her little girl on the top of the head and put Janelle back on Stone's lap, acting like it didn't bother her at all that her child was being a turn coat, she sat on the opposite side of the sofa. It was obvious to both men that Kerensa chose not to be too close to Stone. It was also obvious that she didn't like how emotionally attached to Stone Janelle was getting. Actually, Nate didn't like it either. He just didn't know why. *Well, maybe he did.*

Kerensa waited for Stone to answer her question.

"The sniper," Stone replied.

"So you didn't catch him?" She asked.

*Correction, I didn't kill him.*

"You don't catch a bad guy, Kerensa, you apprehend him, and no, I got to his apartment too late."

"Oh," she leaned back against the sofa and closed her eyes.

Stone felt as though he disappointed her, and it irritated him.

"I just need a little more time, that's all."

She opened her eyes and studied him through slightly hooded lids.

"So what else happened?"

"That's about it," Stone retorted, sending a sidelong glance toward Nate.

Nate knew that look all too well. It was the '*I'll fill you in later*' message.

Kerensa abruptly sat upright, snapping her head so hard in Stone's direction that her curls fell completely across her face. She abruptly pushed them away with one quick sweep.

"That's not what Vance told me," she spat furiously at Stone.

*What the fuck is Vance calling again for?*

He quickly glanced at Nate but he looked just as surprised as Stone was.

Stone leveled his tone until it was smooth and silky. "Oh, and what did he say?"

"Don't play that game with me, Stone. You know he filled me in about the dead guy he found in the apartment with his throat slit." Her tone faltered slightly at the thought of that image.

*The dead guy? And the one He found?*

"Really now, tell me more."

"Why, you were there, weren't you?"

Stone nodded.

"Vance said that he had a good lead on who the sniper was and he said that he was on his way to the guy's apartment. He said that he couldn't get in so he had to call for back up and also the landlord. He said that you arrived right after they gained entry into the apartment."

*That lying sack of shit!*

She stopped talking and stared at him. Somehow she knew there was a discrepancy in her dissertation by the frown on Stone's face. But that frown disappeared immediately into an expressionless cold slab. She narrowed her eyes at him.

"Vance said he's really close to finding the sniper, how about you?"

"I figure Vance can do it, he certainly accomplished quite a bit today."

She kept her eyes steady on Stone but finally shifted her gaze toward Nate. There was enough tension in the room to-, well they could have defied gravity and floated to another planet with the extra heat.

Kerensa caught on quickly, her anger slowly dissipating into disappointment.

"That's not what really happened, is it?"

Stone didn't look at Kerensa. He simply shook his head, *no.*

Kerensa sighed softly.

"You were the one who identified the sniper, and found out where he lived, not Vance. Am I right?"

Stone's gaze caught her eyes briefly. "Does it really matter, Kerensa?"

"Does it really matter?" Kerensa shrieked, jumping to her feet in unabashed fury. She silently threw her arms up in frustration when she saw the frightened look on Janelle's little face. Instead of saying another word, she plucked her daughter from his arms and stomped out of the room.

Nate stared at his partner. Stone's face was void of expression, but it wasn't because he didn't care maybe it was because he cared too much.

"The guy lied to her, Stone. It's obvious how much that matters to her."

"Bullshit," Stone crudely responded. "She knows the guy's a jerk and he's all wrong for her. It's that simple." As an afterthought, he added, "I thought she wasn't talking to him anymore."

Nate shrugged his shoulders, hoping that he wasn't going to ask him if he knew they had connected again.

Stone opened his mouth to ask Nate precisely that, but he clamped it shut again. What did it matter to him anyway?

Instead, Stone began to fill Nate in about what really happened that morning.

When he was finished, Nate let out a slow, panicked hiss. His heart was pounding a little too hard as well.

"Jesus Christ, has Thorne turned into a serial killer?"

"That or she was killed by the sniper. Either way, I think Thorne had something to do with it."

"Thorne isn't allowed to leave his home State of Ohio, which would mean that he either killed her there or afterwards transported the body, or he killed her right here in Florida." Nate paused a moment, contemplating his own theory. "Man, if that sick-o is here in Florida that means we have even more problems than what we've already considered."

"Yea, but it also means that Thorne's issues aren't just with Kerensa anymore, and they aren't necessarily about the money anymore, either. He's an out of control psychopath, and there's no telling what he'll do or to whom."

"So do you think that maybe Vance led Kerensa to believe it was a man found dead in the apartment instead of a woman just to protect her?"

"I can't even begin to think like that hammerhead. The problem now is that he told her enough distortion to make her suspicious about who's really telling the truth." Stone glanced away as he continued, "I think you're going to have to be the one to talk to her."

Nate sprang to his feet with renewed energy, eager to follow through before Stone changed his mind. He had learned from experience that Stone's *no frills* personality got the job done but tended to create a backwash. He knew he could tell it to her in a way that wouldn't have her running to an underground fallout shelter with Janelle and Nana for the next fifty years.

As if reading Nate's mind, Stone replied, "you always did have a way with words, so don't deny it."

Nate laughed. "Oh I'm not about to deny it. You're about as tender as a swarm of killer bees. I'm glad you decided to concentrate on fighting the bad guys and leave the other stuff to me."

Stone scoffed at Nate's incorrect critique of himself. Nate could be downright hazardous when he needed to be. He had saved Stone's hide more times then he could even remember. Stone stood to his feet and strode to the door, but before pulling it open, he just stood there momentarily thinking about what he should say to Chief Donovan. Nate had already left the room, no doubt on his way to schmooze Kerensa with the truth. This was his ideal moment to get the hell out of there before she bombarded him with a thousand questions. Actually, it was Nana he was afraid of. Now that woman was downright dangerous.

Stone chuckled to himself as he locked the door behind him.

# 17

Thorne sat at his computer contemplating his next move. He was trying to calm down, tell himself that maybe the tactics didn't quite turn out the way he intended but he was superior and in charge of the world. He will provide another solution to fit the original plan and he had several of them figured out, down to every little detail. After all, he wouldn't be here and be free if he hadn't manipulated those idiots into believing he was a changed man.

He took several long, deep breaths. He could feel the bile just rising in his throat every time he thought about how Kerensa was still alive. She should have been shot right between the eyes; her body buried six feet under by now.

When he found out that the sniper missed, he was so fucking pissed off he called the woman he had met in the bar the other night. He just wanted to meet her for a drink and hopefully some sex afterwards. He never intended on doing anything else but then he just plain lost control. He was on top of her and looking into her eyes, *what the fuck was her name again?* But he was seeing Kerensa's face instead.

Suddenly he freaked out. He remembered how he grabbed her by the throat and started to squeeze the life out of her. Her eyes bulged with terror, and she began to thrash about. His strength was amazing, even to him. He watched in awe as she slowly became limp beneath him, a tear forming in the corners of her eyes.

He felt euphoric, a cleansing that was both physical and mental. When he finished, he knew it was the best orgasm he ever had. But it was short lived. An hour later, he stared into her cold, lifeless eyes and didn't feel a thing. The anger began to consume him again straight to his soul. He realized that he would never feel true peace until he killed Kerensa Fiori, until he eliminated her existence from this earth and then he could be reborn again. He would be Dr. David Fiori's only living child. He will succeed, and finish what he started eight years ago. As this awareness set in, so did the comprehension that he had to clean her body and get rid of it. So he carried her down three flights of stairs and threw her into the trunk of his car. He drove twenty four hours straight, all the way to Florida. All the way to Kerensa's home town and he showed up on Muhammad's dump of a doorstep.

*He didn't know what else to do at the time.*

He grinned when he recalled how pissed off that son of a bitch was. He started screaming at him to get the hell out. Instead, he dragged her body into his apartment and told him to take care of it. He told Muhammad that he had enough on him to turn him in right then and there and watch him fry in the electric chair. He watched in awe as Ruger pulled out his knife and slit her throat from stem to stern. Then, Thorne left. It was later, much later when her face showed up on the five o'clock news reporting that she was missing.

It was almost twenty four hours later when her dead body was found in another state. Much to Thorne's disappointment, that part never made the news. He found out another way.

Thorne turned his attention to the computer again. He read the instant message of the girl he had been corresponding with for almost six months. Soon, when his window of opportunity opens wide, they will meet each other for the first time.

*Desert green wrote:*

*"I'm so glad you finally got some vacation time granted. I can't wait until you come down and we can get together, I'm a little nervous but it'll be OK. The weather here is close to ninety degrees!"*

"Don't be nervous, baby," he wrote. "I know I've found the right girl in you."

Thorne signed off with his screen name, *Doctors' son.*

\*\*\*

Stone watched Chief Donovan pour him a cup of coffee from a very old, crusty urn. The glass container was so stained; it almost looked like it was a steel pot. Stone snickered as he accepted the Styrofoam cup and mumbled his thanks. He stared at the urn and his thoughts drifted briefly to his last mission when he was captured for almost two weeks in Pakistan. He was sent there to track the whereabouts of a high profile government official who had turned up missing. The man was last seen in a Pakistani jail with a gun to his head.

His captors were demanding that the US release three of their men who were at the top of their *ten most favorite terrorist list*. Stone was sent along with two other CIA agents. They never made it past the first night. Stone wasn't as lucky; they tortured him and left him spoiled, stinking food and dirty water to drink. Stone's mental strength and fortitude was a challenge to them, and they almost won. Stone often wondered if he would have surrendered what he knew for a frigging cup of coffee. It wouldn't have mattered if it was cold, moldy or rancid. It would have been coffee just the same.

He took a sip of the bitter liquid, unaware that Donovan was looking at him. Later, after he rescued the official, escaped from jail and killed his captors, he told the airline attendant on the flight home, to leave him with the whole frigging coffee pot. And she did.

*Top secret government information just for a cup of coffee?*

*That's pretty sick thinking.*

He glanced sideways when he realized that Donovan was talking to him.

"Well son, you're certainly on another planet right now."

"Sorry," Stone murmured, "I was a little distracted. Did you get an ID on the victim yet?"

"Of course I did, we're not some small town hillbillies."

Stone grinned. "Good work, who is she?"

"Her name was Maya, last name Sahara and she was twenty three years old. Last known address was in Toledo, Ohio. She worked for a computer company as an independent consultant. No prior arrests, no record. She was clean."

*And became someone else's sick, displaced obsession.*

"What was the cause of death?"

"Well now, that's the interesting part. According to the autopsy reports, morbidity occurred before she was moved to this location."

"So she was killed somewhere else and dumped in that apartment."

Donovan nodded his head.

"Somewhere else like Jonathan Thorne's apartment. I'll bet that her cause of death wasn't that fancy artwork on her neck. She was killed by strangulation and her throat was slashed afterward. Am I correct?"

Donovan stared at Stone for several moments.

"Why do you say that?"

"There wasn't enough blood, that's why. You slice a person's throat the way she was cut, and the Jugular along with other arteries will bleed a body right out. She should have bled out; instead she didn't look like she lost that much blood."

"Are you a doctor too?" Donovan asked, his tone was sarcastic, but his eyes were dancing.

"No, I hate the sight of blood."

"Yea, I'll bet you do. You're too busy killing them, not healing them."

Stone bristled, he didn't like Donovan's frank attitude. As if realizing he had overstepped his bounds, Donovan put both his hands up in a friendly gesture of surrender.

"Didn't mean to insult you Sergeant Stone, the country needs men like you."

Stone didn't respond to Donovan's comment, he was too busy stuffing any further thought into what he did for a living. Better to concentrate on the thought at hand.

He swallowed past the bile threatening to rise in his throat and nodded his head.

"Thanks for the information."

He spun around on his heels hoping to get away easy.

Donovan's soft timbre caused him to pause in his tracks.

"I have more information."

Stone spun around to face him again.

"Continue, what else?"

Donovan snickered loudly. "Oh, I see you're not so quick to get away from me now." He poured himself another cup of coffee and reached for Stone's Styrofoam cup. Stone gave it up willingly. He watched as Donovan poured another round and thought about a time when he would have been sitting at the bar drinking Tequila instead of caffeine. But that was a long time ago too. Stone took the cup from Donovan and waited impatiently for him to speak.

"I got a phone call today from a guy by the name of Sammy Jackson. Says he's holding important information and he's gotta get it to you." Donovan narrowed his eyes as he pointed at Stone with the forefinger he was using to hold his coffee cup. "Does the name mean anything to you?"

Stone shrugged his shoulders. "Nope, I don't recall that name."

Donovan scratched his gray head. "I asked the guy how he knew that I had any contact with you and he said he didn't. He said he'd been trying to reach you for about a month now and when he couldn't find you he figured you'd be where Kerensa Fiori was. So he looked her up and the local police department."

"What else?" Stone asked, making sure his tone was perfectly calm.

"He wants to see you, in person. Say's he can't talk over the phone."

Donovan peered at Stone suspiciously before continuing, "Why do you suppose that is?"

Stone shrugged his shoulders again.

"I said I don't know the guy. But I hope he has information we really can use."

Donovan drained his coffee cup and threw it into the trash. He turned to face Stone, his features drawn into a tight frown.

"I'm not telling you where you can find him until you agree to take one of my detectives with you."

Stone could feel his heart thump with anger. He knew better than to show that side to Donovan. He knew that the Chief would use it against him on purpose.

"I work alone," Stone responded.

"Not on this case, you're not. When the death of this girl hits the news, they are going to be crawling all over my ass to find out what's being done. I want to be apprised regarding every move you make."

"Don't worry, I'll notify you with every breath I take."

"Not good enough, Stone."

Stone rubbed his temples with his fingertips. Why was he feeling so stressed? He handled cases far more complicated than this one at a day's end.

"I work alone," Stone repeated.

"Not this time, Stone. You'll take Vance Robertson with you or you don't get my cooperation."

Stone groaned aloud. Talk about torturing him. What kind of sick joke was this?

"If I have to take someone with me, it's not going to be Robertson."

"This is Robertson's case. Take it or leave it."

Stone was furious, and he didn't hide it. Chief Donovan didn't let Stone's obvious anger faze him either. He stood still, his small beady eyes just glaring into Stone's.

"Take it or leave it," he repeated.

Stone practiced his deep breathing with his mind. He didn't want to show Donovan how much this deal was affecting him. "I'm leaving in ten minutes, so Robertson better be ready," he snarled.

Donovan nodded his head, taking great care not to show Stone how satisfied he was that he was victorious. "Sammy Jackson is a security guard at the maximum security facility in Elmira, NY. If you plan on leaving in ten minutes, I suggest you get to the airport ASAP. "I'll send Robertson to meet you there."

*Elmira New York? Where Thorne was incarcerated!*

Stone didn't respond, he simply strode to the door. Turning around and facing Donovan, he spoke again.

"I know Jonathan Thorne killed that girl. I expect your forensics team to find his DNA somewhere on her body. Furthermore, I expect you to obtain a search warrant and check out Thorne's place. Keep me as apprised with any new information as you are expecting me to do." Stone paused, and then continued, "And tell Roberson I'm leaving his ass behind if I don't see him in an hour."

Stone pulled the door open and slammed it shut behind him.

Donovan chuckled aloud, shaking his head from side to side and staring at the closed door.

*I wonder how much he already knows that he isn't about to tell me.*

\*\*\*

Stone checked his watch for the hundredth time. It was three minutes to the hour, and he was going to stick to his threat. It looked as though Robertson wasn't going to make it, *glory Hallelujah.* He stood to his feet and headed toward Gate fifteen. All passengers were currently boarding and he was going to make sure he was one of them. *Alone.* He smiled at the airline attendant and handed her his ticket. Just as he was turning away from her, he heard his name called out. But it wasn't Robertson's voice. Stone glanced sharply in the direction of the tone. He observed Chief Donovan rushing toward him, his face was flushed red and he wasn't looking very happy. Stone stepped out of the way of the existing passengers and waited for Donovan to reach him. By the time he arrived he was breathing heavily and gulping air.

"Jesus, Stone," he panted heavily, "You could have met me half way."

Stone smiled to himself. "What's going on?"

"Sammy Jackson is sitting in my office waiting for you."

Stone lifted an eyebrow. "Really?"

"Yea, so I suggest you get there right away."

Stone nodded his head, glancing around the crowded airport. His gaze instantly locked with Vance Robertson's as he was now pushing his way in their direction.

"Your boy is late," Stone declared, motioning toward Robertson who was moving at record speed ready to take out any poor little old lady who got in his way.

Donovan turned his head observing Robertson too. "You were going to get on that airplane without him, weren't you?"

"Damn straight I was."

Donovan chuckled despite the serious look that clouded his features.

"You're going to burn in hell, Stone."

"Don't remind me," Stone retorted.

\*\*\*

Sammy Jackson was a man of medium stature with a dark complexion and small, but expressive eyes. And those eyes were staring doggedly into Stone's at the moment. Stone stared right back.

"Do I know you?" He asked.

"No sir," Sammy responded, "But it's a pleasure to meet you."

Stone took Sammy's hand in his, but he didn't comment. Donovan stood in the corner of the office staring at both of them.

Stone cleared his throat. "How can I help you Mr. Jackson?"

"I have information that concerns Jonathan Thorne." Sammy took a sip of his coffee, appearing nervous. "I have reason to believe that Thorne is plotting to hurt Kerensa Fiori and kill you."

*Hmm, kill me too?*

Stone chuckled softly beneath his breath. "You're a couple days late with that information; however, you could really help out if you tell me the story as you know it."

"Did he already make an attempt on your life?" Sammy asked, looking scared.

"Not exactly, but someone tried to shoot Kerensa."

"Oh man, that's where you're wrong, Mr. Stone, I have a strong reason to believe that Muhammad Ruger is the man that has been hired to kill you both."

Stone paused, deep in thought. "Well, wanting me dead makes sense too. But Thorne would need some serious money to hire someone to kill both of us. I don't even know where he would get the money to hire a merc to kill anyone."

Sammy shrugged his shoulders, glancing upward at Donovan as he came closer into the room. There was a skeptical expression upon Donovan's features, causing his face to form a hard line.

"How did you come upon this information, Mr. Jackson?" Stone asked, ignoring Donovan's expression.

Sammy appeared nervous again. He rubbed his temples with his fingertips, and remained silent for several moments. Finally, he took a deep breath.

"I got in over my head, Mr. Stone. I lied to some people, thought I could handle something I had no business doing."

Stone read between Sammy's *I'm in way over my head* lines.

"Did you get cold feet," he asked.

Sammy's head snapped around. "What do you mean?"

Stone leaned forward, his face just inches from Sammy's. "It sounds like the deal went sour, so you decided to find me and spill the beans."

Sammy's eyes narrowed dangerously. "You're wrong, Mr. Stone. I couldn't find you until now, some folks say you're dead, others say you're a myth."

Stone laughed aloud. "Who's saying this stuff?"

"Some of the inmates at the prison, the ones that have a real vendetta against you, you know?"

*That's it of course; I should have figured it out sooner!*

"No, I don't know, "Stone lied, "who are they?"

Before Sammy could answer, Donovan piped up. "Did you know the sniper could be this Ruger guy?" He asked Stone.

*I was waiting for you to ask that question five minutes ago.*

Stone didn't miss a beat. "Yea, I knew."

He watched Donovan's eyes narrow with the same annoyance that Sammy's did just a few moments before. It didn't even faze Stone, but he knew he would be answering to Donovan sooner or later and he was hoping he could keep the identity of the sniper hidden a little while longer. *Until after he killed him.*

"So who are these men?" Stone asked again, turning his attention to Sammy.

"There are a few men talking; Joey Burns, Jimmy Sipco, Tony Barresi."

Stone thought for a long moment. Tony Barresi…yea, he remembered him. He was related to a punk who ran a major drug cartel in South America and Stone was sent there to take the guy out. The punk also had a brother and Stone's guess would be that the brother had 'Ruger' as his last name too. *Oh yea, it's beginning to make some sense.*

He watched Sammy watching him. "I don't recognize any of them," he lied.

Sammy nodded his head. "They know you real well; say you killed friends and family of theirs. There's a lot of talk about you, Mr. Stone."

Stone didn't acknowledge that statement. He suddenly put the last piece to the jigsaw puzzle together. Finally understood where Jonathan Thorne got the money to pay for the sniper. Actually, there wasn't any money involved. It was a trade off, one life for another, Kerensa's life for Thorne, and his life for Ruger. They both got what they wanted.

"So what is it that you want, Mr. Jackson?" Stone asked bluntly.

Sammy bristled, his soft brown eyes turning dark again.

"What makes you think I want something?"

"You came all this way to tell me something you could have done over the phone or email. So what's the trade off?"

This time Sammy grinned. "I wanted to see if you were as ugly as I heard you were."

Stone chuckled but didn't respond, allowing the silence to grow in the room. Donovan had become completely silent, which was unusual for him too. Finally Sammy sighed loudly and rubbed his lower jaw. Stone knew there had to be more.

"You're right, Mr. Stone. Like I said before-I guess I got in too deep, afraid for my life now that I led Thorne on and didn't follow through with the plans."

"Are you willing to testify against Jonathan Thorne regarding this plan of his?"

Sammy gulped air. "Now wait a minute, I'm not saying I know that for sure, 'cause I don't. I just overheard a few things, that's all."

Donovan glanced over at Stone, a murderous look across his features.

"What exactly are you saying, Mr. Jackson?" Donovan asked.

Sammy's forehead was beaded in sweat. "Look, I don't know for sure about Thorne, I just know that Ruger was the guy who wanted to kill you."

"And you want protection, now that you said too much?" Stone asked, glancing at Donovan again.

"Yea, something like that."

*You don't have anything to worry about; Muhammad Ruger will be dead long before he ever looks for you.*

Stone leaned forward, placing his face only inches away from Jackson's. "I think I know exactly what happened." Stone's tone was low and clipped. "You heard a few things, got to know a couple guys in prison; these guys had it out for Thorne and wanted to see him go down. So you waited till he was free, but somehow everything backfired, and now you're here asking for protection."

Sammy wiped his forehead with the back of his hand and simply nodded his head, *yes.*

"Do you know where Ruger is now?" Stone asked, leaving the other subject open for Donovan to take care of.

"Yes and no. I know where he hangs out, I know how to send a message to him, but I don't think he'll respond now."

Stone could feel his heart begin to pound. "Where does he hang out?"

"A local bar in Miami Beach, a place called *"The Down Under."*

Stone nodded his head, his thoughts already into overdrive. He glanced at his watch, it was almost midnight. The party was just getting started. Stone rose to his feet and headed for the door. Donovan's mouth was gaped open with surprise as he followed Stone's purposeful stride across the room. Stone paused at the door and turned around.

"I want Jonathan Thorne brought in for questioning as soon as possible."

Stone nodded his head at Jackson in *thanks*, turned on his heels and quickly walked out, making a beeline for his truck.

Hopefully he'll be gone before Donovan catches up with him.

The door slammed behind Stone with a big bang and Sammy Jackson sat there appearing stunned for a long moment. Finally, he shook his head and looking at Donovan he replied, "I really thought that guy was dead. You wouldn't believe the stuff I heard about him."

Donovan shook his head back and forth. Yea, I think I would."

# 18

Stone had been gone for two days without sleep. He kept in touch with Nate just to make sure that everything was alright on the home front. It was. That was more than Stone could say for himself. He was past exhaustion, heading down the path to total collapse. *And that was no easy feat.*

Muhammad Ruger was dead and that was the good news. Stone finally tracked him down right before closing time. He silently waited for him in the shadows of the bar, diligently watching every move he made, observing him as he got drunker and drunker and killing Ruger proved to be quite easy. He certainly knew what he looked like, and he didn't have to ask any questions in order to find him. His snake tattoo took care of his identity just fine. And Stone took care of everything else just fine too.

*He never saw me coming.*

Stone picked up his cell phone and dialed Nate's number. When Nate answered, Stone replied, "Is everything alright?"

"Of course where the hell are you?" Nate responded.

"I'm heading your way."

Nate snickered. "You're slowing down, my friend. I expected you twenty four hours ago."

Stone chuckled beneath his breath. "Yea, well it became a little more complicated than I thought."

"Oh yea, how so?"

"You were right about that little red dot being on the back of my head. It seems that Jonathan Thorne and the sniper, Muhammad Ruger, had a little deal in prison. He wanted me dead, and Thorne wanted Kerensa dead. So

Thorne knew that I would be where Kerensa was, he offered my head to Ruger in exchange for Kerensa's."

Nate whistled softly beneath his breath. "Oh man, I hate to say it, but that was pretty damn ingenious."

Stone grunted. "Yea, well it certainly reminds us of how smart Thorne really is. He's managed to lie, and manipulate everyone around him so far, fabricated quite a Smokescreen."

"Well, we'll have to figure out the next move."

"I told Donovan I want Thorne brought in for questioning. I'm sure we can prove that he hired the sniper."

Nate was silent for a few moments. "Fill me in on the details when you get here." Stone agreed, and hung up the phone.

He processed those details after he hung up with Nate. Now that Ruger was no further threat to Kerensa and her family, he was back to figuring out what to do with Thorne again. He was hoping he would have enough to nail him with conspiracy to attempted murder, but Sammy wasn't about to talk and without Sammy's testimony, everything else was considered hearsay. He knew now, without a shadow of a doubt that Thorne was behind the snipers actions, the young woman's death, and the conspiracy to kill him for the package deal. Stone's first inclination was to torture Thorne to death. He could certainly imagine all sorts of creative things to torment him with. However, he couldn't waste his time thinking up such pleasurable things. His moment would come soon enough.

Realistically, he had to go about this as up front and straight as possible. Chief Donovan didn't appear to be the kind of guy that would look the other way. He was already prepared to respond to any questions that may come his way regarding Ruger. *That is, if they ever find his body.*

Stone pulled into Kerensa's driveway shortly before dawn. He cut the engine right before he turned in. He softly closed the door and did a walk around the house just to make sure everything was secure. Of course, it was. He knew how thorough Nate was. Satisfied that he had nothing to worry about, Stone cut the alarm by using his remote control and let himself into the house. He was his usual silent self as he slipped past the kitchen and into the living room. Stone took only one step in to realize that someone was there, ten paces to his left, and standing right by the window. He quickly turned to face the person, his gun already in his right hand. He reached out with his left hand, pulling Kerensa straight into his arms. She let out a small squeal before landing with her mouth against his shoulder, muffling the sound.

Stone sighed.

"Why the hell didn't you tell me you were there?" He hissed into her ear.

Kerensa's back stiffened, but she didn't attempt to pull away. Stone didn't want to let her go either. Instead, he slipped the gun back into his shoulder harness, his left arm never loosening its hold around her waist. God, but she felt so good in his arms. Her scent was intoxicating, reminding him of the tantalizing mix of lingering lilacs on a warm summer night and a rose garden; a glimpse into the bittersweet reminiscence of their past relationship.

"You never gave me the chance to tell you, I turned my head and you were there," she responded, her tone still muffled.

Stone grinned wanly in the opaque darkness, thankful that she never heard him coming. He took another deep breath, consuming his senses with the fragrance of her hair, storing it into his memory. Then, he released her. He felt empty.

He suddenly wondered if she did too, noticing that she reluctantly allowed him to let her go, yet not stepping too far away.

"Why aren't you in bed?" he asked.

She ran a hand through her tousled curls. "I couldn't sleep."

Stone grunted in response. "What's been going on around here?"

"Nothing it's boring as hell around here," she bitterly retorted.

He chuckled softly, grateful that boring meant she was still safe and alive. "How's Janelle and Nana?"

"Equally as bored," she snapped.

He highly doubted that. The house smelled of fresh baked apple pie and numerous other tantalizing scents he couldn't recognize. Stone strolled across the room and sat down on the sofa. Kerensa watched his large body move with a quiet swiftness that reminded her of who he really was.

"Come over here, Kerensa."

She hesitated briefly, before crossing the room and sitting down beside him.

He stretched his long legs, leaning his head back on the cushion. For several moments, neither one spoke. Kerensa could feel her heart pounding swiftly in her chest, realizing how much his nearness would always affect her. It simply was what it was. She found herself leaning her head upon his shoulder. They remained that way for several minutes. When Kerensa's breathing became deep and even, he realized that she had fallen asleep. She was barely a whisper beside him, her unruly curls every which way, her legs tucked beneath her. His chest ached with a tightness he was beginning to get accustomed to. God, how he wished he could change history.

Stone sighed, not wanting to wake her up. He owed her an explanation, actually he owed her an entire ocean of explanations, but he was going to work on just giving her one, one tiny story with a lot of holes in it. *She deserves to know the name of the man who tried to kill her.*

She stirred languorously in his arms, her breasts rubbing against his lower chest. He groaned softly and her eyes suddenly popped open.

"Oh dear, I must have fallen asleep!"

Stone didn't answer; he was too busy trying to control the activity in his groin.

She sat boldly upright then, forcing him to focus on his next step. The part where he had to tell her the nightmare was almost over. *But almost isn't good enough she deserved better than that.*

"So what's going on?" she asked quietly, attempting to study his features in the opaque darkness.

"His name was Muhammad Ruger, and he isn't going to bother you anymore."

Kerensa sucked in her breath, honing in on the word, *was.*

She nodded her head slowly, instantly not wanting to know more. Suddenly understanding Stone's harsh words of the other night as he warned her never to question his actions again. She knew her sniper was dead and perhaps the only two people in the whole wide world who also knew that were sitting together on this very couch. Right now. And the realization of how far away they really were from one another slammed into her gut like an iron fist. *Different worlds, isn't that how the saying goes? They were from two different worlds.*

She nodded her head again, but didn't say anything more.

Stone braced himself for the barrage of questions that never came. He knew why, and the silence made him feel even lonelier.

***

It was Janelle who found her mommy curled up beside Mr. Ick in the morning. She let out one of her piercing screams of glee as she immediately climbed over both of them, forcing Stone to move over so she could shimmy her tiny body between them. She kissed Kerensa, a big wet one on the cheek. Kerensa stirred, her eyes finally opening. Stone was surprised that she still slept so soundly, wondering if he had anything to do with that.

Kerensa reached out to hug her little girl, but Janelle was already wrapping her arms around Stone's thick neck.

"Traitor," Kerensa murmured.

"Good morning princess," he whispered softly. Wondering how

in the world he would leave this little girl when the time came.

And h*ow about Kerensa, how much would she hate him when he slipped away from her again?*

As if reading his mind, he caught Kerensa's gaze intently upon his face. She met his eyes with hers, and then slowly spoke.

"So what's the next step?"

Stone didn't answer her right away, he spotted a movement that was almost behind him, and he knew Nate was there watching them. Stone directed his attention to him first.

"Where were you when I came in?" Stone asked.

Nate chuckled aloud. "It was precisely 4:05Am and you surprised Kerensa, she never saw you coming. *But I did.* Yee have but little faith."

Stone nodded his head, knowing full well that Nate had been in the hallway watching them on the couch. He also knew that his partner wouldn't miss a trick, and it was the other reason why Stone didn't reach for Kerensa in the darkness and make love to her the way he was yearning too.

Stone turned around and their eyes met, a silent but firm message tangling between them. It was a reminder to Stone that Nate wasn't just protecting Kerensa from Jonathan Thorne anymore; he was protecting her from him too.

# 19

Nana seemed unusually quiet at breakfast. She followed everything that was being said, superficial conversation that didn't touch the true topic that was weighing heavy on her mind. Yet she stayed patient, serving everyone home made waffles and fresh blueberries with whipped cream, scrambled ham and eggs and hot buttered toast. It was the first meal Stone had had in two days, and it tasted magnificent. Finally, after everyone had their second cup of coffee, *Stone's forth* and Janelle was complaining that she wanted to go outside and play, Nana turned her gaze full force on Stone. She didn't have to speak, he already knew what was on her mind and he had been watching her for nearly an hour. It was about time he gave her some well deserved answers too.

*And that's why I prefer to work alone.*

"She can go outside and play as long as someone is with her at all times," Stone finally replied.

Nana's eyebrows rose, but she remained silent.

Stone sighed. *Damn but she would have made a good operative!*

"The sniper that shot at Kerensa has been apprehended. *Well, sort of.*" He continued, "There is no reason for Kerensa or Janelle to stay out of sight anymore. But Thorne continues to be our primary concern."

Stone glanced at Nate to include him in the conversation even though he had already given him the details on the side.

Kerensa stepped away from the door, pulling Janelle with her. "Give mommy five more minutes and we can go outside."

"Now mommy," she whined.

Kerensa ignored her daughter's request, and joined the conversation between Nana and Nate. It was her turn to discuss a very important issue that had been on her mind for the last three days. *Well, besides their safety.*

Yes, three days of calling her students and their mothers so she could mislead them into believing that she was too sick to teach that day. Three days of missed practice for competitions and recitals, time was running out and she needed answers.

She cleared her throat, wondering why she suddenly felt like her tongue tasted like saw dust.

"What about my dance classes, can I resume them today?"

Stone stared into Kerensa's eyes, but remained silent. Kerensa waited, hands on her hips in a defiant pose. It made Nate laugh to himself. Kerensa's gaze suddenly landed full force on his face, but he wasn't about to answer her question. It wasn't his call.

"We can resume the classes today, and while you're at it, find out how many prospective students Nate is going to have in his karate class."

Nate's eyebrows turned downward in a quizzical frown.

*My karate class?*

Kerensa suddenly began to giggle, and it didn't take long for Nate to realize that he was the prime object of a very private joke. A few moments later, when neither Stone nor Kerensa were going to let him in on it, he put that together too.

"I take it I'm going to be teaching a bunch of girls' karate?" he retorted.

"Something like that," Stone quipped back.

"So that's what it boils down to, hah?"

Stone chuckled softly but quickly sobered when he saw that Nana remained much too serious for her usual easy going disposition. *She's worried about something.*

"Go call all your students," Stone quickly directed, hoping to get Kerensa and Janelle out of the way for the moment.

Well it worked. Kerensa left the room, and Nate followed behind her. As soon as they were alone, Stone walked over to Nana.

"Talk to me, Mrs. Drago... please."

Nana turned to Stone, tears glistening in her eyes. "When is this going to end, Dominick? When do we get our lives back?"

Stone felt a stirring in his chest he hadn't felt before. It was a sensation nearly foreign to him, yet not lost. He recalled it from his long term memory long before he became an operative. It was the feeling that went along with knowing he must protect his mother after his father died and the realization that he was responsible for his mother's safety.

"It's going to be alright, Mrs. Drago, I promise you that. I realize how hard this is on all of you."

"I'm more worried about Kerensa and Janelle. She's barely hanging on by a thread. She's a strong young woman, but this has become so horrible for her to endure day after day."

Stone sighed. *How do I tell her that there is no end in site yet? But there will be, and she won't approve of how that happens.*

"What about my grandchild? How safe is she?"

"Nothing will happen to Janelle, Nate's been protecting her and he is one of the best. Trust me, Mrs. Drago, please."

She raised her head again to look at him. He was so tall in comparison to her that sometimes he felt like getting on his knees just to see her eye to eye.

"You still didn't answer my question, Dominick, just how safe is Janelle?'

*Man, this lady is brutal.*

Stone ran his hands through his loose hair and shook his head from side to side.

"I can't answer that question," he replied. "I don't know if she's in danger at all, but if Thorne knows about her, there's no telling what his mind is thinking."

"You mean there's no telling what his sick, demented mind will tell him to do."

Stone grinned suddenly, impressed with how astute she was. He nodded his head in response.

"Yes, ma'am, you're right."

"And you're going to make sure that nothing happens no matter what it takes, right?"

*Good grief, maybe she lived a double life as an operative...*

Stone's eyes met Nana's and her gaze was fierce. He knew at that very moment that Nana was willing to risk what was right or wrong, good or bad, sin and evil just to make sure that her family was safe, the ferocious protection of a mother with her children. She was granting him permission through her silent but steady stare. *Kill if you have to.*

Stone cleared his throat. "I understand Mrs. Drago." *I'm way ahead of you.*

This time Nana nodded, and as if on cue, Janelle came running into the kitchen, throwing her little arms around Nana's middle.

"We're going to the dance studio," Janelle chirped excitedly. "Are you coming too?

Nana laughed aloud, and the sound was refreshing. "Sure I am. I'm up to an adventure."

"You are?" Kerensa asked, pretending to be surprised.

"I definitely need to get away from here for a while. Nate, why don't you give me one of your guns, just in case you boys need backup?"

Kerensa's mouth dropped open.

Nate roared with laughter.

*And nothing surprised Stone when it came to Nana.*

***

Kerensa teased Nate all the way to the studio about how excited some of the mom's were when they found out that the karate class was starting today, and some of them signed up for it too.

"Are any of them single mom's?" Nate suddenly asked.

"Maybe."

"Hmm... I think I'm going to like this after all."

Kerensa giggled an evil twinkle in her eye. "Well, actually, they think Dominick is doing the teaching."

"Well that's even better," Nate quickly retorted. "They'll really be excited when they get the better looking guy."

Stone took his eyes off the road long enough to cast a sidelong glance at Nate, but Nate ignored it. Kerensa studied Nate from the back seat. He really wasn't joking about his good looks. His tawny brown hair was cut short and trimmed neatly around his ears. His brown eyes were always more amber than brown, sometimes reminding Kerensa of tiger eyes. His tall, well built muscular frame was deceiving when it came to hiding his true physical strength, but it was his mental and emotional fortitude that always amazed her. He had a sixth sense about others, an uncanny ability to read feelings and understand just what she was thinking. She imagined that he had that ability with other people too. Nate was intelligent and astute with a certain life experience that Kerensa never did explore. Perhaps she was afraid of what she would find out about him too.

When they arrived at the studio, Kerensa noticed that her little girl was sleeping soundly in her car seat. She reached in and gingerly picked her up, trying not to jostle her around too much. She knew that Janelle would awaken in plenty of time to see the girls; she always loved the attention they gave her. Kerensa reached in and gingerly unbuckled the strap, carefully pulling her out and cradling her in her arms. She tried to slam the door, but she didn't have to. Stone was directly behind her, slamming the car door and lifting her child over her head and into his arms. Kerensa looked upward, and smiled her thanks. When her attention focused on the studio, she noticed Nate watching them intently. He had a peculiar expression on his face and Kerensa wondered if there was an issue going on between both men. Stone immediately detected the frown on Nate's features, but he interpreted it immediately. It was Nate's constant reminder to Stone that he better keep his hands off Kerensa.

*I hear you loud and clear.*

She walked in with Stone; Nana was already waiting for them with Nate.

Stone's gaze quickly swept the parking lot, the buildings on either side up and down and across the street. His examination of his surroundings was cautious, meticulously examining every little detail around him and committing it to memory.

Kerensa sighed at the sudden thought that popped into her head. It was so crazy now that an entire production had to occur, equipped with body guards and family, just for her to go to work for a few hours. Life certainly had its way of changing in a heart beat.

As soon as she stepped foot into the studio she began to prepare for her students arrival. She set up the CD player, and proceeded to section off an area for her newest class offered, 'Beginner Karate.'

Nate strolled over.

"So, how many students do I have?"

"I'm not sure, probably around ten."

"You know, Kerensa I never taught Karate, maybe you should hand this little project back to Stone. I know he pawned it off on me."

Kerensa focused on Nate's face. He was wearing that same expression she had seen when they walked into the studio. "Don't worry; I'll make sure that Stone does his share of teaching too."

Nate stood by in quiet contemplation, watching as the students began to arrive. In a matter of moments, their quiet atmosphere suddenly erupted into a full fledged combination of noise and laughter, similar to the decibels one would hear at a rock concert.

Nate held his ears and tried to speak to Kerensa above the chatter of little voices, mommy voices and uncontrollable giggling. "How the hell do you manage to put up with this day after day?" he shouted.

Kerensa shot him a dirty look. "Go sit down over there," she pointed to the other side of the studio, "I'll introduce you in a few minutes."

"Yea, yea, yea," he muttered, glancing around the studio to see where Stone was hiding out and quickly located him toward the back of the hallway by the rear exit door. He was on his knees examining something. "What the hell is he up to now?"

Nate decided to check it out, and wandered over to him.

"If you're trying to hide out so you don't have to teach it's not working, your ass is sticking out."

Stone stood up, brushing the dirt off his jeans. "What do you make of that?" He pointed to a tiny dent on the bottom, left side of the steel door.

Nate stooped downward, running his hand over the little bump. "It looks like someone tried to pry this door open."

"Yea," Stone growled. "But the alarm is sensitive enough to have gone off, and someone should have notified Kerensa. I was meaning to get a better, thicker door for this rear entrance, but I figured I had time."

Nate nodded his head, and speaking of Kerensa, he noticed that she was already motioning for him to come over. He ignored her, speaking to Stone again.

"Whoever did this obviously kicked it in from the outside, because the dent is bubbled toward us. But why is someone kicking the door to her studio in the first place?"

"Well I'm going outside to check it out; it looks like you're wanted over there," Stone responded, pointing in her direction.

"Oh no you don't Stone. I've been thinking about this, and you are much more qualified to teach the 'attitude' that goes along with the Karate."

Stone chuckled, observing Kerensa's angry look from the corner of his eyes.

Nate motioned to Kerensa for five more minutes and turned around before she could refuse.

Stone pushed the door open, and Nate followed. The back door led to an ally that was lined with bushes and weeds. They slowly walked around to the back of the building where the bushes were thicker and the overgrowth much denser.

The early afternoon sun was scorching and there wasn't a breeze to be found. Then that familiar odor drifted over both of them. It wasn't strong, but once you've smelled it you never forget it. Both men instantly drew their guns as they proceeded slowly, checking the brush carefully for any human remains. Then, Nate spotted the tip of a black steel toed boot.

"Hey Stone, over here," he called out.

Stone was there in an instant. He didn't need to see the rest of the DB he already knew who it was.

# 20

Nate managed to teach Karate to a dozen rambunctious ten year olds, and four, very aggressive moms, Kerensa managed to practice every dance with the girls and in four separate classes, Nana supervised each class in between and babysat Janelle who was more unruly than usual, and Stone stood guard on the dead body until the classes were over, the parents were shooed home and Nate could give him the high sign to call the police. When Stone made the call, he made sure they understood that it was to be kept low profile, absolutely no sirens.

Of course Stone knew that his favorite detective duo would be responding to the call and there would be a plethora of questions that he would have to jump through hoops to avoid. Stone was not in the mood to see Robertson since his brainless lie regarding the sniper and the woman's dead body.

Hell, he just wasn't in a mood to ever see Robertson, period.

Stone watched as Kerensa approached him. Her long, dark curls were piled high on her head, and with the glow of the evening sun, they looked like hundreds of cork screw antennas sticking up all over her head. The golden hues of the sun spilled over her cheeks and lips, making her look almost ethereal. *But he knew better.* He stopped her from advancing any further, several yards away from the body.

"What are you doing here?" he tersely asked, attempting to keep the anger from his tone. "And where is Nate?"

"He's inside, talking to Nana," she replied, her voice trembling.

Stone sighed. "Kerensa, you cannot stay out here. I want you to go back to the studio…now."

"Who is he?" she asked, ignoring his request.

Stone noticed that her complexion was as white as her dance top now.

He bristled with irritation. He wanted her as far away as possible from the dead body and his crime scene, away from the police, Donovan and most of all, her idiot ex—fiancé.

Stone glanced away from Kerensa to see Nate advancing toward them. *Perfect timing.* He quickly took Kerensa's arm and escorted her away, before she could object. He knew how angry she would be, but he would deal with that later. Actually, he was about to make her even more irritated. He walked her past Nate with a silent nod of the head, and he knew that Nate would take over for him until he returned.

Stone marched Kerensa right back into the studio, and in the privacy of her office and away from prying eyes, he kicked the door closed with a big bang, and drew her against the wall firmly holding her there.

"Look at me," he demanded, pulling her chin toward him.

Kerensa's eyes slowly met his. She could feel his wrath; see the fury in his dark blue eyes. His tone was smooth, but like raw silk with a deadly edge.

"This is the last time I'm going to tell you this, Kerensa. You are to follow my orders, do not make me repeat myself, and do not disobey me. I cannot protect you if you deliberately ignore my commands. We've been through this once already, Kerensa, and you know what happens when you don't follow the rules. You were told not to come out here. Now, do you understand me?"

His chastising instantly brought her back to yesteryear. He was belittling her like he used to, treating her like a misbehaving child, and it pushed every button she had. Kerensa pushed her body against his in an effort to get away from him, but his grasp was like iron, cold and unrelenting.

"How dare you talk to me like that?" She admonished angrily. "Get your hands off me!"

His grip on her wrists became tighter as he held her arms over her head. She furiously squirmed against him, hot tears forming behind her eyes and threatening to slip down her cheeks. Yet her mind was *shouting 'you bastard, leave me alone'* and her body was instantly responding to the pure masculinity that radiated from the heat of his hands and the hardness of his chest. She desired him like she used to, untainted and innocent, yet shameless, bold and unafraid of rejection. She lifted her face to him, and caught the pure desire that intensified in his eyes.

He only had so much discipline to draw upon. His desire for her was quickly out of control, brazen and yet he knew he couldn't stop himself any longer. All those nights he dreamt of her, wished she were by his side to make him feel whole again, hated the dark lonely pit his heart had fallen into since he left her. And so he kissed her.

Her lips were hot and soft, and joined his lips perfectly. He slipped his tongue into her mouth, forcing it to open. His need was enormous, tearing at his gut and stealing any strength he had. What was it about this woman that made him feel so alive, made him forget how dark the life he had chosen for himself really was. Made him question if that life was really what he wanted anymore.

Kerensa surrendered to his kiss, relishing in the pure heat of him. She felt her self control drowning in the strength of his arms, the hardness of his biceps as her hands caressed his upper shoulders. She always loved to run her fingers down the hard, sinewy, muscles of his arms and chest.

And then she heard sirens. Lots of them. *At first, she thought the sound was coming from inside her head.*

Stone hesitated, reluctantly releasing her. Then, he swore several times beneath his breath.

"I told them no sirens," *Son of a bitch. That's probably Robertson's idea.*

He took her hand. "Come on, I want you safely in the studio right now."

And just like that, their moment was gone.

Kerensa walked quietly alongside Stone; her tender lips still tingling and swollen from his kiss. *What just happened between us, and what exactly does that mean?*

Stone was wondering the same thing, only a little less sappy. *What the fuck was I thinking, am I freaking crazy, or what?*

"Look, Kerensa…"

"Don't say it Dominick," she barely whispered. "I know what you're about to declare, but it's already been said once before, a long time ago. "Please don't ruin that moment between us…again."

Stone remained silent, thinking back to the very first time they were together, yet he stopped them before becoming intimate. He told her that he was out of line and that he had made a mistake. She was so offended and afterward she cried herself to sleep. And she was right, he was about to tell her again that he had made a mistake.

*A great big fucking colossal one.* He had no right touching her, kissing her.

Stone already heard Donovan's voice long before he entered the studio. It was a few octaves higher than it should have been, and it was calling for Stone.

As soon as Donovan focused on Stone, his pitch quieted for a moment, but his face remained diaphoretic and red.

"Sergeant Stone," he bellowed again. "You neglected to tell me that everywhere you go, dead bodies are sure to follow."

Stone decided not to qualify that statement with a remark of his own. *Guilty by association.* His attention was focused on Vance Robertson, and he was already pissing Stone off, even though all he was doing was just standing there.

But he was staring at Kerensa, and trying to get her attention. That was enough for Stone to want to punch his lights out.

Stone turned on his heels and walked out of the studio, figuring they would have to follow after him, and he was right. Donovan stomped out directly behind Stone, and along came an obedient Vance Robertson. Nana was holding a tired Janelle, and although she was dying to go out back to check out the DB, she remained inside with her daughter and granddaughter.

*Thank God.*

Donovan quickly caught up with Stone. "You've got a lot of questions to answer, Sergeant Stone," he gruffly replied, "And the first one being, is the dead guy Sammy Jackson?"

Stone nodded his head, *yes.*

Donovan grunted. "I'd like to know what happened to your sniper, Muhammad Ruger, it's rather interesting that you have Kerensa Fiori and her family outside mingling with civilization again."

Stone glanced briefly at him. "So what's your point?"

"You know damn well what my point is. You'd have her in an underground sanctuary if you thought that sniper was still around."

Stone stopped walking and turned to face Donovan.

"I brought my partner here to help me protect Kerensa. That should be a relief for you since you won't have to call on your own officers to help out."

Donovan scoffed loudly. "I may be a lot of things, son, but I'm not stupid."

"I know that Chief Donovan," Stone responded, thinking about how he called him *son* for the second time since they met.

This time it was Donovan who didn't answer. He was about to when they turned the corner and that familiar odor invaded their nostrils.

They continued to walk in silence to the crime scene. The back yard was crawling with cops, detectives, cop wanna be's and rubbernecks all hoping for a glimpse of the action. Stone located Nate about fifty feet from the crime scene. He had a mega scowl on his sunburned face and Vance Robertson appeared to be the one he had issue with. Stone nearly laughed aloud, it was time to referee.

"I see you've met Detective Vance Robertson," Stone replied.

The recognition was immediate in Nate's brown eyes. "Actually no, the guy was telling me how to do my job, but he never said who he was."

Vance cleared his throat. "I'm Vance Robertson, Kerensa Fiori's fiancé."

Stone's eyebrows shot up in surprise but he didn't have to say a word. Nate said it for him.

"That's funny; Kerensa told me she wasn't engaged anymore."

"Well, I broke our engagement, but I just got a little out of control. I plan on changing that." Vance turned his attention directly on Stone as he spoke in a no nonsense tone of voice. *And just try to stop me.*

There was a roaring in Stone's ears and it took him a few moments to realize that the sound was coming from inside his head. But this wasn't the time or the place to discuss Vance Robertson's delusional behavior. There was work to do and he knew that Nate would handle the situation just fine. *Probably better.*

Stone walked away.

Nate knew he needed to drop the issue too, but not before he threw in one more dig.

"I don't know how you're going to do that without getting close enough to talk to her, because I'm not about to let you alone with her…ever."

Robertson narrowed his eyes. "Who exactly are you, anyway?"

Nate wanted to say something that came right out of a Dirty Harry movie, but he knew better.

"I'm Nate Drake, Stone's partner."

Vance was no fool when it came to reading most people. Nate Drake may have known Stone a long time, but he didn't have what it takes to be his partner. *And that's what Nate always counted on.*

"Look, I may have come on a little strong. I just want to talk to my fiancé and iron things out."

Nate was beginning to hate this guy.

"I don't think you get it, pal. She's not interested in you anymore, so back off."

"We'll just see about that," Vance retorted, his tone curt and challenging.

Nate glanced over at Stone watching him, the detectives and crime scene investigators taping off a significant area and processing the scene. They looked as though they had more than enough help collecting evidence. *But from the look of the DB, most likely there was very little evidence.* Nate could tell that the hit was professional.

He also knew he should head into the studio and see what kind of trouble Kerensa was getting into; it was time to terminate this ridiculous charade of who can carry a bigger club. Arguing with Vance Robertson was getting a little old, and he really did have more important things to do.

Then he saw Kerensa standing near the side of the building.

*Damn, He should have known it wouldn't take her long to stick her pretty little nose into something, especially since Stone told her to keep her ass in the studio.* She spotted Nate and headed toward him. He could tell that she didn't notice Vance until she proceeded closer to both men. Her gait hesitated briefly, but she kept on walking. *That's my girl, Nate thought.*

She marched up to them, directing her attention to Nate. Nate took advantage of that and quickly put her arm in his.

"You know you shouldn't be out here, sweetheart," he replied, deliberately emphasizing his term of endearment.

She narrowed her eyes at him for a second, and then openly smiled.

"So take me back inside, but you're still going to tell me what's going on."

Nate grinned; so far she was playing into his hands perfectly. He nodded his head at Vance and quickly escorted Kerensa away from him. That is, until Vance showed up alongside Kerensa.

"Can I talk to you inside?" He softly asked.

She kept on walking. "Why?"

"Please Kerensa, just hear me out."

Nate could feel her body stiffen but only for a moment.

"Don't you have some crime scene to process or a sniper to catch or something like that?"

Nate nearly laughed aloud.

"Five minutes, Kerensa, that's all I'm asking for."

She didn't speak for a few moments, and they were practically to the door of the studio. Nate could tell her resolve was melting away. *Son of a bitch it's time to intervene. If I can just get her where Janelle is…*

Nate cleared his throat and Vance looked at him.

"Kerensa, I'm going to take you, Janelle and Nana home right now. Stone can catch a ride to your house when he's done here." Nate looked back at Vance.

"I think you're wanted outside."

Vance wasn't about to move. Actually, if he did decide to move, it was probably to punch Nate smack in the nose. Kerensa squirmed uncomfortably under the pressure of both men and their heightened testosterone.

She sighed. "It's alright, Nate, I want to speak to Vance also…in private, please."

*Like hell, in private.*

"I can't stop you from talking to him, Kerensa, but I'm not going anywhere."

Nate faced Vance. "You want to talk, than talk." Nate folded his arms and stared into Vance's eyes. Nate knew how to look mighty dangerous when he wanted to.

Kerensa didn't argue that point with Nate, and it made him realize that she felt better with him there. So he simply stood there in silence.

Vance fidgeted under the pressure, but he realized it was as good as it was going to get. He sucked in a deep breath, and spoke.

"Kerensa I'm really sorry about what happened last week. I've done a lot of thinking, and I made a big mistake. I-I really love you, honey." Vance sucked in more breath. "And I miss you very much."

For some strange reason, Kerensa focused on the word *mistake*. It seemed as though she had the cornerstone when it came to mistakes being made around her, and with her and in her personal relationships. As a matter of fact, it was quite apparent that every major crisis in her life had to do with a man.

And a mistake.

She suddenly realized that she hadn't said a word to Vance. He was still looking at her, a perplexed expression across his features. It was time she faced the truth with him.

"I'm sorry Vance, but everything you said to me last week was true. I really don't know what I want or who I love." She shrugged her shoulders as she forced away the tears from springing behind her eyes. "I can't be your fiancé anymore. It-it just wouldn't be fair to you…or me." She cleared her throat, and chewed on her bottom lip. "I hope you can forgive me."

Nate surmised that Vance was in some catatonic state of shock, because he didn't move, flinch or even blink. Nate was ready to wave his hand across his eyes when suddenly Vance's face turned lobster claw red.

*Whoa, what a bummer. He pours his heart out in front of me and makes himself look like a complete idiot.*

But Vance wasn't finished yet. "Look, Kerensa, I know what kind of pressure you must be under right now, so I just want you to think about this before you make a final decision."

*Oh Jesus.*

Nate saw the flash of anger in Kerensa's thunderstorm eyes. Maybe he better go inside and find Nana and Janelle, he was beginning to need some reinforcements and dependable backup. As if on cue, the studio door opened and there stood Nana, with Janelle in her arms. Janelle squealed when she saw both men, but she tried to jump out of Nana's arms for Nate to hold her. *That's right, Nate.*

He reached out and took her away from Nana.

"Come on, sweetheart, let's go back inside."

Janelle hugged Nate's neck. "Where's Mr. Ick?" She asked.

Vance turned around and walked away from all of them. It was apparent to him that he had lost out on any future with Kerensa. Hell, even Janelle didn't want him anymore.

Nate watched Robertson's retreating back and actually felt a tinge of empathy for him. He studied Kerensa's brave little face and knew that she was going to cry her eyes out *as usual,* as soon as she was away from everybody. But somehow he didn't think her tears were going to be just about Vance Robertson, ex-fiancé.

He followed her gaze as it rested on Stone, ex-heartbreaker extraordinaire.

# 21

They were talking all around her again. Talking about her, making decisions without her input, future plans that she didn't have a clue about, and she felt totally invisible, like she wasn't even sitting there on the couch. Actually, she was indiscernible to them and that's what pissed her off the most. They were all back in her living room and it felt just like ground hog day all over again. Except Nate was there this time.

"Sammy Jackson died from a fatal gunshot wound to the head, execution style. That doesn't match the style of the sniper, Muhammad Ruger..." It was Stone talking and Donovan arguing with him. Of course, Donovan wouldn't be arguing if he knew that Sammy Jackson was killed after Stone killed Ruger.

Really now, how could a dead man kill him?

"...We are dealing with an entirely different situation, and an entirely different killer." Stone concluded, shooting a quick glance in Nate's direction.

It was Nate's cue to chime in.

"Was there any evidence collected at the crime scene?"

Now it was Donovan's turn to look at Robertson. Robertson bristled.

"No, I don't think there's anything we can really work with... well not yet anyway."

*Yea, right, just as I predicted, Nate thought.*

"The back door to Kerensa's studio was tampered with. It should have activated her security alarm. I want to know why she wasn't notified."

There was an unusual silence in the room. Stone's eyes were burning that eerie blue—black light again and they were staring directly at Vance.

Vance refused to be intimidated by Stone. "The call did come through from the security company; Kerensa has me as her backup. When I received the call, I went to the studio and checked it out. There wasn't anything unusual there, or on the premises so I instructed them to reset the alarm."

"There were many 'unusual' clues Detective Robertson, not to mention the dead body about a hundred yards from the back door."

Stone was doing his thing again, pushing those buttons that forced even a saint to commit murder. He was doing a mighty fine job.

"I checked every inch of the premises, and I can vouch that the body wasn't there when the alarm was set off." Vance was trying to stay calm with every fiber of his being, but Kerensa could see his face slowly turning red.

"That dead body was there just as sure as the dent in the back door was there. They planned on dumping the body in her studio but the alarm activated forcing them to dump the body outside and getting out of there as soon as possible. You didn't check the premises well enough, and you damn well know it. You didn't care, Detective Robertson, and you're letting your personal issues get in the way of this investigation." Stone turned his deadly gaze on Donovan.

"I want Robertson off this case."

Kerensa moaned softly beneath her breath. Talk about feeling half helpless and the other half numb. Part of her wanted to come to Vance's rescue, but the other part didn't have the energy to say a word.

Donovan cleared his throat, choosing his words very carefully.

"I realize that Detective Robertson could have made better choices regarding this situation, but I do not feel he lost focus regarding the seriousness of this case. I am not removing him, at least not at this time." Donovan glanced at Vance. "If you make any other inappropriate decisions or any oversights that could cause this case to be compromised, you will answer to me."

Nate could tell by the blaze in Stone's eyes that he wasn't finished yet. He couldn't wait to see what natural disaster was coming next.

"You should have notified Kerensa regarding that alarm; it's her studio, not yours and I expect you to follow the orders of your supervisor."

Stone didn't wait for Vance to respond, he rose to his feet, indicating that their little get-together was over. Vance stormed out the door without even a sidelong glance or a goodbye. Donovan nodded his head in acknowledgement and left behind Vance.

Kerensa continued to remain quiet on the couch, with Janelle finally asleep on her lap. She wasn't feeling very calm inside; her guts were churning like a tub of sour butter. She had an inclination that the real argument was going to occur after both Chief Donovan and Detective Robertson left the house. It was strange how she thought of Vance as a detective first now, instead of the man she once loved. *Well, thought she loved... Whatever.*

Stone sat back down again, this time closer to Kerensa. She knew he was checking off the next item on his *to do* list. She also knew that she was the next item.

"We need to discuss our plan of action," Stone replied, still all business. "I don't know who killed Sammy Jackson and I could only presume I know why. My concern is that the rules have changed and it's difficult to speculate how many agenda's are out there now."

*How many agenda's? I think you mean how many killers.*

Kerensa could feel that churn in her belly again. It was threatening to bring the bile up to her throat. She tried to take some deep breaths, and kissed the top of her little girls head. *Breathe, breathe, breathe, she reminded herself.*

"So what are you trying to say?" she croaked out.

"You're not going to New Jersey, Kerensa; you will have to make other arrangements." And then as an afterthought he added, "sorry."

She sat there motionless and just stared at him. He couldn't be serious, could he?

"You've got to be kidding me, Dominick, it's almost impossible for me to back out now!"

Stone was about as sensitive as a brick wall. "No, I'm not kidding, and you will have to figure out the best way to solve this problem. But you will not be participating in the nationals at New Jersey this year. It's much too risky; Kerensa and I will not jeopardize anyone's life for the sake of a..." Stone was suddenly at a loss of words, but before he could continue, Kerensa finished his sentence for him.

"-Of a what, Dominick? Of a stupid dance? Isn't that what you were going to say?"

Nate looked at Nana and shook his head in frustration.

Stone was at it again, the fox in the house of chickens, devouring everything in his sight. Nate leaned forward, resting his hand on her knee. "Listen to me, Kerensa. I want you to put Janelle to bed, and come back in here and have a decent discussion regarding this issue. Getting upset about it isn't going to make it work out any better."

*And you sure as hell aren't going to change Stone's mind.*

Kerensa sighed, carefully scooping up her little girl and taking her into the bedroom. As soon as she was out of sight, Nate turned on Stone.

"Lighten up; you're coming down way too hard on her." Nate glanced over at Nana and was surprised to see how quiet she was.

Stone wasn't about to be anything but his usual not so delightful, self. "Yea, well you better use that prince charming personality of yours on her then, because if she doesn't agree to this, you haven't begun to see how tough I'm going to be."

Stone glanced in Nana's direction as if to apologize for his behavior.

She nodded her head in agreement, and it was suddenly apparent to Stone that Nana didn't want Kerensa to go to New Jersey either. *Do whatever it takes, Dominick, wasn't that what she had said?*

Twenty minutes later, Kerensa came back into the room with her boxing gloves on. Stone recognized that look on her face immediately. The problem was, he didn't have any more patience left and his bag of tricks had a big hole in it.

She began talking before anyone had a chance to say a word; her tone was sharp as a tack.

"I don't see how Sammy Jackson's death had anything to do with me." Stone bristled, and the air became thirty degrees colder. He responded with an icy stillness to his tone. "Sammy Jackson didn't die, Kerensa, he was murdered, and yes it could have plenty to do with you."

She glared into Stone's back, sending a silent *'please rescue me'* plea to both Nate and Nana.

Nana decided it was time to end this argument. "Kerensa, I don't think you should be arguing with Dominick about going to New Jersey. He doesn't think it's safe. End of discussion."

Nate stared at Nana, impressed with her no frills summation.

Stone was pretty awed too.

Kerensa slumped into the chair, closing her eyes and covering her face. "I can't disappoint these children, what am I going to do?"

"Who says you have to disappoint the children?" Nate asked quietly.

"What do you mean?" there was a scowl across her smooth features.

"Well, you've got friends, don't any of them dance?"

Kerensa pondered Nate's question for several moments. "Yes, my friend Sandra dances."

"Does she teach?"

Kerensa nodded her head, *yes.*

"Then I believe you've answered your own question."

"But that's a lot to ask. She's got less than two weeks to learn all the dances and maybe she'll be too busy or she may not be able to go out of town that weekend or…"

"Jesus Christ, Kerensa, shut up and pick up the damn phone. Call her; we'll worry about the details later."

Kerensa sighed, reaching for the telephone and going into the other room to get the number. Nana decided to head into the kitchen to fix a light dinner and some coffee.

*Stone couldn't help but wonder how Nate could talk to Kerensa like that and get away with it. She would have added yet another year onto his eight year sentence.*

Once both women left the room, Stone started in again. "I'm not finished with her yet, so I suggest you keep up the good cop, bad cop act."

Nate groaned softly. "What other earth shattering news are you going to lay on her?"

"I'm getting her out of here, first flight in the morning."

Nate raised his eyebrows, waiting for the part where Stone was going to tell him what his next assignment was, or if he would be tagging along.

"I'm taking her back to Buffalo, that's where she should have been from the beginning."

"She's not going to go, Stone; I know that for a fact." Nate was shaking his head, dreading the moment when she found out.

"Either she comes willingly, or she doesn't, but she's still going. This situation has spun totally out of control; I don't know whose out to get her, and who's out to get me anymore. I want her in total seclusion."

"What place are you thinking of?"

"I'm going to put a call out to Sebastian North, he owns a little cabin in Springville, and I figure he can pull some strings for us. He owes me one."

Nate remembered Sebastian and a case they had a couple years ago, it was a pretty wild case and he was one tough dude. He also remembered how Sebastian ended up in a whole heap of trouble. *Oh yea, he definitely owed Stone more than just one, not to mention his life.*

"If you need more backup, you can always call Joseph Salvatore; he's still the cop in Alden. He and Sebastian were in the same Seals unit together. Salvatore got married to Kira a year ago, but he's always looking for a little excitement.

"Well, don't look now, but here she comes," Nate commented, watching Kerensa as she was heading toward them. Her curls were more unruly than usual, and her hair practically covered her small face. She was without a doubt having a bad hair day but it was about to get worse.

"So what's the verdict?" Nate asked.

Kerensa took a deep breath, a smile on her face. "Sandra said she could do it. She's meeting me at the studio tomorrow morning and I'm going to show her all the choreography and she'll get a chance to meet the girls then too."

Nate groaned softly beneath his breath, but not silent enough. Kerensa caught on quickly.

"What's going on, Nate?"

Nate lived by simple rules when the heat was on. You keep your mouth shut and act like you don't know a thing and that's exactly what Nate did.

Kerensa's gaze landed full force on Stone who was quietly watching her. He leaned forward, hoping to gain a little patience when he knew she would freak out. He just couldn't seem to care about that. All he could think about was how much danger he feared she was in. Everything else was insignificant.

He cleared his throat; best thing to do was to plunge right in.

"We're leaving on the first flight to Buffalo in the morning, Kerensa."

He watched the color drain from her face. *That was definitely plunging right in.*

"We can't stay here anymore, it's much too dangerous. I have to get you somewhere far away from everything and everyone. We'll be going to a small town about thirty miles south of Buffalo, there's a cabin we can live in until this problem is solved."

"Problem?" Kerensa whispered the color instantly back in her cheeks again. "Figuring out who could take my students to New Jersey was a problem, what to wear in the morning is a problem, forgetting to pick up a quart of milk on my way home from work is a problem, not having enough money to pay the bills is a problem... being stalked, and someone wanting to kill you and those you love is a hell of a lot more than just a problem!" Her voice escalated with every word she said, and by the time she was finished, she was shouting.

Stone remained as always, level and composed. She hated his ability to process a situation, hated the way he could look at her as though she were a crazy lunatic, hated the hard barrier he constructed that never made him fragile, weak or human, and right about now she just plain hated him.

She stood there glaring at both of them and neither man said a word. She could feel herself unravel, one little inch at a time; she was giving in to Thorne's sick, demented plan allowing him to win the game. She was having a melt down.

And that was the worst thing of all. She began to tremble, and within moments, the tremble turned into a full body shake, even her teeth were chattering. She wasn't sure when the room began to spin, because she was instantly shrouded by strong, steadfast arms that gave her immediate warmth and security.

Stone cradled here against him, and murmured soothing words into her ear. She began to calm down again, and think clearly.

Sometime during this episode, Nana returned into the room to announce that dinner was ready. When Kerensa heard Nana's voice, she finally lifted her head from Stone's chest and attempted to stand to her feet. Nana watched Kerensa's unsteadiness while she followed behind Stone into the kitchen.

"You know what you need, sweetheart," Nana clucked her tongue, as she pulled out the kitchen chair. "You need a sugar fix and I think you should eat the apple pie first."

Kerensa giggled, part hiccup, and part laugh at Nana's theory and Nate simply smiled. He was too busy realizing again that there was no force of nature that could keep Kerensa and Stone apart forever. They were meant to be, as much as he hated that very thought, or the possibility that Kerensa could very well never get over him if they didn't end up together.

It was about time that he, Nathan Lawrence Drake, stopped hoping that she would fall in love with him someday.

# 22

Janelle took turns playing with Nate and Stone all evening. She would sit on Stone's lap for a while, and then she would switch over to Nate's. It was quite comical to see how both men enjoyed every minute of her attention. Janelle, on the other hand was quite brilliant, with just a smile, she figured out a way to get them to do just about anything, even if it meant volunteering to hurl themselves over a bridge if it would make her happy. Oh yes, Janelle was working her audience like a pro, and her mommy could learn a few things from her since Kerensa was sulking most of the night.

There was tightness in her chest she just couldn't find an answer for. Perhaps watching both men laugh with Janelle made her even more melancholy than she already was.

*If that was even possible.*

Perhaps too she was a little resentful that they came into her life again like a short-lived cyclone, disrupting every decision she made, just to get back on their white horses and disappear into the sunset, never to be seen again. And this time they would not only break her heart, but Janelle's as well. *That really sucked.*

Kerensa stood up. "Come on my Nellie, it's time to go to bed."

Janelle wasn't interested in any bedtime plans. "No," she wailed.

"Yes, baby," Kerensa said firmly. "Say goodnight to Mr. Nate and Mr. Ick."

Janelle whined some more and didn't budge an inch, that is until Stone put his colossal hand in hers and with his usual amazing gracefulness, rose to his feet and escorted her to her room. The constriction in Kerensa's chest got a whole lot tighter. Her eyes locked with Nate's.

"A nickel for your thoughts," Nate said.

"It's a penny for your thoughts," she corrected.

Nate grinned. "It's Inflation, sweetheart, now talk to me."

She sighed. "You guys come breezing back into our lives, disrupt our worlds and then you're going to vanish again. I hate what that will do to Janelle."

Nate's smile disappeared. He knew how right Kerensa was.

"And what will it do to you?" he softly asked.

This time her eyes filled with tears. Shrugging her shoulders, she turned her back to him. He was about to put his arms around her, when her cell phone rang. *It figures even the forces of fate were against him.*

"Saved by the bell," he murmured. "Let me answer it." *Just in case it's the ex-fiancé from hell.*

But it wasn't. Her voice was sweet, and soft and for some ungodly reason, shot straight to his groin.

"Here," Nate responded, handing Kerensa the phone. "Say's her name is Jade, and she's a friend."

Kerensa's face lit up like a full moon as she grabbed the phone from him. "Jade, how are you!"

Jade laughed, equally as excited. "I'm doing great, and I miss you."

Kerensa nodded her head in agreement as if Jade could see. "So what's going on?"

"I was wondering if I could pick Janelle up tomorrow so she can spend the day with me."

Kerensa hesitated; not really wanting to tell her what a mess her life had become, and yet Jade was one of the few people she could ever trust. She didn't dare look at Nate; she could tell already how intently he was staring at her.

So she decided to tell her the truth, or at least a very condensed version. She left out the part where anyone was trying to kill her; she left out the part about body guards and Jonathan Thorne because that would certainly be a long drawn out fraction of the story, but she did end up telling her that she needed to get away because there were personal problems that may place her and Janelle in danger. She also told her what airlines she was flying out of, and what time. All the while she was talking to her; Nate was in her face making gestures for her to cut off the conversation. She ignored him.

When she was finished, she promised Jade that as soon as she came back to Miami she would call her and then they would make arrangements for Janelle to go over to her house for the day. When Kerensa was finally off the phone, Nate was all over her.

"What the hell is the matter with you?" he asked his tone furious.

"Look, I trust Jade with my life. She's a wonderful friend *and ex-sister in law* and has a heart of gold. Now you sound a little paranoid, even to me, Nate."

Nate could feel the blood rush to his head.

"Did it ever occur to you that a cell phone can still be monitored?"

Kerensa paled. *No, I hadn't thought of that.*

When Kerensa didn't answer with her voice, but instead with the tone of her very ashen skin, Nate sighed.

"Forget about it, Kerensa, I'm just being extremely careful. I suggest everyone turn in early. I know I'm bushed. By the way, did you call Sandra back and tell her there's been a change of plans again."

Kerensa nodded her head, the look in her eyes silently apologizing to Nate for her lack of good judgment. If it had been Stone, she would have worn a big *stupid* across her forehead for the rest of her life. "Yea, I told her that I had to call the students and temporarily suspend the classes for a few days. I asked her if she would be willing to do it next week."

"Good, it's a day by day situation, you know that Kerensa."

"Don't get me started, Nate. I guess I should just say goodnight and get it over with it."

Nate nodded his head and then grinned. "So, is the friend of yours attached?"

"Who are you talking about, Sandra?" she asked with a twinkle in her eye.

"No, I mean Jade."

Kerensa smiled deviously. "Yes and no."

"How much of it is a *no*?"

This time she laughed. "I would say about fifty percent."

"I can live with that. So, what does she look like?"

"She's really pretty in a sort of unconventional way."

*Unconventional way, what the hell does that mean?*

Nate huffed. "Why do women always have to answer that question in riddles? I mean, why can't you just say, yes, she's gorgeous, or no, she's a dog and leave it at that?"

Before she could answer, Stone came back into the room.

"Say yes about what?" He asked.

Nate shook his head. "Nothing, is Janelle asleep?"

Stone glanced at Kerensa. "Yea, she wanted me to tell her a bedtime story."

*Bedtime story? Somehow Kerensa couldn't imagine Stone telling her little girl a sappy bedtime story. It was probably something that included Minnie Mouse and her arsenal of weapons.*

"Did you?" she asked.

"Sort of, at least it was my version of a bedtime story."

"She better not have any nightmares tonight, Dominick."

Stone chuckled softly, but didn't say a word. With a little bit of luck, nobody would have any nightmares tonight.

\*\*\*

*She was running again. This time it was freezing outside, and she didn't have any shoes on her feet. She was dressed in her pink tank top and silk shorts and there was snow on the ground. Lots of it.*

*She was breathing hard too, her breath swirling around her like small puffs of smoke, reminding her of how terribly cold she was. And she was crying. She could hear her voice like it was coming from a distance though, not from her mouth, and it sounded like Janelle.*

*Janelle's voice was begging him to leave her alone too, screaming at him to go away, and the faster Kerensa ran, the closer he came.*

*It was dark outside, only a sliver of a moon and the white of the snow to show her the way. But she already knew the way; she had been through this area already, many, many times. Soon there would be a turn in the path, it would lead downward into a steep gully, and then to the swamp. But she must not get to the swamp, because that's where he'll catch up to her, and this time he will kill her.*

*"No!" She screamed. "No, no, no, no..."*

*She was fighting him, digging her fingers into his flesh and pushing him as hard as she could away from her.*

*"Stop it," he was demanding, "I won't hurt you."*

*His voice, although firm, was gentle and kind...And she knew that voice.*

Kerensa's eyes popped open and she found herself staring into Stone's very blue, very worried eyes.

"Oh my God, Dominick, I was having this horrible..."

"Nightmare, I know Kerensa. I heard you scream so I came in."

She swallowed hard, but couldn't speak another word.

Nate heard her cry out too, but Stone made it to her room first, and the look that exchanged between them was very territorial, a little too territorial.

He was in her bedroom now, instead of Nate, holding her trembling, cold body in the dark. *Why was she so cold?*

"Kerensa, you're freezing."

"I was barefoot in the snow, he was chasing me again."

"Is this the dream you used to have?" he asked her quietly, ignoring her difficulty to connect her dream to reality.

She nodded her head against his chest.

"Who is he, sweetheart?"

She began to tremble more, her small body shaking wildly until finally, she replied, "he's death, Dominick."

Her words kicked him hard in the gut.

"Nobody is going to hurt you, Kerensa, let alone kill you." His tone was thick with sentiment, it was gentle and kind and it helped to soothe her frightened soul.

She began to cry again, and he held her, waited for her to take a deep breath to talk to him.

"This time Janelle was in the dream," she choked out; her tone was so soft he could barely hear her. "And I'm so terrified."

Stone could feel that protective stir in his chest again. It was beginning to have a semblance of similarity and he knew that wasn't a good thing.

"I won't let anyone near Janelle, she's safe," he reassured.

She nodded her head and took a deep breath.

Her nightgown was thin and he felt the softness of her breasts and her hard nipples pressing against his bare chest as she breathed in deeply. It instantly had an affect on him, and he knew he needed to get the hell out of there, fast.

"You'll be alright now," he murmured, his tone almost harsh.

"I know you want to leave, Dominick, but don't…please don't."

*I can't just lie beside you; I want to be inside you.*

"If I stay, I'm not just going to hold you; I'm going to make love to you."

Kerensa felt an instant sensation, a bolt of electricity right down to her toes.

"Then do it. Make love to me, Dominick."

She didn't have to say it twice. Stone groaned softly, and lifted himself off the bed. He quietly pushed her bedroom door closed and turned the bolt. Then he came back to the bed and folded her possessively into his arms.

How long had he fantasized about this moment? His fantasies were all he had for so long, they encompassed every imaginable position he could put her in, he took her hard and fast in his fantasies, and he took her slow and soft, exploring every inch of her. Oh yea, he knew the answer to that question, *probably every single night for the last eight freaking years.*

He found her soft, sweet lips immediately, claiming them hungrily and slipping his tongue into her mouth. She reciprocated with the same need as her hands slowly caressed every indentation, every hard outline of his muscles that spanned across his shoulders and upper chest. He ran his hands through her hair, loving how her curls spun around his fingers and wouldn't let go. His hands traveled slowly across her breasts, her firm belly and the graceful curve of her hips. He slipped his hands behind her, lifting her to him. His lips trailed down her neck, across the soft, silken skin of her firm, round breasts.

*Just this once, he bargained. Let me make love with this beautiful woman just one more time again. Let me hold her in my arms and feel her, taste her, get my fill of her…*

He tugged at her nightgown, quickly slipping it over her head. When he took her into his arms again, he knew he was lost. He also knew something else, and the realization was far worse than he could ever imagine.

He would never get his fill of her, not now, not ever.

***

Nate lay awake in bed in the room next to Kerensa's. He heard the door as it quietly closed, heard the latch on the door lock the world outside. Lock him outside.

*Son of a bitch.*

He was pissed, and it took every ounce of his being not to kick that door down, not to drag Kerensa out of that bed and take her somewhere else, anywhere else, as long as it was safe and not with Dominick Stone. This was the first time since Nate met Stone that he passed judgment on him. As soon as that door closed, it gave him the fucking right to judge him. And Stone had better make damn sure that he did right by Kerensa this time, because this time Nate Drake would be watching and this time, Nate Drake wasn't going to let Dominick Stone get away with anything.

*Not this time.*

***

Kerensa never actually did fall back to sleep, perhaps because they never actually did stop making love. It was nearly dawn when he slipped out of her bed, barely making a sound. She awoke instantly, a sudden feeling of loneliness washing over her like a tidal wave. Her eyes fluttered open when he softly kissed her on the cheek, reminding her much too clearly of the last time they spent the night together. Yea, the last time he probably kissed her on the cheek just like this, and was gone for eight years.

*Geez,* she was certainly batting a zero.

*Stupid-stupid-stupid-stupid.*

There were hundreds of other adjectives for her to choose from, what was she thinking, was she out of her ever loving mind? And that came to her mind too.

They all but devoured each other all night. She still had the scent of him on her skin, she could still feel his strong, masterful hands as they aroused her past any self control, stimulated her into another dimension…

Fucked her, that's what he did. Say it was making love, hell, call it anything you want to, deny it all you want, but she needed to face the truth. And she knew what that was. He simply fucked her, and left her. Again.

It would be different if she wanted it that way too, but she didn't. Even if she tried, she could never settle for Dominick Stone to come and go as he pleased in her life. She deserved better, and she knew it.

She stared at the bedroom door and felt the bed sheets beside her now cool to the touch. She needed to strip the bed, and she needed to get up and take a shower.

She needed to wash him away.

# 23

Their flight was scheduled to leave at ten o'clock in the morning. She had a little over an hour to get her and Janelle packed, Janelle and herself dressed, and eat breakfast. All the while her thoughts were still on last night and if that wasn't bad enough every time she almost thought of the present, the soreness in her body would betray her all over again.

Kerensa sat down at the table, cup of coffee in hand. Janelle wasn't very hungry, and she was barely eating her breakfast. Nana was working, or attempting to work her magic on her. So far, she was unsuccessful.

Kerensa tried to avoid making eye contact with Stone. It was fairly easy to do, since he was avoiding her too. However, evading Nate was another story.

She glanced away from her coffee cup her eyes colliding with Nate's like a runaway freight train. His gaze was hard, and unrelenting. She had never seen him looking like that. It was unnerving, and she recognized instantly that he knew exactly what went on last night. *Oh, dear God.*

She groaned silently to herself. She would eventually have to face the music with him too, but not right now. She didn't have the emotional energy. So she did the next best thing, she pushed away from the table excused herself and practically ran down the hallway into her bedroom to finish packing.

It was no surprise that Nate was right behind her. She tried to remain calm and nonchalant, as she began piling more clothes into her suitcase. That was particularly hard to do since he was two feet away from her and in her face.

"I don't want to talk about it, Nate."

Nate leaned backward against the dresser. "Oh, I'm sure you don't. But guess what? You are going to talk to me."

199

Kerensa sighed, she had never seen him like this, and it was a real eye opener. He suddenly played the role of the ex-marine, gone cop and Stone's tough partner to a tee. He was glaring at her now, his finely tuned body tense and on edge. His arms were crossed, his short sleeved tee shirt showing enough bulging biceps in his upper arms to prove just how well built he really was. He was standing with his legs stiffly apart and he looked downright perilous.

"We don't have time right now," she softly replied.

Nate didn't respond to that excuse, he suddenly reached out and pulled her around to face him.

"I'm going to tell you my piece, and than I will never say anything about the two of you again. Now look at me, Kerensa."

She sighed in resolution, and tipped her head upward, focusing her eyes on his.

"Stone is like an addiction for you, a really bad one. Now maybe I'm being a little unreasonable because I happen to love you too, but there is one thing I do know. He's not going to commit himself to you, not now, and most likely not ever. If the kind of life you want to have involves a knock on your door in the middle of the night and wondering if you just dreamt it in the morning, then by all means knock yourself out. But I'm a little tired of scraping you off the floor every time he falls off that fucking pedestal you put him on. Learn to say *no* to him, Kerensa. You have no problem saying it to me."

Nate dropped his hands from her shoulders, turned on his heels and walked out of her bedroom.

She stared after Nate for several minutes. If she didn't feel discarded before, she certainly felt abandoned now. She was actually too shocked to respond. She stuffed the rest of her belongings without even paying attention to what she was packing into the suitcase. She had to sit on it just to get it closed.

\*\*\*

Stone followed every move Nate made watching him while he followed Kerensa out of the kitchen. He wondered when Nate would confront him about last night too, and he knew it was coming. Although this situation had one hundred percent of both his, and Nate's attention, Stone knew that what happened between him and Kerensa last night was going to be a real issue with Nate. It was complicated for him too, but he put it out of his mind for the present time. He needed to concentrate on this crisis, especially if they wanted everyone to walk away from this situation, alive.

Thorne was out there somewhere and most likely he wasn't leaving his home at all. Owning a computer could change all that. He networked with a lot of people, and he undoubtedly planned several layers of backup to qualify him to the next level. Stone surely never underestimated his intent, nor did he underestimate his determination to succeed in this game of revenge. But he did underestimate his ability to intricately weave a precarious web of deceit, and retribution.

The problem was that Stone had so many fucking enemies he didn't know who they were or how many people wanted to take him out. Thorne took advantage of that, he calculated a major weak spot in Stone's persona and he played it to the hilt. Thorne's plan was brilliant, but like all plan's, it wasn't foolproof. There was a way to bust this plan too, and Stone knew he would. He didn't have a choice, if anything ever happened to Kerensa or Janelle, Nana would never forgive him.

Stone glanced up at the slightest noise as Nate entered the kitchen again. Stone met his somber gaze. He knew why, too.

"So what were you two talking about?"

Nate didn't look at Stone. "The truth…and you know what that is."

"Since when do you actively participate in my business?" Stone retorted, his tone rigid and cold.

"It's not just your business anymore; it became my business every time you broke her heart, it became my business every time she cried on my shoulder, so that makes it my business this time too."

Stone didn't respond, but he kept his gaze level with Nate's. Nate paused, but then continued, his tone stronger. "You know she deserves better."

Stone nodded his head once in acknowledgement, but still didn't respond.

"Make sure you do right by her this time, Stone, and I mean it." Nate's gaze was narrow, his tone deadly.

"Are you threatening me?" Stone asked quietly.

"Yea," Nate quickly retorted, his brown eyes dark as coal. "You're damn right I am."

Stone nodded his head once again, and watched Nate walk out of the room.

\*\*\*

They parked right in front of the American Airlines terminal, the exact location that had a huge sign above it that read, '*No Parking Allowed At All Times.*' Big surprise, because it should have read, '*No parking allowed at all times unless your name is Dominick Stone.*

Nate, Nana, Kerensa and Janelle walked into the terminal, but Stone headed in the opposite direction. Kerensa watched him as he disappeared from her sight.

"Where's he going?" She asked Nate.

"He's going to familiarize himself with the security operations at this airport." *In other words, he's going to start barking orders at everyone.*

Nate escorted them quickly along, following his own orders to keep walking until they arrived directly to the gate where Stone was to meet them. Then they were going to take a private charter non stop to Buffalo, NY. The airport was extremely busy, people crowding in small and large groups, waiting for rides to their gates, and pushing their way to the baggage pick up. Nate put his arms out to Janelle to see if she would come to him, so Kerensa wouldn't have to carry her. But Janelle wanted to stay with her mama.

Then, Kerensa heard her name being called.

Startled, she turned in the direction of the female voice.

"Oh my goodness, it's Jade," Kerensa exclaimed, surprised and delighted to see her.

Nate was suddenly interested to see if she was just as pretty as her voice had been last night. And she was. Then he kicked back into combat gear, and realized this was a little snafu in the plans. *Actually, it could be a big snafu in the plans.* He quickly spoke into his headset.

"Stone, we have a situation."

Stone responded quickly. "What's going on?"

An old friend of Kerensa's is here to see her off; actually Kerensa spoke to her last night and told her when she was leaving and where."

*When the fuck did all this happen?*

"Get rid of her."

"I will."

Who is she?"

"Her name is Jade."

There was a brief moment, it was a split second of time and yet that's all it took to change the course of everything, to change the course of everyone's lives. *Forever.*

"It's a setup, Nate; get the hell out of there!"

Nate reacted instantly to Stone's directive, pushing his way toward Kerensa, hell; he wasn't even twenty feet away. He yelled out to Kerensa as Jade took Janelle into her arms and hugged her. She turned in Nate's direction, a perplexed expression across her features. Then it was like a slow motion horror flick that was played in fast forward. From out of nowhere came a man, he pushed Nana and grabbed Jade with Janelle still in her arms. It took Nate a brief moment to realize that the man was Jonathan

Thorne, older, a little heavier, and ten times more dangerous.

Nate drew his weapon, but Thorne already had his to Jade's head.

She was crushed against him, one arm wrapped around both Janelle and Jade, the other arm raised, the pistol jammed into Jade's temple.

She screamed, alerting everyone around them. Mere moments passed, people started to shout and run when they saw what was happening. Nate was helpless, he couldn't shoot Jonathan, and it was much too dangerous for Jade and Janelle. They were too close to the exit too; if they had been a little further inside, it would have made Thorne's escape harder. But this was easy, too easy, and perfectly executed, as if someone had written the script.

And Kerensa, she was out of control, trying to get to her baby as Nana was attempting to hold her back. It wasn't even ten seconds, that's all it took to be over. Thorne pushed Jade out the door and inside an emergency vehicle that was idling at the curb.

Stone arrived outside just as the SUV pulled away.

*A Perfect plan, right down to the last detail.*

Kerensa couldn't stop screaming, it was partly because she was in shock, and partly because she was so damn helpless. One minute she had her little girl safely in her arms, the next moment she was gone. Her baby was crying, reaching out for her mama and screaming at the top of her lungs.

"Oh my God, my baby!" Kerensa shrieked, over and over again.

There was a flurry of commotion, Nate was nearby but why wasn't he doing anything? Why was Nana holding her back, didn't she see that Janelle was in danger? And where was Dominick, he was supposed to protect them, protect her little Janelle.

"Oh my God, my baby. Oh my God, my baby. Oh my God, my baby…"

# 24

Ground hog day again, the scene too familiar, a crowded living room, Chief Donovan and Vance Robertson sitting on the sofa, Nate, in one corner of the room in a straight back chair, and Stone in the other corner. Nana and Kerensa were sitting on the small sofa in each other's arms. This time they were both crying.

But no Janelle.

*Oh sweet Jesus, no Janelle.*

There was a lot of tension in the room, Chief Donovan was pushing his weight around and demanding that Stone tell him every detail regarding the situation. Stone wasn't saying a word, but he had that '*bad—to—the—bone,*' look in his eyes again. Nate could tell that he was going to do whatever he damn well needed to do to get Janelle back. Nate also knew that Jonathan wasn't going to see another sunrise. He was as good as dead already.

Thorne's plan was now crystal clear. Nate kept going over the circumstances blow by blow in his head. There were a few holes in the picture, but overall, Nate knew that Thorne had factored in one option none of them thought of, another woman, and a friend that Kerensa trusted.

Nate glanced over at Stone again. He wasn't responding to what Donovan was saying, and he sure as hell wasn't bothering with Robertson, he was however, watching Kerensa, just as Nate was. Then Stone's eyes met Nate's. Nate knew that look, and it was time they got rid of the local boys before they got any more bright ideas.

Vance cleared his throat and spoke again. "I'm calling in the FBI we need their help." *Oops, too late already.*

"We don't need the FBI," Stone growled.

Vance kept talking as though Stone didn't say a word.

*Big mistake.*

"We do need the Feds, this is a kidnapping and Jonathan Thorne is now a fugitive. We need the FBI's help."

Stone leveled his deadly gaze on Vance. "I am the FBI; I am the CIA and everything in between including in charge of this investigation. You are also wasting my time right now, so if you'll excuse me this meeting is over."

Stone rose to his feet, looking down at Donovan and Vance like they were two ants in his toy farm. Nate knew Stone couldn't wait to get rid of them so he could find out where Jonathan Thorne, psychopathic freak and future dead man, was hiding out. Fugitive or not, kidnapping or not, Stone wasn't following any rules, and he certainly wasn't taking any prisoners.

Kerensa was lost, although her heart was broken and she was in major denial, she suddenly saw everything clearer than she ever did in her entire life. Her baby was kidnapped by a devious, sick, demented man and she had no control over it. She was helpless, she had to depend on the law to save her child, or she could depend on Stone and Nate, the two man army. Her money was on the two man army. She watched as Stone carried out his usual, '*don't-begin-to-mess-with-me look*'. She watched him stand up, dismissing Donovan and Vance without even a blink of an eye. Kerensa was surprised that Donovan allowed Stone to send him away, and she watched as he dragged Vance out the door with him.

*Once outside, Donovan told Vance that Stone could put together a team that was a hell of a lot more powerful than the Miami-Dade police department.*

As soon as the door closed behind them, both men sprang into action. Stone began making several phone calls and by the tone of each conversation, they varied from connections that were down right scary, to high profile government officials. It didn't make a bit of difference to Kerensa who he was talking to, with each call came the hope that Janelle would be found safe and unharmed.

Kerensa tried hard to focus on the present, tried hard not to think about her baby and where she was. The fact that she was with Jade was a small comfort to her.

Suddenly the conversation between Stone and Nate caught her undivided attention yanking her mind to the here and now.

"It's likely that Thorne will make contact soon. The question is going to be where," Stone replied, drinking his tenth cup of coffee. "I have several internet sites being monitored, there's a possibility he may send some live pictures on some of the more obscure sites."

A small sob escaped Kerensa's lips as she suddenly thought of a live feed of something involving her baby girl, something…horrifying. Both men glanced quickly in her direction, but Nate had a compassionate expression on his face, Stone wasn't so warm and cuddly.

"I'm sorry…" Nate began, but Stone bluntly interrupted.

"If you can't handle this conversation, Kerensa, then I suggest you go somewhere else. I know how harsh that sounds, but I can't worry about every word I say just because you may not be able to deal with it." Stone didn't wait for a response, although he cast a glance at Nana before he turned away.

Nana remained silent and calmed Kerensa down with a quick finger to her lips. Nana knew that her daughter would react angrily to Stone's statement, but there was a time and a place to pick a battle. All Nana wanted was for Stone to concentrate on finding her precious granddaughter and besides that, he did have a good point. They needed to discuss their plans as well as their concerns, freely. *And Nana wanted to hear every word.*

Stone disappeared into the kitchen and returned back with another cup of coffee.

Nana mentally counted the cups and was glad that she had a double pot going, four more cups to go. She settled in, paying close detail to both men. Stone was talking again.

"Somewhere along the way, Thorne met Jade and she must have trusted him enough to feel comfortable with him."

Nate thought for a moment. "Yea, either that, or Jade was somehow involved with Thorne's plan."

"Highly unlikely," Stone replied at the same time that Kerensa responded with, "Jade would never get involved in anything that could hurt us."

Nate looked at both of them, raising one eyebrow.

Kerensa looked at Stone.

"Do you know Jade?" She asked.

Stone cleared his throat. "We met the day I went looking for the sniper, *although the sniper had a name, Stone liked it better not personalizing him.* I went to the building where I figured the shots were coming from. Jade was the security guard there. Now it all makes sense. The sniper had a connection to that building and he somehow had a connection to Jade. Most likely, that connection was through Thorne. Jade never knew or saw the sniper. She must have told Thorne about her job, and the security, even about the camera that was on the roof."

Stone paused a moment, deep in thought. "Picking that building was no coincidence, as a matter of fact, I'll bet Thorne researched everything he could possibly find out about Jade, and once he established that she was single, he knew just how to worm himself in."

Stone turned his head toward Kerensa. She was looking chalk stick, white. "Did she talk about a new boyfriend?"

Kerensa shook her head, *no,* but then remembered something that Jade had said to her last night.

"Jade said that she had a surprise for me, but she wasn't going to tell me what it was. She said I would find out soon enough." Her voice slipped away when she said those last few words, her living nightmare coming back into her cognitive thinking full force. She turned her face away from both men.

Stone swore softly beneath his breath. "I was with Jade about an hour that day, she's smart, damn smart *even if it takes her a few extra minutes,* and she's bold that's for sure. Thorne conned her with that sick charm of his." Stone looked at Kerensa again and it nearly killed him to see the pain that reflected in her eyes.

"Just like the night you met Thorne, remember?"

Oh, but she did remember. She remembered his charismatic smile on the evening she first met him, his attentiveness, and the way he kept complimenting how beautiful she was…oh yes, she remembered, every last crazy detail. She also forgot that Stone was talking to her, and she simply nodded her head in response, swallowing to push the vomit back down her throat again.

Stone was watching her for a few moments before he directed his next statement to Nate. "I know Thorne is going to contact us, I'm just not sure what his demands may be."

"I'm not sure if it's about the money anymore," Nate responded.

"I think you're right," Stone agreed. "It's not about the money. He may demand a ransom but he took a risk now. He violated his parole, and committed a major felony; he knows that when he gets caught, he'll be going away for a long time."

*Actually, he'll never live to see prison.*

Stone suddenly turned his gaze on Kerensa, his eyes intensely blue. "Tell me about your ex-husband."

Kerensa was shocked by his question, her eyebrows rose in silent query, and her face twisted in a perplexed frown. It took her a few moments to respond.

"You met him, Dominick; you know what kind of a man he is. Where are you going with that question?"

Stone didn't answer, and it was his intention not to respond. He simply fixed his eyes on her and waited for her to say more. She hated when he did that.

"I already told you the Connor and Kerensa fairy tale. He never wanted a baby, so when I had Janelle, she was only a couple months old when I packed her up and moved us back in with Nana. Connor may be a real bastard, but he wouldn't kidnap Janelle or hurt her."

Stone turned his gaze to Nana, silently expecting her input too. He wasn't disappointed.

"Connor is just a very superficial, egotistical man, Dominick, but he's not a danger to anyone. I don't think he would hurt Janelle, or strike a deal with Jonathan just to save a few bucks on his child support."

*Bingo! Nana knew just where I was going.*

Stone cracked a small smile. He agreed that Connor didn't seem to be involved in any conspiracy theory either. This meant on to the next puzzle.

"Do you know of anywhere Jonathan Thorne could take Janelle. Think about any abandoned buildings, warehouses, apartments or homes."

*Abandoned, oh my God, that's what I've done. I've abandoned my baby!*

Stone was waiting for her answer, and he could tell she was in zombie land again.

So he swore beneath his breath again. He hated this feeling of vulnerability, even if it would be short lived. He was a powerful man, a man in control, and it wasn't just what he did, it was who he was, feelings of insecurity and helplessness were foreign to him. There was something else foreign to him too. The paternal feeling he had for Janelle. *Oh shit, he couldn't get out of this deep, pit he fell into the moment he laid eyes on Kerensa again; he couldn't get out no matter how hard he tried. He was buried well past the point of return.* Janelle was more to him than Kerensa's little girl. He loved her, just as he loved her mommy.

He studied Kerensa's face, and in one sweeping glance noticed her pale cheeks and blood shot eyes. He could tell she wasn't concentrating on his question; her brain wasn't even plugged in. So he turned to Nana instead.

"How well did you know Jade?" He asked.

Nana only thought for a brief moment. "Fairly well, Kerensa was quite close to her during her marriage with Connor and after they divorced. She visited often."

"Good," Stone responded, "Then Janelle will feel safe with her."

Kerensa heard his statement and was glad that Stone was attempting to make her feel better. She took a deep breath, she needed to concentrate, think about where they could have gone.

208

*Abandoned buildings or warehouses? Think, Kerensa, Think.*

Suddenly Stone's phone rang, and Kerensa's bottom jumped about a foot off the chair.

He pulled it out, checked the ID and replied, "Yea, it's Stone, what's going on?"

"It's Chief Donovan. They found the SUV Thorne used to kidnap them. It's been abandoned on the interstate, about ten miles from Sunrise. The vehicle is being checked for evidence now. They had one of those blue lights that firefighter's use when they're responding to an emergency. It gave them the chance to drive twice as fast and everyone else just got out of the way."

Stone swore again. *There was something to be said about how many times you could say the word, 'fuck', in one breath. Stone was winning the game.*

"Who's the vehicle registered to?"

"A guy who reported it stolen two days ago and he wasn't a firefighter."

"It doesn't matter," Stone snarled. "You can buy those blue lights anywhere. Keep me posted." Stone hung up his phone.

He ran his hands through his loose hair, and spoke, this time directing his attention to Nana again.

"I've got a few guys coming this way; I hope it's alright with you."

Kerensa looked at Nana; she caught the sly grin that landed on her lips before disappearing a little too soon. *Oh goody, more guns.*

She could tell that Stone caught it too, making her smile inwardly for a brief moment.

"When will they be here?" Nana asked.

Stone glanced at his watch, and it was already two o'clock. "They should be arriving by late evening, but don't worry about any sleeping arrangements."

Stone continued, knowing how Nana could switch gears from being axe murderer, Lizzie Borden, to baking home made peach cobbler and ice cream.

Nana nodded her head already thinking about where she could find more blankets and even a sleeping bag or two.

Kerensa was still trying to think about where there may be any deserted buildings and hopeful that Stone believed Thorne wouldn't leave the Florida area. And Nate was waiting for Stone to tell him what that last phone call was about, and what their next plan of action was going to be.

Oh yea, there were so many different thoughts flying around in everybody's heads, but there was a common knowledge on everyone's mind. They knew that time was of the essence now if they wanted to save Janelle and Jade and it was still going to be a very long, frustrating night.

# 25

Jade was trembling and it wasn't because she was cold. She held little Janelle tightly within her arms, cradling her and protecting her against that sick, possessed man, a man she allowed herself to fall for, to trust, and to make matters even worse, the information she so naively supplied him with, became the actual plan for their kidnapping. Could she have been any stupider? Or any less aware of what Jonathan Thorne was really doing while courting her, schmoosing her and making her feel like she was the best thing that ever happened to him. He was laughing as he told her the sick, demented story of his life. Laughing… while he told her who Kerensa was to him and why she didn't deserve to live, why her little girl didn't deserve to live. All the while, Jade kept thinking of how she knew there were people like him in this world, but feeling really naive that she actually didn't have a clue.

She groaned aloud, and Janelle stirred in her arms. She tightened her hold on her niece, softly kissing the top of her head.

"It's going to be alright, baby," she whispered, "I promise."

And she meant that, every single word. She was determined to beat Jonathan at his own demented game, and he really didn't know the real Jade Alexander. She wasn't all soft and mushy and obtuse. She was one tough lady, and this son of a bitch wasn't going to hurt either one of them.

She was already developing her own plan, and with a little help from above, she knew the best way to execute it. But first, she needed to show him she was terrified, that way he would continue to think she wasn't capable of pulling the wool over his eyes. *Fake it till you make it.*

She ran the details of their abduction over and over again, in her head.

After he took them by gunpoint, he pushed them inside an SUV that was driven by a guy she never saw before. But she got a quick look at his face before Thorne screamed at her to lie down on the floor and keep her eyes closed. Shortly after, he crawled to the back of the vehicle and blindfolded her. He tried to do the same to Janelle, but she was screaming so loud that Jade was afraid he would hurt her. Jade convinced him to leave the baby alone and she would quiet her down. Jade didn't know how she managed to do just that, but she did. There were a few guardian angels around her that was for sure.

Then she began to count, every single second in her head until they stopped again, 4,224 seconds. And she did the math. It took her around five minutes of soothing before Janelle calmed down and that was when she began to count. All that figured out, she guessed they were around Fort Lauderdale, give or take a few miles. That was when they stopped again and Jonathan instructed her to take the baby and get out. He half pushed, half shoved them into another vehicle. The blindfold was too tight for Jade to move it so she could see what was going on, but the new vehicle was just as big, and she was pushed to the back of it. If she had to guess, she would probably say this vehicle was a van with no windows in it. They drove for another 2,720 seconds, until they came to another stop. This time, she was dragged out of the vehicle without Janelle. She recalled her panic, and she remembered that she began to scream. It was then, that he punched her, right in the face. And that's when she lost any semblance of time. When she awoke, she was right where she is now and thankfully, Janelle was in her arms again. Her blindfold was still on her face, and her face throbbed terribly, compliments of Jonathan Thorne. But Janelle was alright, and again, that's all that counted.

She was afraid to move, straining to hear if she was alone in the room or if someone else was there. Her guess was that she wasn't alone, but it was about time she found out.

"Jonathan, are you here?" She asked, making sure her tone was deliberately sounding panicked.

It worked, she heard him snicker loudly.

"Yes, poor little Jade, I'm here," he cackled.

"It's so warm in here, I'm afraid Janelle is getting dehydrated. Please bring her some water."

Silence.

"Please, Jonathan, if you plan on asking for ransom money, you know they are going to demand that you prove we're alive. Please, give her some water."

Jade heard movement that sounded like Jonathan was getting off a chair.

She heard his footsteps fade away and a door close. Now, was she alone in the room? Her hands were free, but her legs were shackled together with a chain. She knew she could never remove the shackles but if she could adjust her blindfold enough to see anything, just a little piece of where she was, she could memorize it. She practically had a photogenic memory.

She quickly reached up to pull the blindfold upward. It was so tight, and it hurt. She inched it slowly, until she could peer out of the bottom. She raised her head, bending her neck as far back as possible to see through the little opening. The room was darker than she thought so it had to be late afternoon. She was alone in the room too, which surprised her. She slowly turned her head to either side, trying to catch a glimpse of the room. It was empty, but clean, and it looked like an apartment. Jade turned her head again, and tried to glimpse a piece of what was going on outside. It was nondescript, a couple skinny palm trees and then another building. But it still spoke volumes. She now knew that she was on the ground level, she also knew that she was in a small building and it had to be within an urban area because the other building was too close to them.

Jade detected a sound and she quickly pulled the blindfold over her eyes again, glad that she hadn't taken the time to untie it. She would never have tied it again in time.

"Here," Thorne said, pushing a bottle of water into her hand. "You better drink it slow, because that's the only thing you're going to get."

Jade felt for the top, grateful that it was sealed. That solved the problem of the possibility of the water being drugged.

"Will you take the blindfold off me so I can see what I'm doing?"

Thorne didn't respond with words, he simply snickered and Jade knew he wasn't about to fall for that request. She sighed.

"Here, sweetheart, drink some water."

Janelle lifted her head from Jade's chest, and Jade had to feel around to find Janelle's mouth. *Oh God, please don't let this water spill.*

\*\*\*

Kerensa stood by the window in the back patio just staring up at the sky. It was a clear night with plenty of bright, shining stars. She was praying for her little girl again, asking God to please save her precious baby. It seemed as though nothing mattered but Janelle and Jade's safety. She felt brainless and guilty for caring so much about Nationals in New Jersey. That life seemed a world away now, a lifetime that didn't have any real purpose to her. She wondered how it ever did. Crisis and tragedy, she supposed, had a way of putting everything into perspective.

She heard the front door open, and voices, plenty of them drifted her way. They were muffled, all of them speaking in low tones. The army had finally arrived. Stone's army and it was apparent to Kerensa that his army wasn't like any law enforcement she had ever known. It was also crystal clear to her now that she and Dominick could never end up together either. They really were from different sides of life. And so was Nate. She saw another side of him now too. He just knew how to candy coat everything like M&M's and chocolate covered bonbons. Stone was more direct, like whiskey on the rocks. And she had no business thinking about any of that right now, anyway.

She said a final prayer *at least for the next five minutes* and turned away from the window. It was time to meet these so called, acquaintances of Stone's.

She closed the patio door and headed to the front of the house, reflecting on the irony of another obvious change. She was allowed to be alone now. It seemed as though she was out of danger now that her child's life was on the line. They didn't seem to be watching where she went anymore.

*However, Kerensa was very wrong. Both Stone and Nate knew exactly where she was and at all times!*

She walked into the living room instantly deciding that she was also in the wrong house. The room had been transformed into suitcases, equipment and oddly shaped bags. There were two other men there, and from the looks of them, she also wondered if she was in the wrong country too. *Like maybe a third world country with lots of machine guns, and very dangerous looking men.*

They stopped talking when they saw her, making her all the more uncomfortable. That is, until she saw Nana, smack in the middle of the entire group. *Ah yes, that was her Nana.*

Stone spoke first, his tone firm and direct as he took two large steps to arrive by her side.

"Gentlemen, this is Kerensa Fiori."

Kerensa smiled wanly, and for some ungodly reason, wondered how bad she must look. Her eyes were bloodshot from crying and she had long given up on her kinked up curls. She certainly wasn't at her best. But, as always, she had no idea how beautiful, yet vulnerable she looked. Every man in the room noticed, and it was the guy to Nate's left that stepped forward and introduced himself first.

"Hello, I'm Sebastian North; it's nice to meet you."

Kerensa nodded her head, and smiled briefly. Then, the other guy stretched out his hand.

"And I'm Joseph Salvatore."

She nodded her head again then sat down on the sofa. *That seemed safe enough for the moment.*

She studied both men. They were around the same height as Dominick, and the same build. Sebastian had dark hair and very black eyes, and an accent she couldn't identify, Russian, perhaps?

Joseph on the other hand, looked very Italian. He had smooth, handsome features and a kind face. He reminded her of the kind of guy you would see at a fund raising benefit, selling cupcakes and hotdogs so his kids could go away to Boy Scout camp for the summer, unlike Sebastian who appeared much more intimidating. Speaking of dangerous, she never in her entire life had seen so many threatening but *sexy* looking men in one place. She didn't even know that men like that existed, and they were downright scary looking. *But still, very, very sexy!*

She decided to look at Nate, kind, caring Nate, to help ease her fears; except he resembled the rest of them. He was leaning up against the wall, his arms crossed, his eyes intently checking out everything and everyone.

*Oh dear God, if they can't save my child than nobody can.*

Stone cleared a space off on the couch, and sat down beside Kerensa.

*Mirror, mirror on the wall, who's the most dangerous of them all? It was still Stone.* Now why was she thinking about such a silly nursery rhyme?

"What do we do now," she softly asked him.

He stared at her for a long moment, wanting to take her in his arms and hold her again.

"We wait," he replied.

She was afraid he was going to say that.

***

They moved again. This time, it was her idea, and he fell directly into the heart of her plans. Everything was happening exactly the way she hoped for, well almost exactly. She did have one tiny kink to the equation. It wasn't going to be just the three of them anymore. Thorne called in a few of the guys involved in this operation, and they would be arriving soon. She was still confident that she could pull off her plan just the same. Thorne had blabbed his mouth about how he had used her to pick the building where the sniper had shot from. So she put two and two together, figured out that Stone was part of this entire situation too. Knowing that he would be in on the case, made her much more comfortable with knowing she would be rescued too. She had watched him in action, and she knew he would figure out her message.

So she still kept up the scared act with Thorne; made sure her voice had that edge of hysteria, and even begged him to take the blindfold off again, even though she knew he wouldn't. Janelle was drifting in and out of sleep and Jade knew she had to move on her plans quickly now, otherwise Janelle may not come out of this alive.

*It was all about Thorne's need to control, and she knew exactly how to handle that.*

Oh yes, everything so far was moving right along, she only had to get him to do one last thing.

Make the ransom call. Get her in contact with Kerensa, and Stone.

She took a deep breath, making sure she sounded hopelessly desperate.

"Jonathan, are you here?"

"Yea, what do you want?"

"I was feeling a little weak, and I was wondering if you would feed us. Janelle has to eat something," she paused momentarily. "Please."

"I'm not feeding you anything," he replied angrily.

"Then please make that ransom call, before Janelle gets too sick."

Silence.

*Good, he's thinking.*

\*\*\*

Kerensa had her head on Nate's shoulder. She would drift off to sleep, and as soon as her body became too comfortable, she would suddenly startle awake. It was around four o'clock in the morning, and still no contact, no phone call, no nothing...

Stone, Sebastian and Joseph were monitoring the internet with some high tech equipment Kerensa had never seen before. She figured it was Nate's job to baby-sit her. She could tell a few hours ago, by the look in Stone's face, that they thought she was going to loose it. They were probably right, but when Nate sat down beside her and still didn't move to join the rest, her hysteria was replaced by anger, which was probably a good thing. *At least Stone thought so. He much preferred a woman's wrath over a woman's tears.*

Then, suddenly, her cell phone rang.

Within moments, every man was in the living room and in her face.

"Answer it," Stone instructed.

Kerensa froze for a brief moment and then pushed the send button.

"Hello."

There was silence for several moments, and then Kerensa heard Janelle's voice. It was faint, but it was there. She wasn't talking to her mommy though, she was just talking. Stone had the headphones on and he was tapped into the line. She could tell he heard it too. Tears filled her eyes, but she refused to cry. She had cried enough, it was time to get her baby home. Then she heard Jade, her tone was much louder, and she was talking to Janelle. "Where is that silly brown weasel toy? You know the one I mean, Janelle, the one with the pink tutu on."

Suddenly she heard Thorne's voice. "You were supposed to talk to her, you bitch." Then, there was silence. The line was dead.

Kerensa held the phone to her ear for a long time afterward. Finally, Stone took it out of her hands.

"Why didn't he demand anything?" Kerensa asked her tone nearly frantic.

"I don't know," Stone replied, but let's play the message back.

He disconnected the equipment, and played the tape recorded message. Everyone heard it this time.

Then, Kerensa began to think about what Thorne said. He wanted Jade to talk to Kerensa, but instead she kept talking to Janelle. She knew that Jade wanted Kerensa to know that Janelle was still alive. But she knew Jade well enough to realize that she was trying to send her a message too... Kerensa kept repeating the conversation over and over again in her head, oblivious to the conversation going around her. *But the brown weasel didn't have a pink tutu...*

"Dominick," she quickly replied, "I think Jade was sending us a message!"

They all looked at her as she jumped to her feet and ran out of the room. She returned just moments later with the furry weasel. "Look, it doesn't have a tutu on. It-it never did..."

"Where did Janelle get this from?" Stone quickly interrupted.

"Jade bought it for Janelle; right after my students had their first recital. We were celebrating the success of the dance studio and..."

*The dance studio! The last place they would have thought of searching.*

"Does Jade have a password to your security alarm too?" Stone asked, his eyes taking on that strange glow when he was about to react or attack.

"Yes, as a matter of fact, she was my backup person they were supposed to call her if they couldn't find Vance."

"How about a key to your dance studio, does she have that too?" Stone asked, glad that he never changed the locks to her studio doors.

Kerensa slowly nodded her head, *yes.*"

The reaction to her statement was instant as she watched the room spring into action. Nate was on his feet at the same time as Sebastian. Joseph and Stone were already standing and they were arming themselves. Kerensa watched in amazement as various weapons were pulled out of every imaginable bag. And if she thought these men looked menacing before, she was certainly mistaken, because now, they were petrifying her.

Nana remained surprisingly silent while she watched in hopeful confidence that her granddaughter would come home. *And of course, she was already thinking that the more guns, the better.*

Kerensa stood to her feet, suddenly panicked that something could go wrong. She remembered her dream, recalled that it was her little girl's voice she had heard this time. *What if it was a message from her father?*

Stone was watching Kerensa; he noticed how her face paled again, and how she could barely stand up.

He gave the men his instructions and the plan of action. When each one of them filed out, Stone remained behind. He strode across the room and took Kerensa into his arms. "Trust me, sweetheart," he whispered softly. "Just give me one more hour and I will bring your baby home."

She nodded her head, but couldn't say a word.

*He had asked for one more hour. Surely she could handle one more hour. Be careful, Dominick.*

# 26

Kerensa's dance studio appeared deserted, but Stone knew better. Somewhere along the way the vehicle they had taken to transport Jade and Janelle wasn't anywhere to be found. Stone had ditched his vehicle several streets away too and they rapidly and quietly surrounded the studio. They were like little dark shadows moving through the night. *Now you see them, now you don't.* Stone's heart was pounding with that familiar adrenalin rush, his hormones into endorphin overdrive. Nate was behind him about a hundred feet and covering his back, Sebastian was instructed to cover the west side of the building, and Joseph was on the South side. Everyone was instructed to shoot first, ask questions later. They all had earphones on too. Do what it takes to get Thorne's hostages safely back. *Shoot to kill.*

Stone hesitated momentarily as he spotted a shadow near the south side of the studio.

"Joe, it's Stone. Three o'clock to your left."

Stone watched as Joe disappeared right behind the guy, one swift butt of the gun to the head. One down, but how many more to go was the question?

Stone turned around and spoke to Nate into the earphone.

"I'm going in through the back door."

Stone was sure that there would be at least one person guarding it. Stone was right. He could barely see the shape of his shoulders, but he knew he was there. Stone showed up behind the guy so fast, the guy never even knew anyone was there. One minute he was standing, the next minute he was gone.

Stone stepped over him and kept on creeping to the door. And then he paused.

He knew he had only two choices, either sneak in until he knew what was up, or barge in, shooting every bad guy in sight. The problem was, there could be the chance of a stray bullet. And he couldn't take that chance, not with Janelle and Jade.

So he slipped through the back door, effortlessly and swiftly, and paused once the door was closed. He snuck by Kerensa's office, now certain that Thorne had his captives in the back studio. Stone crept close to the floor and around the corner before pausing to detect any sounds or voices. Then, he heard Janelle's voice and glory halleluiah she was crying which meant she was alive. Stone paused again waiting for any other response. He heard a gruff voice, but it wasn't Thorne's. That meant there were at least two of them.

"Where are you, Nate?" Stone's tone was barely above a whisper.

"Right behind you, I just came in through the back door."

"Two subjects," Stone whispered again. I don't have a visual, but I will in a second."

"Roger."

Stone crept closer and closer. He could finally visualize the studio, and he could see where Jade and Janelle were. Thorne was about twenty feet away from Jade, and there was one other guy next to Thorne. That was all he really needed to know.

He burst into the studio, and shot two bullets, one for each man, and it was over within five seconds. Both man had a bullet in the head. It seemed too merciful a death for either one of them, especially Thorne.

Nate was in the studio by the time he heard the gunshots. He was glad it happened that way, which meant he could actually say that he never saw a thing. When he spotted Jade, she had Janelle in her arms, but she had a blindfold on her eyes. *How perfect was that.*

Both men rushed to Jade's side, and Stone lifted Janelle from Jade's arms. Janelle clung to Stone, whimpering softly and hugging his neck. Janelle knew something bad had happened, but with a little tender loving care, counseling and love, she would forget everything.

Nate carefully took the blind off Jade's eyes. She was trembling and in shock, but she was able to respond to his questions and she was oriented. Nate was taken back when he saw how bruised her face was. A strange feeling washed over him and he was glad Thorne was dead; he would have wanted to kill him all over again. *Now where did that feeling come from?*

Jade focused her eyes on him, even though they were swollen.

"Now who are you?" she asked.

"I'm Nate Drake and we're going to get you out of here."

"It's about time," she quipped. "I sent you guys that message over an hour ago."

Stone was standing behind Nate and he started to laugh. Jade turned her sarcasm on him, her tone getting stronger by the second. "I thought you were some big cheese, FBI guy. You should have been here forty five minutes ago."

"Sorry Jade, we needed to secure the scene."

Jade looked at Janelle who continued to cling to him and smiled.

"Ditto that," she replied softly.

Nate pulled out his cell phone and made the first call, it was for Emergency Services. When Jade heard him call them a rescue squad she had a fit all over again.

"You need to transport Janelle and have her checked out, I'm fine."

"You need to be checked out too," Nate retorted firmly, wondering what it was about this woman that frustrated him so much. "You haven't looked at your face, have you?"

"I'm perfectly capable of knowing if I need any medical help. I'm also capable of taking care of myself, including how to use a gun."

She looked over at Stone again. "Tell him, Mr. FBI."

Stone chuckled softly. "Yea, she's pretty good; just don't give her too many things to hold all at once."

Jade wrinkled her nose at Stone, remembering how she dropped his ID.

Stone pulled his cell phone out and made his first call. It was to Kerensa. When she answered he simply handed the phone to her little girl.

"Say hello to mommy, honey."

Janelle spoke softly into the phone. "Hi, mommy."

Kerensa began to sob, and Stone could hear her crying. It was the best sound in the whole world. He took the phone from Janelle, and spoke quietly to her.

"Stop crying and come to your studio. Make sure you take Nana with you."

Kerensa managed to agree through her tears.

"Drive safely, Kerensa."

Stone terminated the conversation and made his final call, the one he waited till last for a good reason.

It was to Chief Donovan.

*** 

Kerensa arrived in record time, probably around thirty five minutes later.

She ran in the door, her eyes darting frantically about until she spotted Jade with Janelle in her arms again. They were in her office, along with several emergency personnel. They were checking Janelle out. She rushed up to all of them and made the announcement that she was Janelle's mommy. She really didn't need to do that because Janelle was already howling for her mama anyway. Kerensa hugged Jade and Janelle together, and took Janelle into her arms. And then she cried some more.

It wasn't until several minutes later, when she looked out the window and began to survey the scene and its details. She saw the two rescue squads parked in front wondering how she missed them when she pulled up. She left her office, Janelle still in her arms and headed to her studio except it was roped off in yellow tape and she knew she couldn't get anywhere close to it.

Nate and Stone were standing together but neither Joseph nor Sebastian were anywhere around. Kerensa surmised that their absence was a planned event. They were probably at her house, collecting their equipment and doing what they did best after a case. Disappear.

The place was crawling with cops, detectives and crime scene investigators. She recalled seeing blood on the ground before she entered the building, and figured out the rest. There wasn't one little piece of her heart that felt sadness, as a matter of fact, she was hopeful that Thorne was dead. She would feel remorse for her thoughts later.

*Maybe.*

She looked up to see Vance walking in her direction. His expression was beyond angry, and she braced herself for the verbal confrontation.

"This is an official crime scene investigation, what are you doing here?"

She looked incredulously at him. Was he for real?

"Picking up my baby, who was part of your crime scene," she furiously retorted.

"Exactly," he continued, "and that means that you can't pick her up until she is officially allowed to go."

*Officially allowed to go?*

Suddenly Stone was behind Vance. *It was one of those usual moves of his. Now you see him, now you don't.*

"Take Janelle to the emergency room to have her checked out, Kerensa. The emergency services will take you. Then go home." Stone was directing his orders to Kerensa, but his eyes were staring doggedly into Vance's.

She somehow knew the very moment she looked at Stone that his patience had finally run out. It was too bad that Vance didn't realize it.

"I can't believe you would let these vigilantes handle this kidnapping", he continued, his tone dripping with sarcasm. "You're damn lucky she's still alive and I don't know why I ever thought you had any brains in your head at all." *Oh boy, Stone's one last nerve was severed.*

Stone grabbed Vance by the collar and pushed him against the wall, hard. His eyes were glowing red if you looked close enough. With his face just inches from Vance's he spoke again.

"You've been trying to piss me off since we met, and it looks like you finally did it. This family is safe now, and they don't need your involvement nor do they need your harassment." Stone gave him one last push before he let him go.

When he turned around, he almost stepped on Donovan's feet.

"Sergeant Stone," Donovan evenly replied, "I want you to take your hands off my detective."

"I did," Stone growled. "Now get your detective out of my way."

Donovan nodded his head, and spoke again. "I see there are more dead bodies."

"Yea, a few," Stone responded bluntly, attempting to calm his anger down. "It couldn't be helped. You'll receive my report within twenty four hours."

"I expect it within four hours, Sergeant Stone, and not a minute later than that." Donovan turned toward a very red faced Vance.

"Follow me, Detective Robertson."

Vance shot one last glare in Stone's direction before he walked away, *hopefully forever.*

Stone turned to Kerensa again. "Ride with the rescue squad, and take Jade with you too. Nana can take your car, and then she can pick all three of you up."

Kerensa nodded her head. He began to turn away, when she stopped him with her hand on his arm. He turned around to face her again.

"Thank you," she said her tone barely above a whisper. "You saved my child."

Stone grinned for only a moment. "I promised you I would, didn't I?"

She nodded, and their eyes met. And then she knew.

She knew that he would be gone by the time they got back home. She knew that he was making his last arrangement for her to get safely home. Actually, for all of them to get safely home. She knew that all she'd have left behind was another memory. She'd walked this path once already; he disappeared soon after she was rescued from the warehouse eight years ago too. It was several months later that she went to find him, that she took the risk of telling him that she loved him. But she wouldn't do that this time, this time she knew better. Sadly enough though, she guessed Nate wouldn't be staying behind like he did before, either. He would be gone with Stone.

But she was suddenly O.K. with that, she was grateful that she was still alive, grateful that her baby girl was unharmed and grateful that everyone she loved had also escaped, unscathed.

She stood before him, her gaze locked with his. Then, she reached out and put her arms around him, and kissed him, long and passionately. Without another glance behind her, she left him standing there.

# 27

Kerensa was back at the dance studio with her students again, and everything was back to normal within a few days. *Or was it?*

Despite the fact that they tried to tone down the story, it became front page news anyway. It was only one week till Nationals in Wildwoods, New Jersey and Kerensa was going to cancel her students until next year. But they begged her not to. With that in mind, she called each parent and asked them how they felt about it. Only a couple moms's had a problem with their safety, but after discussing it further, they changed their minds too.

So it was decided that they would go to Nationals and give it their best shot.

She had been right about Dominick, when she returned home from the emergency room that night, all his things were gone and so were Nate's. She knew she could reach Nate, because he left his calling card behind. Stone didn't leave anything behind. Well, maybe he did. But it wasn't in the form of a phone number.

Nana never said another word about the kidnapping, nor did they discuss anything more about Stone or Nate. Janelle woke up screaming for three nights in a row, but the past two nights she slept peacefully. Kerensa didn't have any further nightmares herself, but she didn't have any sweet dreams, either.

She watched as her students filed back in from their break. Once they were all inside the studio, she put the music back on again.

Five-Six-Seven-Eight, she counted as the girls began to dance their jazz number. When they were finished, she showed them what mistakes were made.

"Alright, girls, we're going to do this again." She turned around and pushed the button for the music to begin, and then she heard the girls giggling behind her.

She whirled around and there was Stone. She blinked, thinking that maybe she just imagined him there. When she opened her eyes, he was still in front of her, bigger than life and so damn handsome. She took a deep breath and smiled at him, but she didn't move a muscle. Then, he strode over to her, picked her up in his arms and twirled her around before setting her down and kissing her.

"Oh, Miss Kerensa!" Her students teased, as they giggled and laughed.

Kerensa blushed, and started the music up again.

"Girl's, I want you to practice this without me and I will be right back." Then, she took Stone's hand and left the studio with him.

They headed to her office where she promptly closed the door and put her arms around him again. His lips hungrily found hers and he kissed her hard this time, and for a lot longer. Finally, she pulled away from him.

Touching her fingertips to her tingling lips, she eyed him suspiciously.

"Why are you here, Dominick?"

Stone chuckled. "One of my guns was missing, and I figured Nana had it."

Kerensa laughed aloud. "I wouldn't doubt it if she did."

He suddenly sobered, and their eyes met again.

"Why are you really here?" she softly asked.

Stone took a deep breath. "Because I'm in love with you, Kerensa, and I can't walk away from you a second time. That would be just plain, insanity. Although I have been there before, I can tell you it's not a very pleasant place."

She felt her heart flutter like feathers in her chest. "What about everything else, though, your job, the government or whatever you want to call it?"

Stone chuckled beneath his breath, and she had already forgotten how sexy it sounded. Then he became serous again.

"I keep asking myself a different question. I'm an assassin Kerensa, you're a dance teacher. Do you see a common denominator here? I don't think you truly understand what I really am or what terrible things I've…"

Kerensa put a hand up to stop him. "Please don't say anything more, Dominick, you don't have to. I understand a lot more than I ever wanted to admit. You warned me not to ask a couple times already, and believe me I've become a little less curious now." *To say the least.*

"What I do care about is whether or not you will come and go in my life. I can't handle that, and neither can Janelle. We either have you or we don't. I won't just have a part of you. And there is a common denominator between us, as sappy as it sounds, its love…I love you Dominick Stone…That is your real name, isn't it?"

Stone grinned at her but he didn't answer her question.

"I'm retiring, Kerensa."

She peered suspiciously at him again. "Somehow I can't believe you would do that and not get bored to death."

"I'm retiring from the government. Does that make more sense?"

She nodded her head. "Maybe, so what are you going to do?"

"I'm just going to run my private agency. I'm sure it will keep me busy enough."

"Are there people out there still trying to kill you?"

Stone's eyebrows rose in thought, but shook his head, *no. At least, not that he was aware of.*

"Will it be enough for you, I mean, this is going to be a semi-normal life..." she suddenly blushed. "You know what I mean, right?"

This time Stone roared, and pulled her to him again. He gently cupped her face with both his hands, brushing the stray tendrils of hair away with his fingertips.

"I have a feeling I will be plenty busy, and in more ways than one. How's Janelle?"

"She's doing better every day, but she keeps asking about you."

Stone became silent again, a tight feeling in his chest as he continued to gaze into her eyes.

"Marry me, Kerensa," he softly whispered into her ear. "You have my word I will never leave you again."

She didn't want to cry again, geeze, that's all she ever did these past couple months. *Cry, cry, cry...* But the tears came anyway, and she allowed them to slowly slide down her cheeks.

"I guess I could say yes, after all it took you eight years to ask me."

Stone didn't respond to that remark, he simply kissed her.

**THE END**

Dear Lynn,

Thank you for
reading. Hope you
enjoy.

Linda

Miranda Lu 9/10/06

Printed in the United States
56131LVS00004B/331-378